THE 17th LETTER

It's the height of World War II. Mary and Paul Strong keep house in their Greenwich Village apartment and look forward to the letters from their friend Max, a news photographer on assignment in Iceland. But when the next letter arrives it turns out to be a series of blank pages with a Canadian theater program inside. That evening they hear the news—the boat Max is on is torpedoed by a German sub, with all hands lost.

Paul knows something is terribly amiss, but can make nothing of the strange clue Max has mailed them. Mary herself is very suspicious of their new upstairs neighbors, then learns some very startling information on her own. Paul decides to catch the next ship to Iceland. Mary decides to stowaway on Paul's ship, and both of them are headed for the adventure of their life.

"Disney presents interesting characters, lots of action and cleverly devised plots."
—*20th Century Crime & Mystery Writers*

**Dorothy Cameron Disney Bibliography
(1903-1992)**

Novels:
Death in the Back Seat (1936)
Strawstack (1939; reprinted as *The Strawstack Murders*, 1944)
The Golden Swan Murder (1939)
The Balcony (1940)
Thirty Days Hath September (1942; with George Sessions Perry)
Crimson Friday (1943)
The 17th Letter (1945)
Explosion (1948)
The Hangman's Tree (1949)

Short Story:
The Usual Three (*Cosmopolitan*, August 1939)

The 17th Letter

Dorothy Cameron Disney

Stark House Press • Eureka California

THE 17TH LETTER

Published by Stark House Press
1315 H Street
Eureka, CA 95501, USA
griffinskye3@sbcglobal.net
www.starkhousepress.com

Cover design by Jeff Vorzimmer, ¡caliente!design, Austin, Texas
Text design by Mark Shepard, shepgraphics.com
Proofreading by Bill Kelly
Cover art by Onzi Brown from *True Detective*, February 1953.

First Stark House Press Edition: September 2024

Battling with the Baron

Dorothy Cameron Disney and *The 17th Letter* (1945)

By Curtis Evans

On January 21, 1941, Franz Xaver Freiherr von Werra, a German fighter pilot and flying ace who had been taken prisoner after his plane was shot down in England on September 5, 1940, daringly grabbed his big chance with both hands. On a transport train en route to a prison camp in Ontario, he escaped from Canadian custody (he had arrived in Canada with other prisoners just a few days previously) by leaping out of a window. Freiherr (i. e., Baron) von Werra, a charismatic cosmopolitan fluent in both English and French, hitched his way to the city of Ottawa, had lunch at a diner and then made his way to the American border town of Ogdensburg, New York, at the final stage of his journey paddling with his hands over the St. Lawrence River in a stolen rowboat. At Ogdensburg, American immigration officials took him into custody, charging him with having made an illegal entry into the United States (which was then a neutral country) and turning him over to the local German consul. Canada lodged charges of theft against von Werra concerning the purloined rowboat and commenced extradition proceedings to have the wily German airman returned to Canadian custody. Instead, however, with the connivance of German diplomats, von Werra made it over the southern border into Mexico and from there in stages to Rio de Janeiro, Barcelona and Rome. On April 18 he finally reached Nazi Germany, where he received a hero's welcome and was awarded the Knight's Cross by none other than the Führer himself.

The exploits of the Baron von Werra—whose movie star smile and handsome Nordic features made him a veritable poster boy for the "Master Race"—were prominently featured in American newspapers and magazines throughout the winter and spring of 1941, months before the attack on Pearl Harbor propelled the U.S. into the ever-widening war. Photos of the Baron grinning, his frostbitten ears heavily encased in bandages, were seen around the country. Unfortunately for the intrepid escapee, however, his luck would run out on October 25, when his plane, having suffered engine failure, crashed into the North

Sea off the coast of the Netherlands. Although his body was never discovered, von Werra was presumed dead. Fifteen years after his recorded death, his story was chronicled in a book, *The One That Got Away*, which was adapted under the same title into a popular 1957 war thriller starring the late German actor Hardy Krüger.

Americans Dorothy Cameron Disney and her husband Milton MacKaye were politically conscious popular magazine writers who certainly would have been aware of the von Werra affair. A reading of *The 17th Letter*, the seventh of Dorothy Disney's nine published crime novels, makes clear that when writing it in 1944, the author drew heavily on the von Werra story, though in keeping with her country's engagement for the last several years in the Allies' liberty-or-death struggle against the Axis powers, she patriotically portrays the Baron's fictional alter ego as an unadulterated Nazi villain. For their part, Disney's protagonists, a young New York married couple named Paul and Mary Strong, bear a certain resemblance to the author and her husband of two decades earlier, when they themselves were young and "just married."

Paul Strong, for example, is a magazine writer. He and Mary have a mutual war correspondent friend, Max Ferris, in Reykjavik, Iceland, who, after some nine months abroad, is due to return to the States, yet when his passenger plane arrives in New York, he is not on it. Instead, the couple receives a piece of mail from Max, which would be his 17th wartime letter to them, except for the fact that there is no actual letter sealed in the envelope, just some blank sheets of paper and a theater program from Halifax, Canada detailing a performance of Henrik Ibsen's play *The Wild Duck*. Then the Strongs learn to their dismay that Max has been slain in Iceland. Eventually through a series of unfortunate events. the couple, armed with knowledge of an imminent deadly plot against the allies, find themselves in Halifax, desperately on the run not only from malevolent foreign agents but the police— specifically, the Royal Mounted Canadian Police, familiarly known as Mounties. Will they ever be able to get out of this mess and prevent a catastrophic enemy strike on the home front?

Espionage thrillers, fashionable fiction since the world had become engulfed in total war, marked a change of pace for Dorothy Cameron Disney, who up to this time had produced a half dozen much-praised American crime novels in the classic style of mystery godmother Mary Roberts Rinehart. More precisely, *The 17th Letter*, which enjoyed a serial run in the *Saturday Evening Post* before seeing publication in hardcover novel form, is a flight-and-pursuit thriller, in the tradition of John Buchan's landmark novel *The Thirty-Nine Steps* (1915) and Geoffrey Household's more recent *Rogue Male* (1939), not to mention any number of Alfred Hitchcock films, including Hitch's own adaptation of *Steps*, and Scottish crime writer Michael Innes, who made a specialty of these sorts of suspenseful tales with such books as *The Secret Vanguard* (1940). *New York Times* crime fiction reviewer Anthony Boucher, a great fan of Disney's, regretted the author's momentarily taking leave of the field of straight mystery to moonlight in spy mayhem, wryly declaring of the events in the tale: "coincidence waves more long arms than a Hindu god." Nevertheless, he praised the novel's "agreeable writing" and "vivid picture of wartime Halifax." Other reviewers were less modulated in their praise. Margaret Sim in the *Montreal Gazette*, for example, pronounced the novel "one of the most exciting of the modern mystery-spy thrillers" while E. B. P. in the *Raleigh News and Observer* warmly summarized *Letter* as "a tale of furious action in which an attractive American couple find themselves both the pursued and the pursuers in a spy plot both unusual and fiendish." Kester Svendsen at the *Daily Oklahoman* found the novel "about as thrilling as [spy novels] come," adding enthusiastically: "the minor characters are extremely well done, even down to the dog Bosco. You can't go wrong on this one."

Canadian reviewers were especially charmed by the author's scrupulously rendered depiction of wartime Halifax. Disney herself informed reviewers that she had personally traveled to the Canadian city to do on-the-ground research. In newspaper interviews she later claimed that from personal observation she discovered two ways in which a person might be able to stowaway on a loaded transport ship, incidentally turning this information over the American and Canadian security authorities, who promptly took corrective action in the matter before her book went into print in February 1945. Here was a mystery that evidently had some actual practical real-world impact!

□ □ □

Born on Friday the thirteenth in November, 1903 in Atoka, Oklahoma (then Indian Territory), also the native town of a contemporary, Choctaw mystery writer Todd Downing, Dorothy Cameron Disney would enjoy a run for thirteen years as one of her country's most successful mystery writers, though from mid-century onward she became better known as a newspaper advice columnist. Had Ann Landers switched mid-career from murder mongering to marriage counselling, she could have been another Dorothy Cameron Disney.

Dorothy, who moved with her family to Muskogee, Oklahoma when she was a child, was one of three children of Loren G. Disney, a boisterous Oklahoma attorney, oil company promoter, former "Rough Rider" in the Spanish-American War and a player in progressive Republican politics nicknamed "Hell-roaring Disney" (his daughter attested to the accuracy of the adjective), and Nettie Vansant, the daughter of a farmer from Topeka, Kansas and granddaughter of a blacksmith from Libertytown, Maryland. Loren Disney, apparently the natural son of an unwed mother, had been adopted by Alfred Adolphus and Clara Arabelle Disney—no relation to Walt—after the couple concluded that after five years of barren marriage, they were not going to be able to produce any children on their own. Unexpectedly however, Clara gave birth to a boy a year after Loren's adoption, with four more children rapidly following. Bitterly Loren always felt that his adoptive parents—who never gave him a full middle name, just an initial—were far more partial to their blood children.

Loren's daughter Dorothy, along with her brothers Loren, Jr. and Stanley, grew up in happier circumstances. After graduating from Central High School in Muskogee in 1920 at the age of sixteen, the bold and outgoing Dorothy spent one year at Washburn College in Topeka College, where she worked on the college newspaper, the *Washburn Review*. Then in 1923 she moved to Washington, D.C. to work as a clerk in the Justice Department's formidably titled Office of Alien Property Custodian. For three years she labored there while also attending classes in history, literature and theater at George Washington University under the distinguished and rather pretentiously named professors Robert Whitney Bolwell, Elmer Louis Kayser and Dewitt Clinton Croissant (!); yet she never graduated from the college. Her son later stated this was on account of her adamant refusal to enroll in any science classes. Six years after she left Washburn, the *Review* vividly recalled her from her single, freshman year, as a fearless, "most individualistic girl" of great talent but mercurial temperament:

> There was one thing she could do and that was write. When it came to hunting up news she took her place as a man, and asked no odds because she wore dresses. And when she turned in the copy it was readable.

Dorothy was active in politics; particularly she endeavored to help one of her girlfriends be selected as editor of the *Review*. Dorothy alone almost carried the law school, but her friend lost the race. The next year Dorothy was not at Washburn.

In Washington Dorothy first encountered native Iowa newspaperman Milton Angus MacKaye. A couple of years older than Dorothy, "Mac," as he was inevitably nicknamed, was then a staff writer with the *Washington Daily News*. His parents, Methodist minister Donald McKay and his wife Mary were native Nova Scotians of Scots descent. Halifax being the provincial capital of Nova Scotia, the nativity of her McKay in-laws suggests another reason why Dorothy partially set a novel there. (For some reason Mac altered the spelling of his surname.) Like a version of a rom-com "meet cute" scene in a Hallmark Christmas film, Dorothy and Mac had an acrimonious initial dustup, when as a judge in a newspaper competition, Mac awarded Dorothy second prize. Dorothy, who stoutly insisted that she deserved first place, indignantly refused, despite the urging of friends, to actually meet her adversary in person.

The same year Mac moved to New York City to take a position with the *New York Evening Post*. Dorothy herself relocated to New York 1926, settling among the Bohemians in Greenwich Village. In the Big Apple she attended classes at Barnard College and Columbia University and held a bewildering succession of jobs: a stenographer in three New York publishing houses, a movie extra, a nightclub hostess, an advertising copy writer, a companion to elderly women and a receptionist to a salesman of fraudulent stocks.

When Dorothy finally met Mac in person in New York, the pair, again like a couple in a rom-com film, decidedly hit it off. Together they compiled a party game book of word puzzles that became a rage among the city's highbrow set. Drolly they entitled the book *Guggenheim*, ostensibly in (dis)honor of the city's reputed worst player of the game. The forward to *Guggenheim* was written by future famed Hollywood film director and producer Nunnally Johnson, then a colleague of MacKaye's at the *Post*. The book sold some 2000 copies in New York in its first week of publication in April 1927. Five months later, shortly after Dorothy's twenty-fourth birthday, she and Mac wed in Manhattan.

The next year, Mac, possibly reflecting Dorothy's influence with Doubleday, Doran, published the true crime book *Dramatic Crimes of 1927*, a complimentary annual offering to members of the publisher's newly launched Crime Club crime fiction imprint. Under an alias, Dorothy herself began submitting fiction to magazines in 1929. Like her younger brothers Loren, Jr. and Stanley, she had long wanted to write, though belying her bravado, had lacked confidence in her abilities. Many years later she credited her husband with much of her later success, modestly telling a newspaper interviewer of Mac in 1951, "He is my most severe critic, a wonderful editor, and he actually taught me how to spell."

During the 1930s the couple independently achieved popular success as magazine writers, Dorothy making a special home for her work under her own name at *Ladies Home Journal* and *Woman's Home Companion*, Mac at the *New Yorker*, where he wrote a succession of profiles of prominent people in politics. (First Lady Eleanor Roosevelt once told him that he had written the best article about her husband's presidential administration.) Both authors also wrote for the high-profile *Saturday Evening Post*. In New York in 1934, Dorothy bore the couple's only child, William Ross MacKaye. Her first novel, a mystery set in small-town coastal Connecticut, entitled *Death in the Back Seat*, came two years later in 1936 and was received with rapturous applause by reviewers. With two successful careers now well-launched, the busy couple, who had resolved to leave New York apartment life behind them, was able to purchase two houses, their main neo-Georgian residence in Washington, D.C., and a summer home complete with working farm near the coastal Connecticut town of Guildford, which had been dubbed "the most charming place in Connecticut."

In D.C., their son Billy, or Bill as he was called when he was older, attended prestigious Sidwell Friends School while his parents kept up their steady flows of lucrative wordage. For four months of the year in Connecticut Dorothy would rise every day at five a.m., pour herself a big cup of coffee and get to work in her latest novel with her pencil and tablet, leaving after three hours of work a mixture of shorthand and longhand scribblings for her secretary to decipher. In 1948, when Bill was fourteen, she freely admitted to neglecting her house "terribly" at those times: "I am not one of those who can run a house beautifully and write three hours a day."

Yet perhaps the give-and-take, with writing doing most of the taking, had become too much of a strain. Dorothy published her final mystery novel in 1949, thereafter starting an advice column in *Ladies Home Journal* entitled "Can This Marriage Be Saved?" Launching the hugely popular column in 1953 and helming it for three decades into her eighties, Dorothy became famed throughout the country for her marriage advice, based on the files of real-life couple counselling sessions. A few years after Mack died in 1979 at his and Dorothy's third home, their winter residence in Florida, Dorothy retired from the column, finally passing away in 1992 at the age of eighty-eight. Her ashes, along with Mack's, were interred next to a glacial rock under a maple tree her mother Nettie Vansant Disney had planted at the Guildford house in 1950.

For years, other, younger women, like syndicated columnist and author Suzanne Britt Jordan, wrote of their fond memories of Dorothy's marriage column, which they had read devotedly. Jordan remembered, how as a pre-teen and teenager:

> I used to get myself a Coke, sling my leg over the arm of the wing chair in the living room and read Dorothy Cameron Disney's "Can This Marriage Be Saved?"—my favorite feature in my mother's *Ladies Home Journal* … Usually the ending was not completely happy for either side [man or wife] … the situation was not perfect, and nobody ever lived happily ever after. I loved those realistic endings.

Dorothy's *New York Times* obituary, carried around the country, did not even mention her mystery writing, focusing instead on the social significance of her long-running marriage column. Dorothy and Mac themselves seem to have enjoyed uncommonly happy endings in their own marriage, as did their son, a newspaperman like his father and pillar of his progressive D.C. church who passed away just last year at the age of eighty-nine, all of which suggests that when it came to marriage advice Dorothy well knew of what she wrote. If anyone ever had it all, enjoying both professional success and a happy home life, it would seem to have been Dorothy Cameron Disney. Still, let us not forget the author's mystery fiction, where the endings, to be sure, were usually happy too—though not without much tension and travail.

—June 2024

Curtis Evans received a PhD in American history in 1998. He is the author of *Masters of the "Humdrum" Mystery: Cecil John Charles Street, Freeman Wills Crofts, Alfred Walter Stewart and British Detective Fiction, 1920-1961* (2012), *Clues and Corpses: The Detective Fiction and Mystery Criticism of Todd Downing* (2013), *The Spectrum of English Murder: The Detective Fiction of Henry Lancelot Aubrey-Fletcher and G. D. H. and Margaret Cole* (2015) and editor of the Edgar nominated *Murder in the Closet: Essays on Queer Clues in Crime Fiction Before Stonewall* (2017). He writes about vintage crime fiction at his blog The Passing Tramp and at Crimereads.

The 17th Letter

Dorothy Cameron Disney

For William Ross MacKaye
who is indeed my severest critic

ONE

To Mary Strong, working in her sunny kitchen, life seemed very good. She liked the early-morning hours before New York awoke as much as Paul disliked them. Humming softly lest she disturb the sleeper in the room adjoining, she carefully measured out two cups of coffee and plugged in the electric pot Max had given them for a wedding present. It was the most expensive gadget the Paul Strongs owned, and Mary smiled to herself at the pleasure she took in something so small as a coffee pot. Somehow the little things were more important nowadays.

With a slightly guilty feeling that she should be so happy in a world so filled with trouble, Mary leaned her elbows on the window sill and gazed down at the early-morning scene below. Washington Square was almost empty, the clean fresh sunlight glinted on deserted benches, poured in a delicate flood through the lovely classic arch that defined the park and gave it character. The trees looked bare and used, perhaps, from the ravages of winter, but in a few weeks now the maples should begin to bud. Already in late January the first false hint of spring was in the air. It felt warm and sweet.

To Mary the view below in any season meant New York, meant her life almost—the adult part that mattered. She and Paul had done their courting in the park. They'd hunted hard and paid too much to occupy this apartment overlooking it. So many of her memories were focused there; saunters toward Sunday morning breakfasts at the Brevoort or the Lafayette; a solemn conversation held one autumn evening long ago when Paul decided to give up freelance writing and go with *News Review*; that awful time when she'd miscalculated the hazards of champagne at the annual office party and he and Max had been obliged to walk her up and down till dawn.

She recalled another journey through the park, midsummer this time and on that last afternoon before Max went away. The three of them had passed along the dusty, white-hot sidewalks on a day of burning heat, headed toward his hotel so she could oversee the packing. Before they hailed a taxi on the Avenue she and Paul had stopped and posed beneath the Arch, and waited in limp, perspiring patience while Max photographed them. He'd just wangled a brand-new Simplex camera from the business office for his trip; the Strongs must begin the roll to bring him luck. For the thousandth time Mary wished Max had remembered to send back a print.

She'd worn her favorite hat, as new that blazing July afternoon as Max's camera, and the real truth was she'd like to see the straw and feather creation in its prime. Even in maturity it was quite a hat! If it stayed as warm as this, she'd wear the hat uptown to market this afternoon. Madison Avenue, or rather that supercilious butcher in the fanciest shop in town, should be impressed.

Mary reached absently into a drawer and pulled out the ration books. She'd saved both their tickets for weeks, worked miracles with fish and eggs, and sure enough acquired sufficient points to buy a steak.

She was still admiring the delicious color of the accumulated ration tickets, when a moving van turned the corner on the street below. With lively interest, she watched the van pull up at the service entrance of the apartment house. The apartment over them must be gone at last. Downstairs Mrs. Bentley was probably in her element. Even in times like these she made an occasion of renting the five-room suites.

Behind her the coffee pot began to bubble. She glanced quickly at her watch. Simultaneously the alarm clock in the bedroom set up a horrific clamor, a clamor that was abruptly hushed. The bedsprings creaked, and then all was blissful silence. When Mary went in to look, Paul was fast asleep.

"Paul," she called.

He moaned and burrowed deeper in the blankets. His head was almost covered. His tousled hair was exposed, one eye that was stubbornly shut and an area of faintly troubled forehead. Watching, Mary felt the wave of emotion that often came to her when she looked at Paul in his unguarded moments. She leaned forward, and lightly touched the nearest wisp of hair. At once the faint lines of trouble disappeared.

"In a minute," he mumbled. "Or better, make it five. I love you, darling."

And then the usual morning phenomenon took place. Almost before the mumbling ceased, Paul was deep in sleep again. He wasn't shamming. The hand that clutched the coverings was quite relaxed. The tumbled bedding was absolutely motionless. Mary never ceased to marvel at the swiftness of the transition.

"There'll be times," Max had told her once, "when you'll think the bastard's dead. Only thing is, he keeps on breathing. Once he is awake, of course, he's more awake than most of us ever are. It's quite a guy you're getting, Mary."

"You're quite a guy yourself," she'd said to Max, and meant it.

Breaking up a bachelor establishment wasn't always easy for the girl who accomplished it. Not that Max Ferris was the sort who would openly sulk and gloom because his best friend had found a wife, and his roommate had moved out on him. Max was far too clever for that. His withdrawal would have been delicately managed. But there had been no withdrawal, no break in the friendship that meant so much to both men. Max had become a part of her life too, exactly as she had hoped he would. Mary sometimes wondered fleetingly just what would have happened in the early stages of her knowing Paul if Max Ferris hadn't liked and approved of her. Being a wise woman, three years married now, she never voiced the wonder audibly.

Looking down at her peacefully sleeping husband, Mary thought to herself that she had missed Max almost as much as Paul did—if not quite so consistently. She glanced across the bed toward the desk that held his letters, neatly filed in their own pigeonhole, the numbered envelopes in order.

The letters that at first had looked so odd with their changing foreign stamps flanked by the blue-ink insignia of the censor packed the pigeonhole. To Mary's secret surprise, Max had kept his promise and written faithfully every second Sunday. His *News Review* assignment had been to make a picture story of a convoy trip to Murmansk, and long ago he had acquitted it triumphantly. His striking photographs had been published in a special supplement, so good they were. In the past seven months, the Strongs had followed the traveler all the way to Russia and back as far as Iceland. There for six long weeks Max had been firmly stuck. In that chill and distant outpost of the world, he had been held up awaiting transportation home. The most recent of the letters, the fat thick envelopes numbered fourteen, fifteen and sixteen, had come from Reykjavik, of all places! Number sixteen would be the last, thought Mary, smiling. The series was done. The Clipper was coming into the airfield sometime this evening, and Max would be aboard.

"Paul!" she leaned over the bed and called. "Paul! It's really very late. Big doings tonight. Anyhow today is Friday. Remember?"

"Friday?" the blankets mumbled.

"Press day, darling. The public and the printers wait."

"If there's a spark of human pity in your heart ..."

"It's exhausted, my slothful sweet." Mary took firm and expert hold of the coverings.

"I'm up." There was a tremendous upheaval of blankets and pillows, a tan tousled head emerged, a pair of lean freckled shoulders, and finally, abruptly and miraculously wide awake in a second, Paul Strong was sitting up. He grinned at his wife. "If we journalists love our work, it must be because we meet such interesting people. Eccentric wenches like you who leap from bed on Fridays with sun-up, and take a savage pleasure in torturing their normal husbands."

"Normal? I'm wondering," Mary said severely, "how you ever managed before you met me."

"Before you, Mary?" Paul repeated, as though the words surprised him. Suddenly he looked up unsmilingly and wonderingly at his wife. "Do you know it's hard for me to remember before you. But I remember this: I was always lonely in a certain way before I met you, Mary. I've never been lonely since."

Mary leaned down and put her arms around him, and laid her cheek against his hair. "Nothing nicer will ever be said to me. I'm not lonely either, Paul."

He kissed her hard and let her go, and broke the moment with a little laugh. "But I haven't told you how I managed getting up. This is how. I just got there late."

"And they never fired you?"

"Never. It must be," Paul said reflectively, "that I offer more valuable attributes, like a quick, sharp mind, say, an ability to grasp what others can't. Strong receives few complaints. Don't I smell coffee?"

She was in the kitchen when she heard his feet thump on the floor. Good! She'd let him get a start, before she carried in the trays. As she cut the bread for toast, Mary listened subconsciously for the familiar series of whirlwind sounds that should follow—the hang of the bathroom door, the indignant scream of the tap that needed a new washer, the quick whir of his electric razor. Once up, Paul didn't dawdle. The bedroom was suspiciously silent. Had he gone back to sleep again?

Mary stepped to the door, and stopped in surprise. Paul was up all right, but he wasn't dressing. He had moved directly from bed to the desk, and was seated there as though he had unlimited time at his disposal. Paul had pulled Max's letters from the pigeonhole. They were spread on the blotter before him.

"Paul," she said.

He jumped guiltily, and turned around. Then, seeing her, he relaxed. He even grinned. She was not deceived.

"Something's gone wrong, Paul. Something about Max."

He did not deny it. She leaned against the wall to compensate for the sudden weakness of her knees.

"There's been an accident, and you were afraid to tell me. When? Where? What happened?"

"Darling," he said, and got up quickly from his chair. "Don't be absurd. How could I keep a thing like that from you? In point of fact"—and then he hesitated—"the Clipper got in from Iceland late yesterday."

Yesterday? The Clipper had got in yesterday. Then where was Max?

"Still up in Reykjavik when last heard from," Paul said dryly. "The managing editor is having fits. A few days before the plane took off, and without a word to the office, Max turned over his seat to another passenger."

She stared at him in astonishment and dismay. It had taken six long weeks to get that seat that Max had casually given away. Weeks would pass before he had another chance. Why? What was keeping him? It could not be work. Max wasn't accredited to Iceland, he couldn't go wandering with his camera around that bleak, mist-swept country where everything was a military secret.

Her eyes fell upon the scattered letters. Her bewilderment increased. Max hadn't found Reykjavik attractive or comfortable. There was only beer to drink, the movies were two years old, the girls looked like goddesses, but they smelled of fish. Max wasn't even staying at a hotel, so overcrowded was the harbor city with the military. He was stopping at the waterfront home of Danish fishermen, a father and son named Thorgsen. Respectable enough people, according to Max's account, but gone all day at their hazardous occupation, and not especially diverting company in the evenings. Whom else had he written of? Only one other person on all of Reykjavik had really interested him—the other lodger at the Thorgsens'. For no particular reason, Mary shivered.

"He's ill," she said suddenly. "He's ill, Paul. Max is just like you. He never takes the slightest care of himself."

"Apparently Max was well enough last Thursday to show up and surrender his Clipper ticket. I think myself," Paul said slowly, "he may have stumbled onto some—story."

"What kind of story? Max isn't a reporter; he's a photographer. I thought he was badly needed here."

"I don't mean anything for the office necessarily."

"Then what do you mean?"

"I don't know exactly," Paul said irritably. "I wish you wouldn't jump at me like that. There's nothing to worry about. Max will cable when he gets around to it. He may have cabled already. Any personal news takes a hell of a time coming through nowadays. All the wires are clogged, and then the censorship ..."

"I do wish ..." began Mary, and stopped abruptly.

Paul surveyed her gloomily. "You needn't look so smug and tactful, my good wife. I haven't forgotten your suggesting that we work out a private code to cover emergencies, and that Max and I overruled you."

"I'm a natural lawbreaker," said Mary guiltily. "It doesn't matter, anyhow. If Max puts his mind to it, he can write his way around the smartest censor. But I can't help thinking ..."

"If you must know"—Paul did grin now—"I have a strong suspicion one of those emergencies has arisen. It seems to be the only answer. This is no boyish prank, that's certain. Max isn't that kind of a fool. Something important kept him off the Clipper."

From the kitchen rose the smell of burning toast. Mary exclaimed, and rushed to the rescue. For the next few minutes everything went wrong. The toast was burning merrily. When she flipped the toaster, a blazing slice of bread fell on the floor and scorched the linoleum before she could dash a glass of water on it. She pulled the toaster plug and burned her hand. When she flung up the window to let out the fumes a gust of wind came in. The ration books promptly blew out the window and went sailing to the sidewalk.

A soldier, who had paused below to watch the moving van unload, caught one neatly and scooped the other from the curb. He looked up. Mary gestured in frantic pantomime and darted from the kitchen.

Without a hat or coat, wearing a kitchen apron, she reached the sidewalk.

The soldier was middle-aged and lonely and in a mood to consider the ration books a letter of introduction. Afterwards she remembered that there was something puzzlingly contradictory about his appearance— he was neatly shaved and very clean, but his coat and trousers were shabby and in serious need of pressing. With his neat mustache and his shifty eyes, the unsoldierly soldier seemed at once painfully respectable and yet vaguely furtive, like an absconding bank cashier.

"My mother's name was Mary," he began with a gold-toothed smile. "You don't look twenty-four. I see you've been saving up your tickets. Is Paul your husband?"

"Yes," said Mary, taken aback. She murmured thanks and gathered her books from his reluctant hands. It was cold outside, and she was in a hurry. She was not to escape so easily.

"Paul's older than you, ain't he?" remarked the soldier. "Thirty-two. How long's he been in the newspaper business? If I'd had the education,

I'd have liked to be a newspaperman myself."

Mary was tenderhearted. Suddenly she felt sorry for him. Lonesome and with no place to go—trying to strike up an acquaintanceship out of nothing. He couldn't help his looks. Paul was waiting for his breakfast, but she could spend a moment. The man's uniform was unfamiliar. She glanced at the insignia on his collar.

"Australian?"

"Canadian," he said, and his narrow face warmed. "The finest country on earth. Why, I could tell you things about Canada that ..." He stopped abruptly. The warmth died from his face.

"I've never been to Canada," Mary said.

They were standing near the moving van, where, in leisurely fashion, several men had gone to work. One of them shouted. They stepped aside as three stout ropes were lowered from a window above. Dangling in the winter air the heavy twisted ropes made a vaguely sinister design, like ropes suspended from a gibbet. But Mary was looking curiously at the soldier.

"You ought to go to Canada sometime. Tell your husband it's a nice place to visit," he said, with a kind of strange insistence. His shifty eyes gazed briefly into hers, and then they fell. His tone flattened. "I wonder— have you got a match?"

There was a packet of matches in her apron pocket. She gave them to him, suddenly glad to close the conversation. As she was hurrying into the lobby, anxious to avoid Mrs. Bentley's lifted eyebrows—Mrs. Bentley believed that all real ladies lived on private incomes and wore clean white gloves in public—Mary glanced back. The Canadian soldier was still standing at the curb, and he wasn't smoking. She saw him fold up the paper packet and put it in his pocket. He'd asked for the matches to get rid of her, when at first he had wanted to keep her talking. Curious. She shrugged the incident away. But when she was in the elevator she glanced at the ration books. Her eyes opened. Her name and Paul's name and both their ages were printed on the pasteboard covers, but Paul's profession wasn't indicated.

TWO

Mary heard the telephone ringing in the living room as she left the elevator. Paul was probably in the shower. She began to run. But Paul was on the phone when she went in, and waving her to silence. His expression told the news. Word from Max!

A cable filed in Reykjavik on Thursday, the day Max had surrendered his Clipper ticket, and delayed in transit, had just come in. Paul had written out a copy of the message and was checking back with the operator. She could hardly contain herself until he hung up.

"Well?"

Without comment he handed her the scribbled sheet. He watched for her reaction. Her eyes raced through the words.

MY SEVENTEENTH LETTER IN THE MAIL
BE UNDERSTANDING, MY FRIENDS.
                    MAX ICARUS FERRIS

She read the message twice. This was not an explanation. It didn't even sound like Max. She raised puzzled, disappointed eyes.

"Understanding? Why wouldn't you be understanding, if he's got in a—a jam?"

"For a smart girl, Mary, you can be extremely dense at times. Think again."

"Oh!" she cried. Realization rushed upon her. She saw the hidden meaning, the other way to read the message. Her eyes began to dance. "Oh! Oh, of course! 'Understanding' is the key word."

"Be smart, my friends, is what Max means," Paul said, smiling at her delight. "For God's sake, be smart, my friends, when you get my seventeenth letter. Pay attention; don't overlook the tiniest clue. Max is going to tell us what he's got himself involved in, what kept him from coming home. In his seventeenth letter he's gone ahead and tried to write around the censors. But you've missed a second key word, dear."

"Where?"

"You didn't notice Max's signature," he said.

They had moved on into the bedroom, and she was seated at her dressing table. She looked down again. Max Icarus Ferris. She frowned. Max had no middle name. Why choose such an extraordinary one to complete the message? Icarus?

"Icarus isn't a name at all," protested Mary.

"Indeed it is, though I'm surprised at Max's classical education. You ought to know the legend yourself; it's in all the copybooks. Don't you remember the young Greek boy who put on a pair of wax wings and went flying off to see what lay beyond the sky?"

She shook her head. "You're the scholar of the family, darling. What happened to Icarus?"

"He fell into the sea and drowned," Paul said.

Mary went a little pale. Suddenly the pleasant ordered bedroom seemed cool, the ardent morning sunshine a little dimmed, as though a breath from the Aegean, salt and chill and ancient, had entered through an open door somewhere. Terror, Mary thought confusedly, is an emotion as old as man. Had the young Greek boy's father been frightened too, as he looked across an empty ocean and upward into an empty sky, over two thousand years ago? The unknown, she told herself, is more frightening always than the known. They could trust Max in his mission, once they got the letter and learned what it was.

"You suggested he had stumbled onto a—a story, Paul. The signature may be a gag, Max's way of telling us that he's looking into something secret—beyond the sky which could mean beyond the eyes and comprehension around him.... It's the secrecy he's stressing."

"I could wish he'd hit upon a merrier signature."

Irritated at a heavy sense of foreboding in himself, irritated at the way Mary kept on staring at the words scrawled on the paper, Paul took it away from her. He crumpled the scribbled sheet, and tossed it toward the wastebasket. The paper ball landed lightly, teetering back and forth like a little ship. Mary sighed and rose. A few minutes later she brought in fresh toast and coffee from the kitchen.

"I suppose there's nothing to do but wait."

"Nothing that I can think of offhand. Reykjavik isn't exactly Kansas City. I hope Max cabled the office something sensible. J. G. was pretty sore."

At that moment a heavy object bumped the ceiling overhead. The electric light cord in the bedroom swayed gently. Startled, Paul put down his coffee cup and looked up.

"People moving in upstairs," supplied Mary. At his look of surprise, she smiled. "I saw the van downstairs. I hope they're nice. The air raid meetings have made us all so clubby."

Another dull thud shook the ceiling. "It sounds as though they've brought along a herd of elephants."

"That would be the piano," said Mary absently. All at once she remembered something. "Oh, I meant to tell you. I met a soldier and …"

Mary's street adventures usually amused him. But he was thinking of something else. His mind had never left the main problem—the puzzle of Max.

"Look," he said, "if the letter was mailed last Thursday, at the same time Max filed the cable, and came by air …"

The Clipper had left Reykjavik the following Tuesday. The Clipper had arrived in port the day before. Simultaneously the thought struck them both. In a moment that was like one of those moments in a dream where everything falls into place with a beautiful, unearthly logic, with an almost supernatural precision, Paul and Mary heard their doorbell tinkle. Mrs. Bentley had sent up the elevator boy with the morning mail.

In one wild rush they reached the door. Max's seventeenth letter looked like all the others—fat and bulky, scarred by travel. His familiar handwriting raced across the envelope with vital energy, the number scrawled beneath the canceled airmail stamps was bold and definite. Seventeen—the very figure was like a promise. But as Paul closed the door on the grinning elevator boy, Mary suddenly held out the envelope, loathe to open it.

"It's addressed to you."

"That hasn't stopped you in the past," Paul began, and broke off in the middle of an old joke of theirs.

In silence he took the envelope. For a moment, he, too, felt the same curious sense of reluctance to proceed, as though the letter had come too quickly and was too simple, as though it wouldn't be the answer to the problem after all. He shook off the feeling, stepped to the desk and picked up the letter opener.

Very precisely he slit the envelope, moving the knife along the gummed transparent tape which closed the ragged opening made by the censor. The tape gave easily. The sheets of paper crowded inside, tightly creased together, formed a compact parcel.

Paul smoothed the pages flat. The inside page, which should have been the beginning of the letter, was blank. With unsteady fingers, he cast the blank page aside. The second page was also blank. As he snatched for the third page something creased between the folded sheets slipped to the floor—a glossy little booklet.

Max had written nothing—not so much as a single word. There was no letter. The envelope contained eight blank pages of paper. Eight blank pages of paper—and the booklet lying on the floor.

THREE

Bumping heads, Paul and Mary stooped for the booklet. He rescued and laid it flat upon the desk. With a mixture of amazement and disappointment, they saw what the booklet was. It was a theatre program—a theatre program nearly five months old.

On September 13th, there had appeared at the Princess Royal Theatre a revival of Henrik Ibsen's *The Wild Duck*. It was quite an ordinary program. The cast of characters, twenty-three people, were listed conventionally in the order of their appearance. Paul and Mary ran quickly down the list of names. Max had mentioned none of these people in his previous letters, long letters where he had taken the trouble to write in detail of his fishermen landlords and had spent paragraphs upon the brief pathetic history of the other lodger.

Because the Strongs had joyfully accepted the passes that came their way and liked a poor show better than none, they were well acquainted with the theatre. No member of this company was in the least familiar. The star of the production was a stranger to them. They had never heard of her.

There was a photograph of her on the cover—a dark woman with a haggard, lovely face, wearing a heavy hat that cascaded ostrich plumes. She wore a white-fox fur wrapped around her long, slender neck. Her name was Lisa Tennevant and she was costumed for the role of Gina. On the following page a tiny note announced that Madame des Brizac of 27 Queen Street had dressed the ladies of the cast, that Alexander Campbell of Marbury Lane had done the company's printing, and that Frome & Frome of 199 Archer Place had generously lent the furniture used in the first and third acts.

"Be understanding," Paul said with a short laugh. "I must say Max puts a lot of trust in us. He expects outright genius. Unless ..."

He leafed quickly through the program, looking for the lightest pencil mark, any sign or clue Max might have left for them. There was nothing.

"Invisible ink?" Mary suggested hopefully. "Where would Max get a supply of invisible ink? No, my darling."

"Why a theatre program anyhow?" demanded Mary, puzzled on another score. "Max detests the theatre. We could never drag him to a show."

"Max wasn't wrestling with Ibsen on the 13th of last September."

Paul reached toward the letters lying on the desk, found the one he wanted, found the proper date. "On the 13th of September, he was on the water, headed for Murmansk."

Paul picked up the program again, and looked at it. His eyes and fingers told him something. The program was crisp and clean. Obviously no theatregoer had crumpled it or handled it five months before.

"I wonder if there is a Princess Royal Theatre in Reykjavik," he said slowly. "I can probably find out that today from our research department. Those girls eat up work. I can also have the cast looked into. This is going to take time, Mary."

Rising, he stuffed the program in his pocket. As he reached for his wallet, his hand brushed the scattered envelopes. He started to replace them, and then didn't.

"You might run through the letters we've had from Iceland, if you have a chance. Don't bother looking for anything connected with the cable or"—Paul grinned wryly—"with the communication we just received. It won't be there."

"What am I to look for?"

"Start fresh. Try to feel the way Max was feeling when he sat down in Reykjavik and wrote us; try to think what he's been thinking these last six weeks. You'd rather read between the lines than on them anyhow. The only unusual thing I recall is …"

"The other lodger," Mary said at once. "I mean to concentrate on him."

"Do."

Paul then kissed her hurriedly, grabbed his hat and coat and rushed uptown, as though belatedly he was glad it was press day and other things would necessarily occupy his mind. Left to herself, Mary slowly sorted out the letters they had received from Iceland, pushed the others back into the pigeonhole. Sighing, she pulled out a chair.

And then on sudden impulse, she slipped on her coat, tucked the letters in her purse, and left the apartment. It was a wonderful day, far too fine to spend indoors. She would do her reading in the park.

She walked down the service stairs from old experience. In their apartment house it saved time in the long run. On the stairs she met with a distraction—a tall young man climbing up. In her preoccupation she wouldn't have given him a second glance if he'd looked like a canvasser, but most visitors and tenants mulishly waited for the elevator. Obviously he wasn't a salesman who had escaped the myopic doorman; he was much too self-assured. She would have guessed him at her own age or even a little younger, except that something about his complete self-possession made him seem more mature, as though he'd been brought up in an older society. His hair was red and thick, his eyes a pale shining brown. He climbed swiftly, with the easy grace of an athlete. On the whole the effect was quite attractive, decided Mary vaguely, and then became aware of how she was staring.

The young man had noticed, and looked secretly amused. Embarrassed, she dropped her eyes and nearly lost her balance. To her annoyance the stranger cleared the intervening distance, and caught her by the elbow.

"Thank you," she said politely, and gently disengaged her elbow.

"You live here, madame?" he said inquiringly, slowly, as though he found the language difficult. All signs of haste had left him. "I'm afraid I've lost my way. Please, you can direct me?"

His voice, with the vague, indefinable foreign accent, was soft and pleasant. It was also a trifle overfriendly. He had a good opinion of himself, Mary thought, still inwardly annoyed with herself.

"I look for the manager, madame? Where is he?"

Mary stared. Mrs. Bentley's office was directly beside the apartment entrance, was marked plainly, and if the young man had passed through the lobby he could scarcely have missed the sign. She hesitated. She didn't especially want his company down the stairs.

"We just move in," the young man said, "my mother and I. We stay in Milwaukee that is in Wisconsin, and now we three move to your beautiful city of New York."

Three? thought Mary.

"My mother is unwell," he said obligingly, and exactly as though he had read the question in her mind. "She has trouble with the heart. We travel here with her nurse."

So this was the new tenant. Ordinarily Mary would have said something friendly to any newcomer to the house, but she felt she'd done enough to welcome this young man already. For a stranger he was a shade overeager and expansive, a bit too ready to put himself on familiar terms. She had a vague impression that his English could have been less stilted had he chosen to make it so. Some foreigners cling to a charming accent. His nationality was difficult to place.

"You may find Mrs. Bentley in the carpenter's shop," she said at last, ignoring the fact that this was most unlikely. "It's on the roof. Twelve floors. I'd really advise the elevator."

"I like the exercise," the young man said, softly and pleasantly. The steady gaze of his pale-brown eyes—they were almost the color of sweet champagne—was disconcerting. The eyes looked very much amused now, as though he guessed she'd deliberately withheld any mention of the office in the lobby, and knew why.

"It's good you don't mind the climb," said Mary crisply, definitely. "Our service is inclined to be erratic; the boys are always going off to join the Army. I hope you and your mother find your new home comfortable."

"Thank you, madame."

Mary passed him then, and quickly went on down. She was too proud to look back, but she had an uncomfortable feeling that he waited on the landing, watching until she disappeared from sight. With relief, she reached the lobby. There she glimpsed Mrs. Bentley, a fat, fussy, perpetually worried woman in charge of an apartment house not so smart or well-staffed as it once was. Mrs. Bentley was just turning into her office. A pang of conscience smote Mary.

"Your new tenant is looking for you, Mrs. Bentley. I sent him to the carpenter's shop—a young redhaired man—I passed him on the stairs."

"I'll go right up," said the manager and bustled forth immediately, headed for the elevator. She then recalled perhaps that she hadn't always rushed to do the bidding of other tenants. Hadn't the Strongs complained several times of a leaky tap? Mrs. Bentley colored slightly, said confusedly, "The Van Andas are such lovely people, Mrs. Strong, a real privilege to have them with us. The mother isn't well. I particularly want to make her and her son happy in their stay; after their misfortunes I do feel the Van Andas deserve a real home. Refugees, you know, Dutch people driven out of Holland by the Nazis."

So the accent was Dutch. Mary recalled the piano, the five-room apartment, the private nurse, young Mr. Van Anda's well-cut suit. She reserved her sympathy.

"Of course, and this is strictly between you and I," said Mrs. Bentley, and dropped her voice in the confidential way that Paul loved to mimic, "I understand that the Van Andas had considerable holdings elsewhere. Indeed I believe the mother, widowed, poor thing, was visiting in this country at the time Holland was invaded. But the son—Hans Van Anda—made a thrilling escape from Rotterdam only recently. A real adventure story. He was a diamond merchant, and of course lost everything. Did you notice that ring of his?"

"He was wearing gloves," Mary said dryly.

"Enormous, my dear, the most enormous stone I ever saw," cried Mrs. Bentley with enthusiasm, and swept toward the elevator.

Mary had noticed the van before, but paid it small attention. Now, as she stepped outside, she gazed curiously in that direction. She frowned and looked again. And then she had a private giggle. If Mrs. Bentley made a careful inspection of the Van Andas' furniture, her snobbish, money-loving soul was due a shock. Possibly the Dutch family had once had considerable holdings outside Holland, but such funds weren't inexhaustible. The furniture, half unloaded on the sidewalk, was all spanking new. But it had been acquired at Gerbers on 14th Street. Gerbers sold the fanciest suites on the installment plan, with the pious hope that the glue and veneer would hold until the final payment was collected.

Quite illogically, Mary warmed to the Van Andas. To her disposition the sketchiness of their financing made a successful bid for sympathy. After all, it wasn't easy to be a refugee, living in a foreign land, putting up a show, impressing people like Mrs. Bentley. Maybe conceit and the enormous diamond were all the young man had left.

She crossed the street and forgot the new tenants—their dubious accents and expensive clothes, their cheap installment furniture. The furtive little soldier had already slipped from her mind—or almost.

In the park it was her usual habit to shop around for a bench that offered the promise of interesting company. This morning she withdrew herself from the Fifth Avenue nursemaids, the Bleecker Street Italian mothers, the children and scooters and baby buggies on the west side of the park.

Mary moved purposefully across the plaza to the deserted east side. She selected a sunny bench, sat down and took out Max's letters. She had the gift of concentration; almost without effort, as she read, she forgot she was in New York and made a swift journey to Iceland.

She cast aside the descriptions of Reykjavik, the bustling, modern city, with its crowded harbor outlined with submarine nets and mine fields, jammed with the variegated shipping of the world. She ignored the paragraphs dealing with casual contacts and casual people. The first letter from Iceland was of no use to her. But in the second letter, the one marked 15 on the envelope, Max told the story of the other lodger as his landlords had told it to him.

The silent, blank-eyed youth was a fixture at the Thorgsens' when Max took up his own temporary residence there. The boy was one of the derelicts of U-boat warfare, one of the bits of human scrap and waste undignified by mention on any casualty list. For many months, quiet and unprotesting, he had lain in bed at the fishermen's home. To the Thorgsens he owed his life, but he showed no gratitude or feeling of any kind. He seldom moved and never spoke. If he suffered, no one knew.

On a bitter autumn day in that region where winter was never distant, far out at sea the Thorgsens had come upon a drifting, shrapnel-scarred lifeboat. It was swamping fast. Stark naked, the single passenger was rolled up in a filthy, oil-stained tarpaulin, doing nothing to aid himself and quite indifferent to rescue. He lay at the bottom of the swamping boat, gnawing ravenously at a putrid fish head. The boy was a hospital case, a mental case, but in Iceland the hospitals were overcrowded too. Uncomplainingly the fishermen had carried home their human catch and tended him as best they could.

No one knew the boy's name or rank, or where those were who wept for him. Those who had shared the battered lifeboat with him, if any had, were dead and buried in the sea. The Thorgsens had copied down and reported the lettering on the splintered stern. It spelled out the name of a Norwegian merchant ship torpedoed in the North Atlantic many days before, a merchant ship that had left behind no survivors except the blond-haired, blank-eyed boy. By some miracle he had drifted several hundred miles without food and with a single tin of water; by some miracle he had not succumbed to freezing cold. He had come through alive, but somewhere on the gray bleak wastes of the Atlantic he had left his mind.

Mary sighed and picked up the last letter. Max had written at length about his fishermen landlords. She almost felt she knew them. Intent and absorbed, she read:

"… Old Thorgsen's got a birch tree planted in his garden that he's as proud of, Mary, as you used to be of that gardenia bush of yours. Trees up here grow only five or six feet tall. The birch is his second pride. The real apple of his eye is his boat—a two-motor job that he keeps tied up in spitting distance of the house. I can see her from my window. She is a little beauty named for the old man's dead wife. The *Irma*, to you. I won't burden you or me with the Icelandic.

"Every day old Thorgsen and Ivar, that's the son, go sailing out to sea as blithely as if those bobbing things that break loose occasionally were rose petals. Thorgsen's a great old guy, a brand-new type to me; these Danes don't shoot off their mouths like us. I was here a week before I heard the history of the other lodger. That gives you a rough idea how chatty my landlords are. Generally they're both so dead beat they fall asleep right after supper. I'll have no old Norse sagas to report.

"Yesterday, as a great honor, the old man asked me would I enjoy to go fishing too, could maybe get some pictures, and quick I had to remember my old *mal de mer*. Pretty as the *Irma* is, the day I step aboard her and go scooting off through floating dynamite on the chance of photographing fish, you'll know I'm as nuts as the poor kid in the next room.

"I wish you two could meet the kid. For my money, he's the fascinating party in the setup, pitiful as he is. Hair as yellow as butter, the curly kind some mother used to love, a healthy, strong-looking kid with those big eyes that watch the ceiling or move toward the door when food is coming in. Grub's the only thing that rouses him. He never speaks and never seems to hear anything except the old dinner bell. He eats ravenously, as though he'd never get his fill, as though each crust of bread might be the last on earth. Otherwise he doesn't move at all. Shell shock, they called it in the last war. They'll have to invent a definition for this war to cover those that get too big a dose of brutal suffering and horror and just shut up shop. I keep wondering what this kid thinks about as he looks at the ceiling, what he sees. Six or seven men probably started in the lifeboat with him, but when the Thorgsens found him he was alone...."

Fascinating? Max had used the word fascinating in connection with the boy. The old Max loved puzzles, and this was the puzzle of a lost and derelict human being. But was it sensible that Max would upset his life, seriously inconvenience his employers, bewilder and distress his friends to solve the problem of a total stranger? Anyhow, if that really were the case, he wouldn't need to hide his intent behind a baffling cable, a more baffling theatre program. Or would he? Intensely concentrated and absorbed, Mary felt that she was groping toward something.

She started when someone spoke from the bench beside her. She turned, relaxed. It was one of the park characters, Professor Throckmorten, who came every noon from N.Y.U. to feed the pigeons. He wasn't a professor, really, he was just one of the janitors, but he had acquired what he fancied was a professorial vocabulary.

"Ah, my dear," he said, "on such a beautiful day, and with those orbs of lovely blue, it's a pity not to use them on a gracious world like ours. Or even on my pigeons. Work is always waiting. But then"—he sighed —"I take it you are one of our students."

"No," said Mary gently, as she had told him many times before. "Don't you remember? I'm Mrs. Strong. You've met my husband. He helped you feed the pigeons last Sunday."

"Of course, of course." The Professor reached into his paper bag, and threw out a handful of stale bread. The fluttering pigeons came surging down around them, settling in clouds upon the sidewalk, upon the bench.

Mary reached out to gather in her letters. The Professor had glimpsed the canceled envelopes, the foreign stamps. With a pigeon on either shoulder and two in his lap, his face suddenly became grave and sad.

"Forgive me, my dear. I am an old man. Sometimes I forget that ours is not a gracious world. A relative of yours?"

"A friend."

"A dear friend it must be that you come to the park to read his letters."

Mary bit her lip. The Professor was a dear old soul, but his wits were not precisely trustworthy and his inferences could be embarrassing.

"It's not quite like that," she said. "He is a dear friend of ours, but I was rereading the letters because …"

"Yes?" The old eyes lit with flattered interest. She had his whole attention.

"We have a feeling, Mr. Throckmorten, my husband and I, that our friend is finding it hard to tell us something about a piece of work he is doing. Now do you understand?"

The Professor caressed one of the pigeons in his lap, then tossed it in the air to fly free, and stooped to lift another. Slowly he shook his head. Suddenly it became important to Mary that he grasp her meaning.

"You've heard of the censorship that makes it difficult for news to come through."

"I was thinking of my landlady's son, Mrs. Strong. I have no son myself. My landlady's son, like your friend, is far away."

"Yes," said Mary, trying hard to follow.

"I know the boy well, as well as you know your friend. He writes his mother often, and she too complains about the letters. Yet if Tim were asked, he would get down on his knees and thank God for the censorship which spares them both."

Mary opened her mouth to speak. But the Professor had the last word.

"If the boy were going into danger, my dear, his mother is the very last that he would want to know."

A cold finger seemed to touch Mary's heart. For the second time that day she thought of Max and—danger.

FOUR

It was late afternoon before Mary returned to the apartment. Thoroughly demoralized in her usual schedule, she had spent the whole day outdoors. She hadn't even carried out the breakfast dishes yet, or made the bed. She rushed through the living room first, skipping the vacuum and making short work of the dusting.

But Paul was usually late on Fridays, and in the bedroom she went more slowly and thoroughly. She liked the bedroom better anyway. They spent more time there, thought Mary, and laughed when she caught her own reflection in the mirror. All alone as she was, she was actually blushing. She'd tell Paul that sometime.

After she used the carpet sweeper and plumped the pillows—the hard one for Paul, the soft one for herself—and got the bed made up, and cleaned the dressing table glass of powder and a smear of lipstick, and washed the window sills, the chaise longue that was her birthday present did look inviting. Accomplishing nothing that day, she still felt tired and more low in her mind than she cared to admit.

She deliberately shook herself free of a depression that was baseless after all. Some small unpleasant task generally improved her morale. She heartily disliked emptying the carpet sweeper.

With the carpet sweeper in her hand, Mary briskly approached the wastebasket beside the desk. She pressed the release that opened the sweeper pans, and then suddenly she frowned and let the release snap back in place. Slowly she put down the sweeper. Her memory for detail was excellent. Why did something seem to be amiss about the wastebasket—different? Since morning the painted tin container seemed vaguely changed, as though something she expected to see was missing.

Leaning on the sweeper, Mary stood reflectively and studied the jumbled contents of the wastebasket—the cigarette butts, the litter of her cleansing tissues, the discarded morning paper. And then she remembered. Paul had crumpled and tossed into the basket his copy of the cable from Max. The crumpled yellow sheet of paper should be perched on top. It was gone. But that was impossible. It must have slipped to the bottom of the basket.

Feeling foolish, rather like a woman who goes back three times to be sure that her door is locked, and distinctly glad Paul wasn't present, Mary removed the newspaper and shook it vigorously. Nothing was caught inside the folds. Again she hesitated, the victim of a compulsion too strong to be denied. There was one way to be sure. Quickly, in almost guilty haste, she spread the newspaper on the floor and upended the basket. She was positive she'd find the yellow sheet hidden somewhere in the debris. It wasn't there. What had become of it?

The copy of Max's cable had no value. Yet while she was absent in the park it had vanished from the wastebasket. Mary looked around the pleasant, orderly bedroom that smelled faintly of tobacco and cologne.

Moving like a dreamer, she turned and lowered the breakfront of the desk. She was then quite sure. The letters from Max, all of them, except those she'd carried to the park, were gone. The pigeonhole was empty.

On the street below a taxi horn squawked and a truck rumbled by. And then from overhead Mary heard the sound of pounding, and, nearby, the gurgle of the hot water pipe in the bathroom. The Van Andas were putting up their pictures, and someone in the fifth-floor bath directly above their own had just turned on the tap.

Like a conspirator, walking on tiptoe, Mary stole into her own bathroom. As her tiptoed steps left the tiles and sank into the mat, abruptly the hot-water pipe stopped gurgling. The tap had been turned off. Someone on the floor above was standing at a chrome-and-porcelain basin exactly like their own. Mary knelt beside the basin, and cautiously leaned nearer to the pipe until her ear was almost touching it. She could feel the warmth against her cheek.

Overhead and down the pipe came the sound of splashing, a nail brush clattered against porcelain. The continued thump of the hammer sounded in the further distance. And then distinctly, as though he spoke directly into her ear, she heard Hans Van Anda's voice. She could almost see him standing at the basin, with his mop of thick red hair, his shirt sleeves rolled to the elbow, splashing water on his strong brown arms, and turning to call through a hall open door into another room.

"Lotte, can't you stop Mamma putting up the pictures? Personally, I think we've done enough to furnish. Americans are an amazing people."

The other voice was too far away to be caught and amplified by the water pipe. Again the pipe began to gurgle, as the water drained from the bowl. In the bathroom above footsteps crossed the tiles, a door banged and that was all.

Mary didn't rise until her heart had resumed its normal beat. Without difficulty she had identified Hans Van Anda's voice, though it had lost the accent that made it charming. The vanished accent did not surprise her. It seemed rather odd that the young man felt he'd done enough to furnish. It seemed odd that his use of English idiom was so excellent. It seemed odd that a woman with a weak heart should be hanging pictures, with a strong son near at hand. But the oddest think of all was Mary's instant, unshakable conviction that one of three people had entered the Strong's apartment, taken the copy of the cable from the wastebasket, emptied the pigeonhole of Max's letters—one of three people, Hans Van Anda, his mother's nurse or his mother.

The conviction and the pure fury that went with it carried her through the bedroom to the telephone. Once there, with her hand on the receiver, she perceived the awkwardness of reporting such a story to Mrs. Bentley. This wasn't a matter of complaining about a cockroach, or demanding the services of the plumber. Intuition wasn't evidence. The irrelevant thought came to her that Hans Van Anda had worn gloves when he passed her on the service stairs that morning. How had he got in? She knew she had locked the apartment. Slowly her anger died, and she felt the first cold touch of fear. Her fingers tightened on the receiver.

And then the telephone rang sharply. It was Paul. "Heavens, darling, you must have been sitting on the phone!"

"I was about to call ..."

"Me?" he said, and, without waiting for a reply, rushed ahead. "I've been trying to reach you all afternoon, but you were busy gadding. You hausfraus do lead soft lives."

"Paul ..."

"We've got to make this quick. Why don't you put on a long dress, dear, and come uptown and we'll eat here? I've had hell's own day, and will feel like celebrating when it's over. I spent my lunch hour in—in the library."

Through the sudden caution in his voice, she heard the clatter of typewriters. He was calling from his desk and didn't want to start a chain of office gossip concerning Max.

"Good results?" she asked, wondering what Paul had discovered about the theatre program. He had discovered something.

"I'll tell you later. The 57th Street Longchamps at eight o'clock, and do try to make it."

Very quickly he hung up.

Not until she replaced her own receiver did she realize that she had told him nothing about the new tenants in the house. Abruptly she became aware that the pounding had stopped. Everything was very quiet.

Opening directly into the living room where she stood, was the small apartment entrance, a foyer more by courtesy than in fact. A mirror placed above a narrow bookcase reflected the outside door. In a sudden access of nerves, as quickly as though someone had knocked, Mary went to the door. Being friendly, unsuspicious people, the Strongs almost never used the peephole. With quick, slightly tremulous fingers, Mary dropped the round metal disc, stood on tiptoe and peeped out.

Across the angle of the outside hall, a flurry of movement caught her eye. The door to the service stairs was just closing. Without thought or plan, she darted into the hall and ran lightly to the service stairs. She pushed aside the heavy door and looked down and then up. A floor above another heavy door was softly closing. The long, uncarpeted flight of stairs was empty.

Mary returned to her own apartment. For a moment, pausing in the hall, she inspected the door, half expecting to find scratches around the lock, minute splinters. There was nothing. The door had been freshly painted in the spring, and the painted surface was unmarred. The door, then, had not been tampered with. She stepped inside. But before she went to dress, she took a precaution that never in her life had occurred to her before. She put on the chain.

When Paul specified eight o'clock on press day, he often meant half past eight. Mary armed herself with the evening papers before she got the subway. For once Paul himself was early. He got up a little wearily as she walked into the restaurant, and then he smiled at the bundle of newspapers that made such an oddly practical accessory to her sweeping dress.

"I see you didn't trust me. It looks rather quiet inside." He glanced through an archway toward the dining room, and back at his pretty wife. "Would you rather go for a gayer, louder supper spot? I've got to run back to the office a minute afterwards."

"We're here," Mary said, content. Paul pretended he liked gay and noisy night spots because she sometimes did. "I'm dying for a martini. I scent you've had one already."

"Two, Mrs. Sherlock. Here let me take your bundles, madame, and we'll make a more impressive entrance."

They moved into the spacious, dimly lighted dining room and their favorite waiter swooped on them and led them to their favorite table. Usually, while Paul was ordering, Mary amused herself by inspecting the dining room in search of other couples as good looking as themselves. It was a game Max had begun, only then they had searched for threesomes and got into arguments. Max's notions of beauty were unconventional. Indeed to protect himself from the Strongs' spirited attack on an occasion when he chose a long-necked greenish-colored woman of thirty-five in preference to Mary, and selected a rat-faced, gold-toothed scoundrel as a beauty compared to Paul, Max had invented a variant of the game which he called "twenty-one." According to Max one person in twenty-one had a striking face, memorable, out of the ordinary, suited perfectly to the camera. "You Strongs aren't photogenic. Even Mary isn't, except to sell soap flakes, maybe, while Paul sells the medium-priced car, when there were medium-priced cars. You're too damn normal!"

Tonight Mary was too intent and preoccupied to play any game. Her own story was going to need careful telling. She was anxious that Paul talk first. He was more than willing. Directly the waiter came and went, he pulled out the theatre program and tossed it across to her.

"I found out several things today, Mary, and decided others. I'll take them in order. There is no Princess Royal Theatre in Reykjavik or anywhere in Iceland—there's something to begin with. The research department checked with the Icelandic Minister in Washington. Now I'll throw in a guess. The city where the theatre is located—even with the street addresses, Archer Place and Marbury Lane and 27 Queen, to work on—is going to be extremely hard to find. But I'll bet right now it will be an easier job than tracking down this talented company."

"Why?"

"Because they're not talented enough. Look at that cast again, Mary. We should have guessed it this morning."

Mary picked up the theatre program. She studied the column that listed the members of the cast who had appeared five months before in *The Wild Duck.* The names were as anonymous, as meaningless, it seemed to her, as a row of names listed in a city directory. Madame des Brizac who had done the costuming suggested nothing to her mind, nor did Alexander Campbell, the printer, or Frome & Frome, who had kindly lent the furniture. And then she understood.

"They're amateurs! It's an amateur company!"

"Of course! Professionals don't borrow furniture. Madame des Brizac, the Queen Street sempstress, is probably still waiting for her pay or else she took it out in advertising. I'll stake my life the company still owes the printer. They are glorious amateurs every one, except of course for—her. She *used* to be a professional."

Paul reached out and turned the program to the cover. Mary looked again at the haggard, lovely face of Lisa Tennevant. It was a strange face, with a curious quality of disillusionment and weariness caught expertly by the camera. The woman wore her plumed hat aslant her sad dark eyes as though the unbecoming angle didn't matter much to her. Beneath the photograph was a printed caption—the picture had been taken in 1932 by I. Sohnne of Vienna when Lisa Tennevant was a member of the Royal Theatre of Austria.

"Vienna, Mary. The graveyard of careers, theatrical and otherwise. The Royal Theatre of Austria closed its doors on the day the Nazis came. That was easy to find out from the clips. The company disbanded, and on March 11, 1938—the day of Anschluss—the actors started for the nearest border. Lisa Tennevant was among them. What's happened to her since, where she is now, how she got tangled with the amateurs, is anybody's guess. It's by no means certain that she's in Reykjavik. But she's the key to the puzzle all the same."

Mary looked from the picture to him.

"Lisa Tennevant is Max's message to you and me. All the message there is. I hunted an hour myself. I can show you in a minute."

Carefully Paul adjusted the rosy-colored lamp that bloomed on the table between them. He tilted the shade, took the program from her, and tipped it carefully. At first she saw nothing except the picture shining in the light and Lisa Tennevant's large dark eyes looking mournfully upon a world that was dark. Paul tipped the program a little more; the glossy page shifted to a slightly different angle, exactly the proper angle.

A pin had lightly scratched the glaze of the glossy paper. The pin had made three tiny dots, and from the dots ran a tiny horizontal bar. The whole formed a minute arrow; the three dots were the arrowhead, the bar represented the shaft. The pin-scratched arrow was in the margin. It pointed straight at Lisa Tennevant.

"This woman knows what Max is doing, or knows—something. The signal's plain enough, if nothing else is plain at all. Max wanted us to know about her. But what interests me is why he wanted us to know so little."

They were silent, as the waiter came again and brought their food. Paul's face was dark and anxious, when finally he leaned across the table.

"Mary, tell me. Is your answer the same as mine?"

"I don't know, Paul." Involuntarily her mind returned to the conversation on the park bench. Her eyes grew darker.

"Max never did intend to tell us what he is doing, Mary. Too dangerous, too risky. He didn't want us worried. But he did want us to be prepared in case his own plans go wrong. In case of trouble, we have the clue. The name of Lisa Tennevant."

It was then that Mary made a connection of her own. She began to tremble.

"Suppose there are things Max doesn't realize. We're not the only ones interested in his affairs. The new people upstairs, the Van Andas—one of them—broke in our apartment today and stole all his letters except those I had with me in the park. They even took your copy of his cable from the wastebasket."

"Broke in the apartment! Someone broke in the apartment! Well, for God's sake, Mary …!"

"Maybe they didn't exactly break in. I'm not sure how that part was managed," and Mary launched into her story.

"Keep your voice down, dear," Paul said suddenly. "You've picked up an admirer in the corner. A tall, redhaired chap who ought to be attending to his family duties is looking over here."

It couldn't be possible! Mary dropped her napkin on the floor. In what might have been only a rather clumsy effort to recapture it, she managed to push it farther underneath her chair. She turned her head. Five tables away, in the shadowed corner, sat Hans Van Anda with his mother and her nurse.

FIVE

Mary brought up the napkin, congratulating herself that she had contrived to avoid Van Anda's eye. She opened her mouth to speak. Almost imperceptibly, Paul shook his head. He was looking casually, incuriously, across her shoulder.

"Get set, darling," his lips framed the words. And then in a natural, slightly lifted voice, he said, "Then you vote for brandy, and damn the expense?"

"You told me once"—her voice was casual too—"that while there was brandy in the world, I could have a pony in my coffee, while there was coffee."

The surprise in her eyes was quite perfect, when Hans Van Anda reached their table. Van Anda's delighted surprise was a match for hers. He sounded boyish and natural.

"I think I recognize you, Mrs. Strong, when you loose the napkin. What an unexpected pleasure!"

"This is my husband," Mary said, taking mental note of the recovery of that vanished accent. Where she should have spoken Van Anda's name, she gave a little shrug of apology and let her voice rise inquiringly. Her eyes, wide and candid, hid inward worry. Had he overheard their conversation, the suspicions she was passing on to Paul? Was he secretly amused at her pretense that she scarcely recalled his existence? Apparently not.

"Van Anda," he said easily, filling in the tiny pause. "Hans Van Anda. A difficult name for Americans to remember. Yours, as I was telling our Mrs. Bentley, are simple for us."

Mary almost admired his adroitness. He was satisfying any curiosity of hers as how he came to be in possession of their name. How natural for Mrs. Bentley, who chattered of everything, to identify the young woman tenant he described as meeting on the stairs. It might even be interpreted as a graceful compliment, a way of saying the newcomer to the house had been interested enough to inquire.

"Don't let me keep you standing, Mr. Strong. Unless ..." Van Anda paused, and with charming diffidence glanced back toward his own table. It was easy, thought Mary, to identify the nurse. The tall, black-haired, flat-chested woman with the face like an unpleasant horse must be Lotte. She was not in uniform, but the set of her backbone and her stiff officiousness took the place of one. Shadowed by her grim companion, the plump, bejeweled patient seemed smaller than she actually was, the high colors of her velvet gown more subdued. Van Anda was saying to Paul, "My mother, I shall explain, has few acquaintances in New York. I was hoping—if this is not an imposition— you and your wife might make her feel less strange, less lonely, and join us for your brandy."

That was certainly cool enough. Paul and Mary exchanged a glance. If this young man had entered their apartment without invitation, and gone away with Max's letters, it was going to be hard to prove.

"I am sorry," Paul began coldly.

At this point Frau Van Anda's loneliness evidently became insupportable. Abruptly she deserted her companion. On short pattering feet—the little woman was shaped exactly like an old-fashioned dinner bell—she joined them. Her hair was red, like her son's, though streaked with gray, diamonds sparkled at her small, fat wrists and fat bosom, and her round face beamed with pleasure. She was a very healthy-looking invalid.

"Are these our new friends, son?" she demanded eagerly. "The people downstairs? I am so very happy to meet others in the house. Will you believe me, Mrs. Strong? I cry my eyes off when we leave Milwaukee, thinking the great city of New York to be filled up with only strangers."

In a quick, spontaneous gesture she laid a fat, diamond-encrusted hand on Mary's wrist. Paul suppressed a start of genuine surprise. Frau Van Anda's type was familiar to him; women like her were his mother's neighbors back in Iowa, dropping in to call on the sick, sewing for the new babies, smalltown women who loved the whole world without reservation and expected to be loved in return. As sure of her welcome as one of these, Frau Van Anda looked anxiously for a vacant chair.

The third chair at the table was piled high with wraps and Mary's purse and newspapers. Cursing himself for a sentimentalist, Paul cleared the chair. And then, as he stepped back with both arms full, he saw that the theatre program was still lying on the tablecloth. Frau Van Anda's small, sharp eyes, bright as buttons, were fixed upon it.

Hans Van Anda had turned his back to pull up another chair. The program was facing Mary, partly covered by her napkin. She was studying the distant Lotte, thankful they weren't to be favored with her company too, when she felt the small fat fingers that overlaid her own tighten convulsively. A varnished, stub-nailed thumb pressed into her palm. Mary looked up, startled, as Frau Van Anda leaned awkwardly across the table. The Dutch woman was clumsy but incredibly quick. The program disappeared from sight. Along with the napkin, Frau Van Anda pushed it from the cloth into Mary's lap. One second it was in view, the next it wasn't.

Hans Van Anda turned around. His mother was smiling placidly. Mary was less successful in concealing her own confusion. She barely grabbed the program, before it skidded to the carpet. Glancing at the table, Van Anda frowned a little.

"You've lost your napkin again, madame."

"It's in her lap, son."

"Don't you want your purse, darling?" Paul asked calmly.

"Allow me."

Hans Van Anda took the jet-and-velvet trifle from Paul and with a quick, stiff bow handed it to Mary. The movement of her hands was hidden by the table, but the crackle of paper was distinctly audible. Mary bit her lip. The program was overlong, it was difficult to fit it in her purse, but at last she managed. Hans Van Anda's pale bright eyes were expressionless. Mary glanced at his mother. Frau Van Anda looked satisfied and relieved, a little smug—like a clever cook who has solved a difficulty among the kitchen staff just as dinner is announced. Placidly she plopped into her chair.

"Please, may it be my party? I shall be honored if my neighbors will drink my brandy."

With a regal gesture, a gesture that showed the cook was rich, she summoned a hovering waiter. The waiter, new to the restaurant, was doing some wondering of his own. Life was strange and perplexing. A five-dollar tip for placing the foreign couple five tables away from people whom they knew so well and expected to join was an unexpected bonanza, but the main question was: need the bonanza be reported to the captain? Whipping out the order pad, he decided the question satisfactorily in the negative.

"Brandy. Your best," said Frau Van Anda, as one to whom the best was as natural as breathing. She had brought along the wine card from the other table, and now she inspected it. "Bring the bottle, if you please. And be quick."

As though he'd been told that the secret of social success was to discuss the other fellow's interests, Hans Van Anda launched into a skillful and well-informed discussion of American magazines. He understood Paul was with *News Review*, how admirably American it was to report the war both in type and in pictures; such a combination was virtually unknown in Europe. Odd when a European invented the camera, that Americans should carry the camera's functions to such a logical and useful conclusion. Smiling brightly, as though she approved all her handsome son's opinions, but had heard them before, the mother didn't find it necessary to listen. She satisfied herself by nodding her head admiringly. Her small hands played with the wine card, creasing and folding until she'd made a neat nervous square of it. Mary leaned forward, listening sharply. So the son was interested in news photography, was he? Any minute now he would be speaking admiringly of Max. She decided to put a stop to it. A half memory came back to her.

"Paul," she said, "what kind of a Canadian uniform has an S.S. on the collar?"

"Security Service," he said promptly. His eyes congratulated her. "Something like our home guards in peacetime, but in the Provinces they're set up for war to look after internal security. They're mostly veterans from 1914-18. You won't see that uniform outside of Canada."

"But I did this morning. Down at Washington Square."

Frau Van Anda's glass struck against her saucer. A little of the brandy splashed on the cloth. Hans Van Anda paused in the act of lighting a cigarette.

"Are you feeling unwell, Mother?"

She turned the glass in the pool of the saucer. Her hand was steady now. "It's been a trying day. Perhaps I am a little tired."

Van Anda rose immediately. Mary frowned at Paul. This was extraordinary. She hadn't expected the rout to be accomplished so easily. Nor was it. As the tall young man helped the small, fat woman to her feet, he glanced at her with a kind of teasing indulgence. He spoke.

"Has Lotte your purse, dear? We don't want to mislay the key again tonight."

Key? Paul's eyes and Mary's met. Hans Van Anda turned to them with his boyish, ingenuous smile. Something seemed to amuse him.

"To add to the general excitements of the moving, my little mother succeeds this afternoon in locking us outside of the apartment by leaving within our only key. Tomorrow we have copies made."

He hesitated as though he expected one of them to comment. Paul and Mary looked at him alertly, intently, but neither spoke. The pause lengthened.

"It was no tragedy," Van Anda said at last, with a little shrug. "I just speak to Mrs. Bentley. She provides with the loan of the—what kind of key do you call it?"

"The master key," Mary said.

Dear Lord, she prayed, let me have a poker face, a face as calm as Paul's. Lifting her half-emptied glass, she took a long, slow sip of brandy. She knew now how their apartment had been entered, knew exactly. The housebreaker had informed them. The master key opened every apartment in the building. It was Mrs. Bentley's duty to follow the master key in its wanderings, but it was plain that her regard for Hans Van Anda had caused her to neglect that duty. Smiling amiably, companionably arm in arm, the Van Andas withdrew. At the doorway the black-browed Lotte joined them. An instant later the strange trio was gone.

The moment the door closed behind them, Paul was on his feet. He shouldered into his overcoat, and held out Mary's wrap.

"Let's move on to the office, and save our talking for later. I want to cable Max about our neighbors."

The newsroom of *News Review* was as it always was on Friday night and as Mary loved it best—quiet and deserted, a place of sudden, unnatural peace after a day of storm and uproar was over. The green-shaded lamps shone down on the paper-littered floor, on rows of empty desks. Only Coles Phelps, the telegraph editor, was about. He didn't lift his elevated feet from the special-feature editor's desk, but he laid down his sandwich.

"Hello, Mary. Evening, Paul. You'll find some proof sheets lying on your desk. Personally, I no longer wonder the advertisers are leaving us in droves."

"How you talk!" said Mary. Coles was a favorite of hers. "What do you hear from your daughter in Des Moines?"

The man's thin, sour face lighted up. "The kid's doing fine, Mary. She looks awful cute in uniform. I've got some snapshots...."

But Paul had already sat down at his typewriter, frowned and rolled in a sheet of paper. It was going to be a difficult message to write. Coles Phelps raised a finger to his lips, and grinned at Mary.

"Sh, genius at work." With which he swallowed the last of his sandwich, rose with elaborate caution and tiptoed off toward the adjoining room where the teletype machines were clicking, unattended. Mary sat down to wait. Paul's typewriter began an uncertain clattering.

"Reach me my cigarettes," he said presently. "Oh, never mind, they're in my overcoat pocket."

Leaning back, he found the cigarettes. His fingers also touched a stiffly folded piece of thin smooth cardboard. Surprised, he drew it from his pocket. It was the Longchamps wine list. Some vague part of his mind recalled Frau Van Anda playing with the wine list, creasing and re-creasing it. She'd sat next the chair where the coats were piled. Absently he undid the creases. He was about to throw the thing away, when he turned it over.

In pinched, meager script, suggestive of Germanic origin, were the penciled words:

> "If you are interested, Lotte and I sail north with Captain Schott on the next voyage of the *Shalimar*.
> My dear sir, I wish you well.
>
> E. V. A."

Mary heard his exclamation, and was at his elbow. Paul spoke first.

"Go ask Coles for the key to the morgue. We'll look up the Milwaukee papers, and see if we can turn up anything on the family. I should have thought of it before. If these people are headed north, Max is going to need all the facts we can gather."

"Why tell you?"

"The Lord knows. But the good Frau is right. I *am* interested."

In the adjoining room the evening news was coming in. Long whirling rows of printed paper were spilling endlessly from machines that seemed to have solved the secret of perpetual motion. The wastebaskets were filled with news, the long tables that lined the room were heaped high with news, the floor lay deep in crackling, rustling news. And still, insatiable and restless, changing with every turn of their whirling drums, the machines clicked on, pouring out the endless cataract of tragedy and joy for someone somewhere, triumph and disaster. London and Cairo, Switzerland and Turkey, Washington and Moscow, Algiers and Tunisia, those were the variegated place names that showed on the turning drums. In this place, Mary had sometimes thought, one stood precisely at the center of the world.

And then she smiled at the grandiloquence of her own imagination. Stationed at one of the machines, Coles Phelps snorted, tore off a length of paper and handed her a tale about a Hollywood show girl who hoped to solve the meat shortage by installing a flock of sheep upon her lawn. She dropped it in the wastebasket.

"I want the morgue key, Coles."

"Hanging on the wall," he mumbled.

A good many keys were hanging there. She started to fumble among them, reflecting that newspapermen were wise to choose independent wives. In the newsroom, a telephone began ringing steadily. Paul wasn't going to answer. The steady ringing made her nervous, and she couldn't find the proper key. Apparently the label had fallen off.

She looked toward Coles. He was still standing at the teletype machine. She looked at him again.

"Coles," she said uncertainly.

Coles Phelps turned around. His thin, sour face, always unhealthy in color, was absolutely white. Clutching his middle, he swayed as though he were going to be very sick and at once. Mary started toward him.

Coles didn't speak. The teletype machines clicked noisily. All at once their incessant chatter seemed to mount until it was like machine gun fire, like the roar of cannon. The telephone in the newsroom rang steadily on. Mary reached the telegraph editor's side. She thought he was about to have a heart attack, and was badly frightened.

"Coles …"

"You'll have to tell Paul—I can't," Coles said thickly. Turning again, with one savage gesture, he ripped a ragged fragment of paper from the machine that delivered news of comedy and tragedy from everywhere. He thrust the paper into Mary's hand, as tears began to run down his face.

She read the brief dispatch from Reykjavik only once. It said:

> Max Ferris, news photographer of *News Review*, killed here late Thursday afternoon, January 26th. More to come.

The ragged scrap of paper dropped from Mary's hand. For a split second, as though shock had sharpened all her senses, she was acutely, agonizingly aware of everything around her. The green lights hurt her eyes, the chattering machines assaulted her ears. The words of the dispatch kept on repeating in her head. More to come? What more could there be to come, if Max himself was gone? He had died on the day he had surrendered his Clipper ticket, cabled them and mailed his seventeenth and final letter. But she had no interest in the details of the tragedy, no curiosity. Her sole instinct was to find escape from the fact itself.

"There's been some mistake," she whispered. "This can't be true. We won't tell Paul yet, we'll cable the Thorgsens …"

"The Thorgsens? They're gone too. There's no one left to cable, Mary.

Look."

The telegraph editor seized her hand, and drew her to the machine. Unresisting, already overwhelmed, she read the remainder of the news dispatch.

Ferris, Lars Thorgsen and son, Ivar, a fourth young man, a mental case identified only as a lodger of the Thorgsens', boarded fishing boat Irma Thursday morning on a fishing trip. Returning to the harbor late afternoon, boat was attacked by enemy submarine and sank at once. All aboard probably died instantly. Unusually heavy shell fire reported. Very little wreckage found. Search for bodies abandoned.

Mary turned then, turned from the message that offered no hope at all. The door from the newsroom was open. Paul had entered quietly, and stood behind them.

Mary walked into his arms without a word. A long time passed while they clung together in grief too deep for speech. Long after Coles had left them she heard Paul whispering.

"Damn them, damn them, damn them! This wasn't any accident, Mary. Don't you believe it! Max was afraid of something like this, he was trying to prepare us...."

"Paul ..."

"German submarines don't hunt down unarmed fishing boats and sink them without reason. They were after Max and they got him. They knew he was aboard the *Irma*, and they got him. Max found out something, and after that he didn't have a chance."

Small disjointed pictures went through his head. The time Max had lent him fifty dollars. A national convention they had covered together. Max's joy when he started off on the trip that had ended with his death.

The six weeks in Reykjavik had killed him. With time on his hands, Max had stumbled upon an—occupation. Paul was certain of that. He had no evidence with which to impress the authorities. But he had his own sure knowledge of his restless, reckless friend. Max hadn't mailed the theatre program lightly. He had meant it to be acted upon in case ...

"I'll start arrangements tonight," Paul said. "I'm going to Reykjavik, Mary. I'm going to find out exactly what it was that Max learned, why it was worth the Nazis' while to attack and sink an unarmed fishing boat. Frau Van Anda and her son fit in somewhere...."

"If Frau Van Anda and her nurse are going north themselves ..."

"I don't know why the women are headed north, but I'll know before the trip is over. I'll be sailing on the *Shalimar* myself. I'm going to finish Max's job for him. I mean to track down Lisa Tennevant and find out everything."

"Take me too," her heart said. Her stiff lips were silent.

Paul was already moving toward the telephone.

SIX

Cold wet New England snow was falling when Paul and Mary reached the waterfront. On a slippery cobbled street worn with holes and ruts until it felt like a country road, their taxi squeezed along beside a double line of street cars, disputing every inch of the way with lumbering trucks. Warehouses and marine shops and tea importers and wholesale houses in fish and wool and the spices of the Orient huddled together, or broke unexpectedly apart to reveal stretches of high steel wire fence and beyond the fence the blowing water of the harbor. Paul took out his passport for the dozenth time. In a few minutes now he would go aboard the S.S. *Shalimar*, and be on his way to Reykjavik. Looking at him, Mary knew that he was gone already, that their real farewells had been exchanged at the hotel.

They rattled across a viaduct, turned sharply. As the soot-encrusted warehouses fell stragglingly behind, the traffic on the street thickened. The trolley cars, caught in the middle, were squeezed from either side. On the right side they were crowded by trucks and trailer trucks loaded so heavily with the stuff of war that their springs almost dragged the pavement. The rattling monsters on the left, headed back toward the plants and factories which had disgorged them, were empty. In the confusion somewhere ahead, everybody's objective on this dismal snowy afternoon, was Pier Seven.

Mary rubbed a hole in the frosted window. This part of the New England city, this section of the waterfront, was given over now to the Army and the Navy. Paul's convoy would be leaving some time soon. Tonight? Tomorrow? When? There, half a block ahead, was an abandoned woolen factory converted into a barracks. That sodden sea of mud must be a parade ground. Two sailors splashed happily across it, nine years old again, not grave responsible nineteen. Workmen ran back and forth along the narrow sidewalks adding to the confusion, yelling directions, shouting instructions to each other. The sailors turned into a garish little restaurant, already brightly lighted at five o'clock, the one gay spot in the strident gloom.

Ahead and to the left were the shipping yards. A clutter of buildings, enclosed in the high steel wire, shut off any view of the pier and the harbor. Lost and hidden, blocked out by the fence and the huddled buildings, were the boats that lay clustered on the water. The top of a swinging crane high and harsh in the distance suggested the activity of longshoremen, told of a ship at anchor that was being loaded. The *Shalimar?* If she'd stopped at that office building back a dozen blocks and climbed to the fifteenth floor, thought Mary, she'd have had a better chance of seeing the vessel that was to carry Paul away. She had no harbor pass. They wouldn't let her through the gates.

Again she surveyed the mass of traffic in the street. In a tumultuous tide it was converging toward the gates. Horns squealed, brakes crashed, bumpers scraped. A truck loaded with oil, a dangling chain behind flashing static electricity, swung sharply over, triumphantly crowded their taxi to the curb. A grinning face showed briefly. The taxi driver swore beneath his breath.

"Some people haven't got the manners of a hog," he observed with no particular rancor. Paul glanced nervously toward his bag. Down the block at the inspection house, the shipping company agent was waiting. The driver was philosophical. "Must be a fair-sized convoy putting out of here. Mostly food and oil it looks like, but I seen some pursuit planes. I hear they're heading for Iceland, by way of Halifax. Anyway, that's what I hear."

"Do you?" Paul said politely.

"Ain't you going with the convoy, mister?" asked the driver, surprised. He looked at the suitcase. "I thought ..."

"Did you?"

The driver got the point. His face and neck reddened, and he was silent. Paul handed a bill up front, seized his bag, and said, "I think we'd better walk, Mary. It isn't far now."

It was close indeed. Three short minutes carried them to the entrance that was barred to her. In the shadow of the inspection house, which rose like a traffic tower between the harbor gates, they paused. Like two bewildered strangers, diffident and awkward and shy, half stunned by the confusion and the noise, they stood there on the sidewalk. In a clamorous endless stream the traffic came sweeping forward, split at the inspection house, halted to show admission passes, crashed on into the forbidden murk beyond. They could hardly hear each other's voices. And what was there to say?

"Be careful, darling."

"I will, I will. I'm keeping in close touch with the office, of course, God and the censorship willing. They'll look after you if you get in trouble. Promise me you'll call on them."

Mary could only nod. Unbidden, the thought had come—the only kind of trouble she could get in would be his trouble. In the fraction of a second, so swift is imagination, she projected herself into the future and was receiving another message from Reykjavik. She was holding an envelope she dared not open. She had never really believed this moment would arrive, even when *News Review* had rushed through the passport, the necessary credentials. Well, here it was. Paul held her hands more tightly.

"Mary, nothing is going to happen to me."

"Nothing can," she said.

"Did I tell you the captain's nickname? They call him Lucky Schott, because the torpedoes always miss him."

"Yes, you told me," Mary said, and thought with a pang that the nickname had its grimmer side. The Captain Schott whom neither she nor Paul had ever met must have earned his sobriquet by the narrowness of his escapes. Lucky Schott, the torpedoes hit fore and aft him....

"Darling," Paul said, "try and think of this as an ordinary assignment. If that won't work, think that no one nowadays is safe. No one. I've got to know what Max was doing, and why he died. I've got to find Lisa Tennevant. Max counted on me."

"Paul, I want you to go. But being left behind isn't easy."

Paul was thinking bleakly that Max had handed both of them a pretty rugged assignment. In a queer way, however, he admitted to himself he was almost glad of that. Glad of his own part, that is. The obligation to finish the work Max had begun, whatever it might turn out to be, had lessened his personal grief, made it unimportant. Emotion was useless. He needed all his resources for the job ahead. He had no doubts of ultimate success. Traveling with Frau Van Anda, he hoped to learn a great deal before they ever arrived in Reykjavik.

Aloud, he said, "If we stop long enough in Halifax, and I get any kind of chance, I'll try and wire you. Otherwise keep your chin up, sweet. Now let me see you smile."

She smiled for him, a wavering smile that made him kiss her quickly. The pavement shook beneath their feet as another truck rumbled past them. Suddenly she could stand no more. "Everybody's going in but me. Goodbye, darling. I'll be seeing you—sometime."

She laid her hand against his cheek and was swiftly gone, as she was always gone when tears were close. She crossed the crowded noisy street. At the threshold of the waterfront restaurant, she whirled around and looked back. Paul had already disappeared. The harbor gates had swallowed him.

She felt strangely empty. Empty and quite hopeless, as though the expedition would come to nothing and Paul was gone forever. The failures and discouragements of the past two weeks arrayed themselves in her mind. They had hoped for further news from Reykjavik, but none had come. *News Review's* cables had dropped into a well of silence. If the German submarine that had attacked and sunk the helpless *Irma* had in turn been hunted down and sunk, they wouldn't learn it until the war was over. If anyone in Reykjavik was suspicious that anything unusual had led to Max's death, if anyone up there suspected he had been engaged in some undesignated task of his own, Max's friends and employers had not been advised. Iceland as a long way off; apparently the Icelandic authorities had more pressing problems.

Mary's thoughts passed to the Van Andas. They hadn't seen the Dutchwoman or her redhaired son since that night in the restaurant. A long and tedious investigation of Milwaukee newspaper files, with particular attention paid to the society pages, had turned up nothing except that Frau Van Anda's reputation was impeccable. She had lived in the Middle Western city since 1939, moving in respectable Dutch circles, contributing to Dutch charities; it appeared that the Dutch consul had been a classmate of the elder Van Anda, a prosperous merchant dead some years before his unhappy country was invaded. Paul had been unable to discover why Frau Van Anda and the black-browed Lotte were traveling north, why Elise Van Anda had deliberately informed him of her plans. It was impossible to guess.

The theatre program was another disappointment. They had counted on it so much. Even with the expert help of the research staff of *News Review*, they had failed to locate the Princess Royal Theatre or to find any trace of Lisa Tennevant. Paul hoped to pick up the actress' trail in Reykjavik.

Suddenly, with unwilling honesty, Mary realized that the real cause of her depression lay in herself. If she were aboard the *Shalimar*, she would feel quite differently. It wasn't in her nature to stand by on the sidelines. She had begged to go along. What had Paul said?

"I'm not running you into danger."

She sighed, gazed across the street a last time, turned around and walked into the restaurant. It was near the supper hour. The place was crowded, filled with cheerful bustle, loud with talk. A jukebox was playing, a group of sailors clustered at the sandwich bar were engaged in a pinball game. The service was laggard. She found an empty table herself.

The New Jersey trucker had the booth behind her. She never saw his face, but his voice was unavoidable and the troubles he was sharing with a waitress gradually impressed themselves upon her. She began to listen deliberately, wishing to forget herself. Around the walls of the restaurant, thumbtacked everywhere, displayed above the sandwich bar, above the door, above the pinball machines, bold-faced placards warned the public against the perils of careless conversation. Apparently the New Jersey trucker couldn't read. She learned a lot about him.

The New Jersey trucker was tired as a dog, had been on the road with cargo since morning. The cargo was still on his hands, and, from the looks of things, he wouldn't get back in line for hours. And then Mary grew tense and rigid. She had caught the name of a ship, the only ship in the world that meant anything to her at the moment.

The undelivered cargo sitting down the block was bound for the S.S. *Shalimar*, would travel north with Paul. Abruptly she finished the last of her sandwich and reached for her check. Her hand paused.

In the noisy busy restaurant the middle-aged soldier was attracting neither attention nor sympathy. Across the aisle, down several booths, he sat sunk in solitary woe. Empty highball glasses surrounded him. In front of him, strewn across the table, were scattered scraps of paper that looked like a torn-up letter. His head was buried in his hands. Tears crawled through his fingers. He seemed deeply immersed in a crying jag.

But suddenly he picked up a newspaper in the seat beside him and got unsteadily to his feet. In a flash Mary recognized him—less because of his narrow face, his neat mustache and his weak, moist eyes, than because he wore the shabby uniform which should have stayed at home. It was the Canadian soldier she had seen on Washington Square, the homesick Security Guard who had tried to draw her into conversation and then had borrowed matches to get rid of her.

What was he doing here? She looked up startled, as the soldier reached her booth and halted. He clutched the edge of the table to steady himself. Something told her that he was truly wretched and that he wasn't as drunk by far as he wished to be. The liquor had failed him. Leaning over, the soldier whispered:

"People oughtn't to talk so much. Talk's dangerous. I could talk myself if I wanted to."

She was astonished enough to find him here, and that he apparently remembered her. She was dumbfounded when he said, "I thought I told you your husband ought to go to Canada. There's nothing for him in Reykjavik. The old woman knows less what it's all about than I do. Your husband should go ashore at Halifax."

Behind them the waitress laughed. The drunken man was in a mood where every laugh was directed at him. His eyes filled up again. Even in her confusion Mary perceived that the impulse which had brought him to her table was dying fast. The important thing was to hold him.

"Halifax?" she said. "Is Halifax your home?"

The narrow face darkened. "What's it matter where I live? I'm trying to help you, ain't I?" and he pushed his newspaper at her.

It was the *Halifax Chronicle*, dated some days earlier, bought back in New York at the Times Square newsstand where out-of-town publications were vended. A stale old newspaper, tattered and worn. She saw that in a glance. And then she saw the advertisement. It leaped out of type at her.

It was an ordinary advertisement run on the *Chronicle's* theatrical page by a Halifax motion picture house. Flamboyantly phrased, typical of its kind. Afterwards Mary was never able to recall the name of the film or anything about the glittering attractions offered by the stage show. But she was never to forget the moment when she located the theatre where Lisa Tennevant had played in *The Wild Duck*. The Princess Royal Theatre, No. 25 Barrington Street, was in Halifax.

"See," said the soldier pointing. And then he leaned across the table and his whiskey-laden breath stirred her hair. "Your husband will have to work fast. Something is set up there for Saturday. Something big. I think myself they're after the convoy."

"After the convoy!"

Mary reached out for him. But he snatched his newspaper, shook off her hand and was gone. As he was staggering out the door, she saw the cashier call him back. He had forgotten his luggage. A traveling bag weaving at his side, the soldier disappeared.

A waitress was already clearing the table across the aisle when Mary got there. The girl put the glasses on the tray, but she had pushed the torn scraps of paper on the floor. She was grumbling to herself.

"What people you meet! That fellow was batty, if you ask me. Drunk as a coot, of course. Sent a telegram two hours ago and sat in here blubbering about it ever since."

Mary was staring at the floor. The scraps of paper weren't a torn-up letter. Nor were they the draft of a telegram. The scraps of paper had once been a theatre program, identical with the program Paul was carrying to Reykjavik.

This program was ripped to savage bits, as though the soldier was taking a curious kind of vengeance for his own miseries. The lettering could never be put together. Lisa Tennevant's face that had decorated the cover lay on the dirty floor in a dozen pieces.

There's nothing for your husband in Reykjavik. He ought to go ashore in Halifax. Something is set up there for Saturday. I think myself they're after the convoy.

Five minutes later Mary was across the street in desperate argument with the harbor guards. There was no time to phone New York. She had to do this on her own and at once. Without Paul, she was only half herself. Paul would know what steps to take, exactly what to do, once she talked to him. She had hopes at first. But the guards wouldn't let her through the gates. Well then, she would send in a message.

"Sorry, lady."

"You don't understand. This is an emergency. I must get word to my husband immediately."

"Our regulations say …"

"He's inside, I tell you. Paul Strong, correspondent of *News Review*, sailing with Captain Schott on the *Shalimar*."

"Never heard of it," said the guard.

"It's going with the convoy. My husband …"

"What convoy? You talk too much, lady. The Governor himself couldn't get through these gates without a pass. Move along, now, or I'll have to run you in."

"Look," said Mary, frantic now. "I've got to see my husband. I must! I must! I think the convoy is in danger."

She had expected a positive reaction. The guard looked at her with a mixture of sympathy and annoyance.

"Lady, sailing in convoy ain't no picnic. I know all you girls are worried about your men folks but I can't permit you standing here and …"

"I tell you this is real! I was talking to this soldier, I don't know his name, but we were in that restaurant across the street, and he told me …"

"Them soldiers talk all the time, lady, and they don't know from nothing. He ought to be ashamed of himself, working you up like this. Go on home now. You'll feel better in the morning."

Beyond his stolid bulk, distant in the confusion of the yards, Mary saw the moving arm of a derrick boom. They were still loading cargo. It was then that she remembered the New Jersey trucker. Somewhere on the other side of the street was cargo that had yet to pass through the gates.

She found the New Jersey truck quite easily. The twelve-ton monster, further increased in size by an open trailer, squatted in the mud near the deserted parade ground. Night had fallen. Overhead the sky was thick and bleak, the moon was lost in clouds. The street, where the traffic still swarmed in restless motion, swam with moving light. But the trailer truck had pulled off the street into the shadows.

The cargo was a broken-down airplane. The engine and body of the plane, the boxed propellers, rode inside the truck, sheltered from the weather. Contained in crates wrapped in heavy paper, looming like giant coffins, the truncated wings reared high above the trailer and projected considerably beyond it.

Mary took a last quick look along the sidewalk. Sure the vehicle was unoccupied, she approached it boldly. A dozing helper at the wheel spoke sharply.

"What you want, Miss?"

Shock almost undid her. Shock and—guilt. She heard her own voice speak, a little shakily but convincingly.

"I expect I'm lost. I'm looking for the streetcar stop."

"You're headed in the wrong direction," said a sleepy young voice. In the darkened cab she couldn't see his face, nor could he see hers, but he guessed that she was young and troubled. "I think it's the other way down the block, Miss. I wish I could help you look, but my orders are to stick here."

"Thank you. I can find the way myself."

She turned around, walked quickly past the sodden parade ground and out of sight. The chilled and sleepy boy at the wheel heard the diminishing clatter of her heels, and dozed again. Like a shadow, circling and approaching this time from the rear, Mary returned.

The trailer was built like a boxcar, open at the top. The two giant crates, marked L. Wing and R. Wing as the pieces of a child's game are marked, were secured against the walls. She climbed into the trailer with little difficulty. Crawling as far back as she could go, her shoulders brushing on either side, she tried to squeeze behind the massive cargo. It was impossible. In the jammed and crowded place, where she had hardly room to move, there was no real concealment. They would surely catch her at the harbor gates. Unless … She reached up and touched one of the crates—the crate marked L. Wing. The heavy wrapping paper that was thick as cloth gave a little. It was wet and soggy, weakened by rain and snow. Underneath one of the binding ropes, she punched a tiny hole. The crate wasn't solid. It was a skeleton crate, knocked together out of slats to hold the metal wing deep within. Cotton waste and wadding padded the crevices. Mary's exploring finger withdrew.

Hunched there awkwardly on the floor, she set to work in frantic haste. She slipped the rope that tied the heavy paper and pulled one edge free. Catching the edge she folded the paper back swiftly but carefully, neatly, as she had seen her mother fold back the wrappings on a Christmas parcel. One corner of the crate was now uncovered. The slats that made up the enormous box were loosely latticed; almost immediately, fumbling in the dark, she found a space large enough to receive her hand. She reached inside. In reckless handfuls she pulled out waste and wadding, piled it around her on the floor, and then pushed it out of the trailer. Again she thrust her hand inside. Her arm disappeared above the elbow before she felt the cold, chill touch of metal. Exultant, she recognized the curve of the great wing, and evaluated the depth of the space. She was small and slender. There was room enough!

She had only to enlarge the opening. She got both hands around a slat, braced her knee against the side and jerked with all her strength. The slat bowed out but it didn't break. She tried again and then again, changing position, applying every kind of pressure. Her hands burned and stung with fiery pain. The latticed crate remained impregnable. She wasn't strong enough to break the wood. And then, groping on the floor, in search of any kind of tool, she came upon an auto jack handle. It was not a perfect tool. But when she felt the sturdy handle her heart leaped up as though she'd found a treasure.

With the jack handle as a pry, she went back to work. Stout nails held the slats in place. The nails squealed and groaned, yielding slowly. They gave all at once. The slat burst from its supports with the sound of an exploding popgun. Horrified, the jack handle gripped in her throbbing hand, Mary crouched against the crate. Nothing happened. In the street beyond, the traffic surged on. In the darkened cab ahead, the youthful helper yawned and leaned his head against the wheel. She listened, set her teeth, and resumed her labors. Ten minutes later she pried the last slat loose.

The hole she meant to enter was ready. Like a mole she burrowed into it. The cotton waste made her cough and choke; she pressed it down and twisted herself around. Then came the hardest part of all. It was fairly easy to replace the slats in something like their original position, but, working from inside the crate, she had to reach out and unfold and smooth the paper wrapping flat again. No sense guided her save touch. Once when she felt the paper tear, she began to cry from nerves and desperation, and then stopped the tears immediately and went on working. She heard no sound from outside.

At last she finished, realizing she could do no more. The outer wrapping paper was folded back in place, but was crumpled and wrinkled now. A close examination would probably reveal that the crate had been tampered with. She could only hope and wait. Worn out from exertion, bedded in darkness beside the airplane wing, tightly squeezed in the trap she had made for herself, Mary settled in the black silence to wait.

Some time later the New Jersey truck passed through the gates of Pier Seven. There was no delay. The truck was hurried forward and ahead to the tally clerk. Most of the cargo had already gone aboard. The vital confusion in the yards had slackened.

The convoy was small. There were twenty-seven ships, the battered survivors of four long years of war: Dutch, Norwegian, English, American and even one pathetic tanker thick with rust that flew the flag of Greece. A large part of the convoy had dispersed, sailed down the harbor and anchored to await the starting hour. Rumors were being whispered. They were sailing at midnight. They were sailing at dawn. Five destroyers were escorting them. No, it was one old-type destroyer and three corvettes, and that was not enough. They were joining a larger convoy at Halifax. No, they would bypass Halifax and meet the larger convoy at sea. British men-of-war would join them the fourth day out. A German raider had been reported on the Iceland route.

So it went, as everybody talked to ease suspense. The first mate of the *Shalimar* was waiting at the cargo inspection depot. Nearby at anchor lay the *Shalimar*, 4,000 tons, ugly in her dun-gray camouflage, built for southern waters and converted to North Atlantic travel. Between the shed and ship reared the tremendous triangle of a derrick boom. Half a dozen grease-grimed stevedores were gathered at the hoisting engine. The first mate of the *Shalimar* saw the tally clerk check in the New Jersey truck and wave it over, and was galvanized into action.

"She's here!" he turned and shouted to the chilled and weary group around the derrick. "Let's have some action now—and quick. What became of the carpenter?"

The truck pulled up beside the shed. Three stevedores ran forward. Three were enough. They worked in perfect unison. Their movements were quick and sure and beautiful to watch. Two crawled aboard the trailer, one stood below and tossed up the sling. As a child might net a butterfly, they captured one of the enormous crates, bound it firmly in the sling.

Yards away the hoisting engine began to throb. The lifting cable pivoted on its great supporting arm, shot down. With swift precision the sling was securely fastened to the cable. The three stevedores stepped back. As winches squealed, the harnessed crate was plucked gently from the trailer and whisked aloft. And then, as effortlessly as a housewife lays a paper of eggs on her kitchen table, the crate was lowered to the dock. Blurred lights shone through the harbor mist, cast strange complicated shadows from men and machinery, but the bold crayon lettering was visible—L. Wing.

The dock carpenter appeared. With a stout hook in hand, he approached the crate. The New Jersey boy had climbed out of the truck to see the operation through.

"Cargo inspection, sonny," said the carpenter, grinning at the youngster's grave absorption.

Quickly, anxious to be done, he glanced around, saw that the necessary witnesses were present. Bending over the trussed-up crate, the carpenter caught the heavy wrapping paper with his hook, and tore a gaping hole. He forced his fist into the hole, jerked out a handful of the cotton waste, exposed a recognizable portion of the metal wing. The cargo was okay. He scrawled his mark upon it.

Again the hoisting engine throbbed. Suspended in its sling, the crate swept upward from the dock—almost as though already the imprisoned wing was in flight. The giant arm spun around. For a second, poised and tremulous, the great box hung high above the deck of the *Shalimar*. The watching boy was filled with pride and anxiety.

"They ought to be careful. That's a bomber wing, ain't it?"

"Hell, no. That's a pursuit, sonny. Watch her go!"

Tense, the boy's eyes followed the downward plunge of the crate. From the dock he heard a muffled thud, as one end struck the deck. He winced as though the jar had injured him.

"They ought to be careful," the New Jersey boy muttered to himself. "That's a pursuit plane. That's mighty precious cargo."

SEVEN

Far out at sea, the convoy was moving silently in triple file. Stealthy clouds hid the pallid winter moon, as the darkened ship slipped along in furtive procession. The thump and throb of Diesel motors, resonant and regular, pulsated in her ears. Mary came back to consciousness, wondering languidly at the sound and motion. When she tried to sit up and could not, she began to struggle, and then she remembered. She had a lucid thought. The crate must be on the after deck above the engines.

She dozed and woke again. Slowly her thinking cleared. Sensation returned more quickly. She became aware of a furiously aching head, of a back that felt broken. A painful exploration proved it wasn't broken, that her skull wasn't fractured, after all. Her hat and hair had probably saved her. The Strongs were hard to kill, thought Mary, trying vaguely to recall a spinning fall through space, a thunderous crash that had preceded hours of nothingness. But her memories were confused and mixed, and she soon gave up. That part was in the past. She had got aboard, all right, and out to sea, and now what next?

Pressed against the airplane wing, imprisoned in the crate that was like a coffin, Mary lay sunk in nightmarish meditation. She couldn't stay here forever. She had to find her way to Paul. Slowly, torturously her stiffened fingers began plucking at the cotton waste, fumbling at the slats and heavy wrapping paper....

Captain Schott prepared to leave the bridge just as the watch was changed. Captain Lucky Schott was a big-bodied man who looked a little like Santa Claus. At first glance, that is. He had a loud jolly laugh, a soft sweet voice, and his step, like the good saint's, was remarkably light and sure for his weight. The Captain, who had been on the bridge for hours, hated to trust anybody's seamanship except his own.

When the mate walked in, however, Captain Schott suddenly decided he'd had enough. His bright-blue eyes ached from hours of peering into blackness through the narrow slits cut into the sheet steel which replaced the shining expanse of glass that once had enclosed the bridge. When his eyes went bad, the Captain's round fat stomach bothered him. Indigestion upset his nerves; and traveling in convoy, creeping ahead at a snail's pace, skulking and cowering in the dark along with riffraff better left behind in drydock, always had affected his nerves unfavorably for all that he seemed so placid on the surface.

To tell the truth, his nerves hadn't been in tip-top shape at the beginning of the voyage. Perhaps that was only natural. This particular voyage was to be the Captain's last. Lucky Schott had informed no one yet, but in his own mind he had decided definitely that with this trip he was done. Done with danger, done with war, done with all the rest of it. After all, the Captain had told himself, he was nearly fifty-four. Much too old a bird to play the fool and push his luck too far.

"You're looking tired, sir," said the mate.

"Am I?" said the Captain coldly. About to retire to his quarters, he changed his mind immediately and stepped outside to take a turn on deck. Not that it was any satisfaction in his present mood and in this damned perpetual blackout. Sometimes it seemed to Captain Schott that his ship had changed as much as he had, with the war.

Hooded anti-aircraft guns turned up their ugly snouts from her bow. High-octane gasoline sloshed below in tanks that once had carried coconut oil; the deck—once scrubbed and immaculate, his special pride— was jammed with a fantastic litter of cargo, battened down, stuffed everywhere, so that the *Shalimar*, once the queen of southern waters, or so her master sentimentally remembered her, was like a traveling tinker's wagon. Swerving in the darkness, automatically following the faint almost invisible glimmer of a silver line painted on the deck, Captain Schott plowed on his way. Twice around, and he'd have his nerves in order. Suddenly he paused.

"Who's there?" he called sharply.

Mary crouched against the bulkhead. She'd just reached an opening of some kind; her groping fingers had found the handle of a door, when she heard the footsteps, heard the voice.

"Who's there?" called Captain Schott again.

Again no answer. There was someone ahead. Someone with no business there. Lucky Schott wanted no one wandering about *his* ship. His big body tensed. Noiselessly he padded forward.

Mary didn't hear the stealthy advance, but she sensed it. Retreat was quite impossible. The slightest noise, and she was lost. If she stayed very still, flattened against the wall, there was a chance she wouldn't be discovered. But the faint silver glimmer, the dim line of aluminum paint that had guided her safely if very slowly from the rail to the forward housing, now was guiding someone else. The unseen figure was coming closer. She fancied she heard breathing.

Stooping silently, she slipped off one of her shoes. With a quick jerk, she tossed it far behind her. The shoe landed, clattering. The trick was old, but it worked. Growling, Captain Schott rushed past.

Instantly she was through the door. Blackout curtains, hanging in thick, bewildering folds so that no light should leak out on deck, stopped her momentarily. The draperies clutched at her, swirled and parted on the dimly lighted companionway. Opening off both sides, ghostly and still, were the public rooms. In the library a single lamp was burning at a distant desk. Was someone sitting there? She didn't pause to see. The passengers should be quartered somewhere near, down the corridor perhaps, around the corner. Paul was in cabin number 12.

Hobbled by the single shoe—she'd been a fool not to remove them both—Mary ran. As she shot around the corner, the blackout curtains behind her split a second time. The trick hadn't worked for long. Unfortunately the rumpled, ruined coat she wore was the brightest in her wardrobe—an eye-compelling crimson that Paul had chosen. Mary looked wildly down the blue-lit corridor that stretched ahead. Lined with numbered doors, it seemed endless, but the final number stopped at nine. At the farthest end, around another corner, must be cabin number 12. Behind her, hidden by the bend, she heard running footsteps, an angry shouting voice. The footsteps seemed to hesitate at the public rooms, to slacken infinitesimally, only to race on. She hadn't shaken off pursuit, or even delayed it much. Moving with energy and speed, the footsteps reached the turning. With a silent prayer for luck, Mary stepped into Cabin 5.

The door wasn't locked. In the fraction of a second it opened, the dim blue light shone in, was gone with the swiftly closing door. The darkness became absolute, that blackness of a small, closed-in space which can be more troubling and intense than the darkness of the open. To Mary, the darkness was friendly and welcome, offering blessed respite. In the fraction of a second she had glimpsed an empty berth, empty hangers against a teakwood wall, an uncluttered washstand. Cabin 5 was unoccupied. She had it to herself. Sick with relief, she sagged against the door.

Outside the footsteps pounded by. She listened a moment, heard nothing except the subsiding beat of her own heart. It was safe now. Safe? Suppose her pursuer knew a trick himself, and was waiting in the corridor, watching for her reappearance. She dared not risk it yet. A few minutes' delay—five minutes, she'd count them off—and then she'd pull herself together and make another run for it.

All at once she knew how tired she was. Through darkness, her knees shaking so that she could hardly stand, she felt her way to the berth. She sat down and took off her shoe. From head to foot she felt bruised and beaten, weary beyond endurance. The temptation to lie back and close her eyes was almost overpowering. The steady motion of the boat was like a cradle, the hum of the motors distant and far away, like a lullaby. She fought with drowsiness, felt herself sinking down, down. Her arm relaxed, slid along the berth. Suddenly she sat bolt upright, wide awake with shocked surprise.

Placed on a rack below the level of the berth was a Gladstone bag. The bag lay open. Snatching away her hand as though it were burnt, she touched socks and neckties neatly balled, a shaving brush, a drugstore flashlight like the one she'd bought for Paul.

Cabin 5 was not unoccupied. It was merely temporarily deserted. There was an enormous difference, a difference that brought her scrambling to her feet. She didn't reflect on the present whereabouts of the missing occupant, or think it odd he should be wandering about the ship at such an hour, or even wonder why he had opened his bag and gone away not bothering to unpack. Her sole concern was to avoid a meeting. In panic she fumbled for her shoe. Surely she'd left it on the berth. No, she'd put it on the floor. The shoe eluded her. She scrabbled for several seconds, before she recalled the flashlight.

By then, between the motion of the boat and her own disordered, nervous searching, she'd got herself turned around. The Gladstone bag was lost, along with the berth itself. Somehow she had blundered all the way to the other wall. Something then occurred which confused her further. She stepped into newspapers, spread for some extraordinary reason upon the floor, a deep rustling layer. They hadn't been tossed there carelessly, they lay evenly and smoothly; whispering in the darkness. The newspapers must be spread to the right of the door, in that side of the cabin which she hadn't seen. The berth was to the left. Oriented, but in some queer, cold way unreassured, Mary found the door again and then the berth. A second more, and the flashlight was in her hand.

She jumped with the jump of the light. Swift as a dagger it leaped across the open unpacked bag, across the washstand—a silly teakwood thing matching the walls—and fell upon a trunk. In that first confused glimpse of Cabin 5, she'd missed a lot. She hadn't seen that large black trunk upended so that it fitted neatly in the corner, an elderly trunk worn and battered by years of travel, with old-fashioned brass mountings and a scrolled, elaborate, old-fashioned lock. Where had she seen a similar trunk before?

Mary stared. She had seen a trunk like that not so very long ago. Brass initials that had been fastened beside the lock had been pried off, and the spot freshly painted. Beneath the single hurried coat of paint the flashlight picked out the dim indentation of the vanished initials.

E.V.A. Elise Van Anda!

Mary remembered then quite clearly. She had seen Frau Van Anda's trunk not so very long ago on the moving van outside the apartment house on Washington Square.

What was Frau Van Anda's trunk doing here in an empty cabin along with a man's unpacked Gladstone bag? Why had the initials been taken off? And then, as Mary moved, her eye came to rest on something else that she had overlooked. Shadowed by the trunk, squeezed in beside the washstand, was a chair.

The occupant of Cabin 5 hadn't cared to disturb the hangers on the wall, but he had removed his coat and arranged it very neatly upon the back of the chair. It was the coat of a shabby Canadian uniform—with the letters S.S. on the collar. Heaped below the coat, arranged on the chair with a kind of fussy tidiness, was a pile of American bills. Several hundred dollars' worth of bills, weighted down by a little pile of American coins, left lying there as though the owner who had gone away had no further use for money.

Mary turned around. The flashlight dipped in her hand, but she didn't let it drop. In complete detail and all at once she saw the scene—the more shocking because it had been so carefully prepared. The occupant of Cabin 5, in his drunkenness or in his despair, had reverted to the training of his youth and tried not to leave behind a mess for others. In the end the liquor he had drunk to give him courage had not failed him.

He had spread the newspapers to protect the floor, laid his stale old copies of the *Halifax Chronicle* very tidily in a thick, absorbent layer, allowing slightly more than the height and width of an average man. He had stepped upon the paper carpet, and faced the wall. And then quite neatly, he had shot himself through the head.

He had fallen exactly as he intended, his gun still clenched in his relaxing fingers. Blood that had soaked into the newspapers was still faintly damp. Blood stained the suicide's thinning hair, but his wispy little mustache was freshly waxed and he had shaved since she saw him last. His eyes were open and mildly startled, as though he hadn't dreamed that death would be such a simple answer to all his problems. It was the soldier who had advised Paul to visit Canada, but he himself was never going home.

She heard a little strangling sound in her own throat, and stopped it short, and thought "I must be calm," and imagined that she was. Slowly, painfully, inch by inch, edging along the berth, Mary left the cabin. She remembered to open the door a crack and peek out. But when she saw the companionway was empty, her illusory calm deserted her and she was outside and running in her stocking feet.

As she came abreast the turn that led to Cabin 12, she thought she caught an echo of muffled sound. Someone knocking at a door? But she had already made the turn. She went around the corner and then she stopped. Only a few yards away, so close that she could almost touch them, two people stood in the open doorway of Cabin 12. Their backs were to her.

The man was Paul, a Paul just aroused from sleep and for the second time that night, heavy-eyed and with rumpled hair, a bathrobe over his shirt and trousers. The second figure, frizzled red locks done up in a boudoir cap, wearing her diamonds even in semi-night attire, a life preserver strapped around a flannel dressing gown, was Frau Van Anda.

"I came to tell you," she was saying, "that Captain Schott is rousing all the passengers, looking for a stowaway. We're around the corner in Cabin 9, you know."

Paul did know; he even knew that she'd had dinner served in there. In vain he had watched for her appearance in the dining room. Paul was fully awake now, his nerves alert, electrically aware. Ever since he'd come aboard that afternoon he'd been planning for this meeting, wondering how to see this woman without her nurse, and now Frau Van Anda herself had made the opportunity. Bless her devious heart, thought Paul, with rising elation. So she wanted to tell him about the stowaway, did she? Her impulse was rather late in coming. At least fifteen minutes ago Captain Schott had stopped at Cabin 12, searched it hurriedly and gone on his way. Obviously his present visitor had some other reason for knocking at his door, some hidden purpose. Well, they couldn't stand here talking. Paul took Frau Van Anda's arm.

"I insist on giving you a nightcap," he began, and glanced across her shoulder.

The surprise was complete.

In the dim blue lights of the corridor, Mary's coat made a blatant patch of crimson that was almost purple against the naked wall. The coat was soiled with grease and dirt. Her hat was pushed awry, her hairpins had slipped their moorings so that her long, tangled hair was tumbling down over a white face. In shock and consternation, they stared at each other.

He recovered himself before she did, saw that she was literally too numbed to move. Her feet seemed rooted to the floor. He had to jolt her back to action, and fast. To Frau Van Anda, who was looking at him with puzzled eyes, he said the first thing that came in his head.

"Cabin 9. Oh, yes, yes, I remember someone saying that you were just *around the corner*."

Immediately Mary began a noiseless retreat. He held his breath. She was going to make it. And then he perceived that Frau Van Anda had noticed something. She was about to turn around. At once Paul checked that. Stepping forward, lurching with the motion of the boat, he trod heavily on her toe. He saw her wince, and commenced a stream of profuse apologies. Mary slid out of sight; before Frau Van Anda stopped nursing her toe, the corridor was empty. Paul said nothing more about a nightcap.

"Sure you're all right now? I'm so sorry. You must let me see you to your cabin."

"It's just a step," said Frau Van Anda. "Please don't trouble yourself. I …"

Frau Van Anda had no chance to say that for many reasons she preferred to go unaccompanied. Paul ignored the fact that her cabin was directly around the corner. Murmuring that he'd like to stretch his legs a bit, gripping her arm so tightly that it hurt, he swept her off on a complete circle of the ship. The way was long but there was nothing leisurely about their progress. They went headlong through the narrow twisting corridors, past the officers' quarters, past the galley, past the ghostly public rooms, with him hurrying her along so fast on her short, stout legs that she could hardly catch her breath, much less glance behind.

Afterwards Paul remembered that curious journey in the terms of his own emotions. Even as he pulled her along beside him, he had forgotten Frau Van Anda's existence and the things he'd hoped to learn from her. His mission, Max, the seventeenth letter and all the rest of it, had vanished from his mind. His sole concern was what to do with Mary, and how best to conquer his own wrath before they met. Indignation— now that his wife must have reached his cabin safely—had supplanted his initial shock. He was so angry he could scarcely see, an anger perfectly comprehensible to all happily married couples, and fed by love and deep concern. Only Mary could have made him quite that angry.

Hadn't Mary the wit to realize that stowing away in wartime was a prison offense? The Captain had spoken of ten years. Ten years, and the soft, deceptively gentle voice wasn't joking. This wasn't the kind of thing that could be laughed off. In peacetime *News Review* might have successfully intervened, got Mary off with a warning and a reprimand. War changed the picture; easy excuses wouldn't do. If Mary were caught, she'd surely go to jail. Somehow he had to get her out of this, keep her hidden in his cabin. Somehow he had to smuggle her ashore when they reached Halifax.

"Here's my door," said Frau Van Anda with considerable relief. "Mr. Strong ..."

"Good night," said Paul.

Mary was waiting in the cabin. She had pulled off her hat, and stood before the mirror trying to pin up her tangled hair. Her hands were fumbling and unsteady; she was making a dismal job of it. He guessed that she'd hurried to be done before he returned, that she'd begun with her hair and overlooked her dirty face, and—that was so like Mary. Suddenly his anger died. He'd been afraid it would. Their eyes met in the mirror. And then, with a start, Paul realized that his own thinking hadn't been very straight. Mary had some reason for her action, a reason that seemed important to her. Otherwise she wouldn't have risked spoiling everything. This was no time to ask questions. She was shockingly pale, on the point of collapse.

"What you need," he said, "is the brandy Frau Van Anda didn't get."

She still stood beside the mirror. He put his flask in her hands. Her hands felt icy cold. It wouldn't do to take her in his arms; she would probably fold up completely. Only nerves were sustaining her. "Drink your brandy now. Take a good stiff jolt. And for God's sake, darling, sit down before you faint."

He pushed her toward his berth. Obediently she sat and drank from the flask, coughing a little as she always did. He made her take another swallow, and then stepped in the tiny bath and got his toilet case and a washcloth. He wet the cloth. Returning, he sat down beside her. With movements deliberately slow, he washed the dirt from her face and gently bathed her hands. Her knuckles were scratched and swollen, and her palms raw and blistered. He helped her out of her coat and tossed it on the chair beside her spoiled, crushed hat. When he saw the bump on the back of her head, he got angry again, sick with alarm at something over and done with, but he made no comment.

"I expect you'd better do your hair yourself," he said. "It wants combing before you pin it up."

"I was in a hurry," she said meekly, and took the brush. Her hands felt warmer now. A little color had come back into her pale cheeks. "Paul, you've been awfully good to me."

"Happens I'm rather fond of you."

"I thought I heard you call me darling."

"What I wanted to do at first," he admitted, "was drop you overboard and let you swim for land. My God, Mary, what possessed you? Don't tell me now. Comb your hair, while I decide what's to be done with you."

At last she smiled.

While she got her hair in order, he appraised the possibilities of the cabin. Somehow he must hide her there. If he had judged Captain Schott's temper correctly the whole ship would be turned upside down in pursuit of the stowaway. Now that he came to think of it, Captain Schott, who looked like a roly-poly Santa Claus, hadn't struck him as either a jolly or a gentle man. Fortunately, however, he had visited Cabin 12 already; fortunately, too, the Captain didn't know that he was looking for a woman.

Paul examined the two chairs, the hangers on the wall where he'd hung his hat and topcoat, his half-unpacked bag, the covered porthole. The bathroom was closet size; it didn't even possess a tub. The cabin was extremely small, small and bare, singularly deficient in hiding places. The only possible place was underneath the berth itself. A shallow sliding drawer, filled with extra life preservers, was fitted in below the springs. He leaned down to pull out the drawer, looked up at Mary.

"Where are your shoes?" he said suddenly.

Appalled, she stared at her feet. One of her shoes was lying somewhere on the deck. The other shoe was in Cabin 5, where the dead man lay.

EIGHT

Paul's first thought was to get back the shoe. His first and strongest instinct was to spare Mary. She had hardly begun her story when he was on his knees beside the berth, clearing the drawer, throwing the life preservers behind him. There wasn't a minute to waste. Captain Schott, his solid heavy body moving on those quick light feet, was making a round of all the cabins. It might be too late now to visit Cabin 5. This was going to be an unholy mess. As he shoveled out the drawer, Paul's mind was working like a machine, grappling with this latest development, trying to make some sense of Mary's shaky, stumbling words.

The suicide wasn't an isolated incident, something to be forgotten with the recovery of the shoe. It had to be considered in all his future calculations. A lot of information, information that Paul badly needed, had died with the man in Cabin 5. The middle-aged soldier had owned and torn to pieces a copy of the theatre program. Why? Why had he killed himself? The man had recognized Mary, had known Paul was aboard the *Shalimar* on his way to Reykjavik. He had known of Paul's interest in the Princess Royal Theatre, and had advised him to go to Halifax. Again how? Possibly if he got a chance to examine the suicide's papers, Paul thought grimly, he might discover how a complete stranger had obtained such intimate knowledge of their affairs and—Max's affairs.

In his haste, he left the life preservers scattered on the floor. The last one flew behind him. Later he could probably stow them in his bag, or stuff them in the cabinet underneath the basin. The drawer was thick with dust. No time to make it clean.

"Now you can hand me a blanket, and both the pillows."

"You'd better keep one yourself," Mary said.

"Give me one then," he said, and suddenly smiled to himself. Her voice was stronger now. If she were amending his arrangements, again thinking in the present, she'd stand the rough going ahead. His girl had guts. "Darling, pull up your legs. They're in my way."

Instead she slid from the berth. The sickness had passed. "Don't you think I should go along?"

"You're going to hide and *stay* hidden," he informed her. "When we do hit Halifax, I'll manage getting you ashore. After that ..."

"Paul, you've got to listen a minute. I haven't finished the story yet," Mary said uncertainly, as he tossed in the pillow and began swiftly lining the drawer with the blanket. In the sparsely furnished cabin the berth stood out conspicuously with the drawer serving as a baseboard. He was worrying about the lack of air and hardly heard her. "I haven't told you the last thing the soldier said to me. I—I hardly know how to phrase it."

"Well?" he said impatiently.

"Paul, something is going to happen in Halifax on Saturday. Someone up there is out to get the convoy."

"What!"

"The convoy is in danger. Because of something that will happen in Halifax on Saturday. Or—or so the soldier thought. I don't know what, Paul. All I know is those few words he said."

"Oh," Paul said flatly. Very slowly he got up on his feet. His face was almost as strained and white as hers. "Exactly what did this man say?"

She told him.

"Nothing more?"

"Nothing. He was drunk, Paul. But I—I believed him. And now that he's killed himself ..."

Something is going to happen on Saturday. I think myself they're out to get the convoy. "They" were not identified. If Lisa Tennevant knew who "they" were, the soldier had not mentioned it. The words were few and the man who had spoken them was dead. But those words changed everything. This meant, Paul thought bleakly, that his personal investigation was ended before it was fairly begun. It meant in some strange way that he had failed Max. In a very real sense it meant that the Strongs themselves were in serious trouble. Because now they must talk. Mary would go to jail as a stowaway, and he would go with her. But none of that signified. If the convoy was in danger, the authorities had to know it. This wasn't the kind of information they could keep to themselves, no matter what the cost. And Paul knew it.

"Listen to me, Mary," he said quietly. "I'm going to get back your shoe, and keep you in the background as much as possible. Your being in Cabin 5 is strictly our own affair. But the rest of it isn't our affair. This is going to be hell's own mess. You're to let me handle things."

"Paul ..."

"Don't argue. Start getting set. After I get back your shoe, we've got to face the music. There's no help for it, darling. I'm afraid we've got to talk to Captain Schott tonight."

Even then he noticed the curious inversion in his own phrasing. Actually, Paul realized abruptly, he was less afraid of any of the consequences than he was of facing the Captain of the *Shalimar*. And that was odd. Perhaps it was that from their previous meeting, a meeting brief and hurried and perfunctory, he had carried away a vague, instinctive mistrust of Lucky Schott. No, Paul didn't want to talk to Captain Schott. Call it a hunch, call it what you like, but there it was. Mary sensed that curious illogical reluctance of his as she always sensed his feelings. Her eyes grew frightened. Leaning over he kissed her quickly.

"Darling, wish me well. I'll soon be back and then we'll get together and figure out a story for the Captain that covers all the facts he's entitled to, a story that's almost—true."

There was a knock at the door. They looked at each other in dismay. Again there was a hesitant knock. Frau Van Anda's voice didn't match her knock. It was urgent and determined.

"Mr. Strong, please let me in."

Paul cursed silently. He considered saying, "Get the hell out of here," and restrained himself. Instead he called, "Just a minute while I find the light."

Mary turned in panic toward the drawer but Paul shook his head, pushed her toward the bathroom. She barely managed to disappear and close the door behind her. Almost immediately the outer door opened and Frau Van Anda walked in.

The three lights in the cabin had been burning. She caught Paul turning off a light instead of turning one on. He watched her tensely, but she hadn't seemed to notice. He relaxed slightly, and then his eyes opened. Over her arm Frau Van Anda carried, of all extraordinary things, a shipboard basket of fruits and jellies. So that was to be her excuse this time.

"You seemed so unlike yourself when I was here before," she began, "that I thought you might be unwell. I hope you're fond of fruit."

Paul muttered something unintelligible. Much as he would like to, it wouldn't be very bright to throw his guest and her basket out in the hall. She was well inside the cabin anyhow, looking for a place to put her offering. His eyes followed her glance toward the chair. Mary's hat was only partially hidden by her crimson coat, and even in the half light of the one lamp he'd left burning the coat did not particularly resemble an article of masculine attire. He backed hurriedly toward the chair. With equal haste Frau Van Anda deposited her fruit on the berth. She showed no interest in the yawning drawer, the scattered life preservers. To his amazed relief, as though her errand was accomplished, she moved swiftly back to the door. When she reached it, she paused.

"Mr. Strong, do you know a man named Adelbert Griggs?"

"Griggs?" he said, startled. The name was unfamiliar. "Who is he?"

"The dead man in Cabin 5."

Paul sat down on the hat and coat. Reaching in his bathrobe pocket, he got out matches and lit a cigarette. He gave himself plenty of time. The need for haste was gone. Mary's shoe was not to be recovered. In silence he digested that fact, and considered its implications. When he looked up his eyes were calm. Indeed, he saw that he was calmer than his visitor. She seemed poised for instant flight.

"I've never heard of Adelbert Griggs. Why?"

"Captain Schott was just now asking me." She glanced quickly, furtively at the burning tip of Paul's cigarette. It seemed to interest her. "Mr. Strong, you should know the Captain believes you to be acquainted with this man Griggs. There was a packet of matches in his pocket."

"I don't understand," said Paul, confused.

"A packet exactly like that packet in your hand. You will see that the name of your magazine is printed on the cover."

Paul glanced down at the matches in his hand. The paper cover was a minute copy of the cover of *News Review*, with the name boldly printed above a line of advertising. He understood at once, with a despairing lack of surprise, where the dead man in Cabin 5 had got his own supply. Two weeks ago in New York a middle-aged soldier had paused long enough on the sidewalk outside their apartment house to borrow matches from Mary and to complicate both their lives. *News Review*, of course, distributed the packets by the thousand, but that answer seemed hardly good enough. Pausing in the act of returning the matches to his pocket, Paul flipped them casually to the washstand.

"I have just remembered. I didn't realize this Adelbert Griggs was the one. I met him a moment on deck about the time we were sailing."

"I suggested something of that kind to the Captain. He will want your impressions, I am sure. Within a few hours after that, Adelbert Griggs was dead."

It is singularly difficult, thought Paul, to have impressions of a man whom one has never seen. All of his were strained through Mary. What did Adelbert Griggs look like? Dark or fair? What was on his mind as he contemplated death?

"He seemed depressed," Paul said, and immediately regretted it. Far better to have stuck as near the truth as possible, and have had no impressions whatever. In protecting Mary, he'd have lies enough to tell. He added quickly, "It was dark, we couldn't smoke on deck, he borrowed the matches and went back inside. I never thought of him again till now. It seems strange a man on his way home would kill himself."

"Kill himself!" exclaimed Frau Van Anda. Until then her voice had been so slurred and low as to be almost whispered. Now suddenly it rose. "Killed himself, Mr. Strong! Why do you say that?"

Another mistake. Nothing had been said about the way Adelbert Griggs had died. But Captain Schott, who had discovered the body and spread the news, must surely know the truth. Was he attempting to avoid a shipboard scandal and giving out the tale that Griggs had suffered a sudden heart attack? Whatever the cause, it seemed quite clear that the Captain had withheld the facts. Again, thinking of Captain Schott, Paul felt a wave of instinctive mistrust. Something was wrong, something that concerned himself and Mary. Some unknown danger was quivering in the air. For no particular reason, his palms were sweating.

"A stupid guess," he said to Frau Van Anda. "Do me a favor and forget it. With all the excitement—well —I suppose I just jumped to that conclusion."

"But Mr. Strong, you did know the man was Canadian."

Torn between irritation and dismay, Paul paused again to weigh his answer. He wanted to be alone, he wanted a chance to think. What right had this woman to stand there cross-examining him about an incident which had not occurred? Had the circumstances been different, thought Paul, he'd have been asking some pertinent questions himself. Obviously Frau Van Anda herself was better acquainted with Adelbert Griggs than she pretended. Mary had seen in his cabin a trunk which had once belonged to Elise Van Anda. That could hardly be coincidence. The shabby soldier who lay dead aboard the *Shalimar* tonight had been wandering around Washington Square two weeks ago. He had known a lot about the Strongs, and where had he got his information? It seemed highly likely to Paul that Frau Van Anda knew.

Looking at her, he had the baffled, irritated feeling that in her own fashion she was trying to be helpful. Why did she need to be so damned circuitous about it? One thing was sure: a direct approach would get him nowhere with her. She'd laid down certain tacit rules, and for the present he had to play the game her way.

"Yes, I knew Griggs was Canadian. I expect I subconsciously noticed the uniform. Possibly the uniform stuck in my mind because I always supposed that Security Guards were confined to duty in Canada."

"Apparently the poor man had lost the right to wear the uniform some months ago," said Frau Van Anda. She leaned forward. "Mr. Strong, it is important that you understand how really serious is this affair. Captain Schott is greatly agitated. A few minutes ago he received by radio an official inquiry concerning Adelbert Griggs."

"By radio! While we're traveling in convoy!"

"I told you it was—serious. The Canadian Royal Mounted Police are awaiting this man's arrival in Halifax, and will no doubt want to talk to you. Captain Schott thought so."

Paul's heart sank. Of all the damnable complications! If the Royal Mounted got the notion Mary was entangled with a man they wanted that badly, a man now mysteriously dead by his own hand, the affair might prove serious indeed. Unlike many Americans, Paul hadn't got his knowledge of the Canadian Royal Mounted Police from the movies; he had got it from the same newspaper experience that had taught him to be suspicious of coincidence and to trust his hunches. He was fully aware that the Royal Mounties had long since climbed down off their horses to take over the policing of a Canada at war. Shunning publicity and working in secret, charged with the internal security of the country, the Mounties had become a dangerous organization to tangle with. How was he going to convince them of how very little Mary knew about Adelbert Griggs?

With shock, Paul saw how implausible Mary's account of her own actions—even if she told the story absolutely straight—might seem to an outsider. Everything about her brief association with Adelbert Griggs had a phony, unreal quality; her chance meeting with him in the waterfront restaurant, her smuggling herself aboard the *Shalimar*— no policeman would be favorably impressed with that!—the calamitous fact that she had blundered into Cabin 5 and remained there many minutes in the dark. If only she had stayed on shore, if only she hadn't stopped in Cabin 5, if only there were some way he could keep her out of this. If only he, instead of Mary, could do the talking and explaining.

"I'm willing to tell everything I know about Adelbert Griggs!" Paul said, more fiercely than he intended. Actually he wasn't talking to Frau Van Anda. Actually, without his wholly realizing it, he was already fumbling toward some way to take over Mary's story, make her information his. The little that Mary knew about the shabby soldier, he also knew. If the Mounties got the facts, why did it matter which one of the Strongs had talked with Adelbert Griggs?

Momentarily, as these thoughts flashed through his mind, it was as though Frau Van Anda's stout body had disappeared and Paul saw standing in her place a member of the C.R.M.P., a tall, grim-faced, unsympathetic stranger clad in whipcord azure-blue with scarlet stripes. He shook aside that disturbing picture. It was false anyhow. Nowadays few of the Mounties went about in these dramatic uniforms. Nowadays the majority of the Royal Mounties, the dangerous, not-to-be-meddled-with Mounties, went in plainclothes. In plainclothes they lurked in war plants and factories on the lookout for saboteurs, and lounged inconspicuously about Canadian harbors and docks and waterfront hideaways watching for those with no business there; in plainclothes they investigated mysterious lights along the shore, and inland, too—hadn't German submarines gone far up the St. Lawrence? It was the Mounties who were responsible for the safekeeping of thousands of prisoners of war, housed in prison camps scattered throughout Canada. When *News Review*, a year before, had desired to photograph one of these camps and had sent Max to Ottawa, it was the Mounties who'd said curtly—no. Suddenly Paul recalled that the Royal Mounted was a part of the military, commissioned by the Canadian Army, that the Security Guards served under them. If the Mounties were awaiting Adelbert Griggs in Halifax, it was certain that he had been in grave trouble when he came aboard the *Shalimar*.

"What was the man anyhow? A deserter?"

"No, he wasn't a deserter. I understand Adelbert Griggs was requested to leave the service about five months ago. Cashiered out, I think is how the Captain said it. Something about a prisoner of war who escaped last September from a camp where Griggs was a guard."

"But if he went to the United States five months ago, why was he coming back to Canada in uniform?"

"I imagine that is what these Canadian police will want to know. Now, Mr. Strong, you can please favor me," she said in a breathless whisper. "Don't tell Captain Schott I was here. Be very careful when you talk to him, I beg you. Believe me, Captain Schott is no friend of yours."

With that disquieting remark she was gone. At once Mary emerged from the bathroom.

"Paul, what now? Have you decided?"

"Yes," Paul said. "Maybe I'm wrong," he said, "but I'm not going to tell Captain Schott anything at all about—you. *I'm* the one who saw Griggs in the restaurant and talked to him, *I'm* the one who lent him matches. Make sure you remember that."

"My shoe …"

"Let Schott worry about the shoe and the stowaway. He doesn't know anything about *you*. When we reach Halifax and the Royal Mounted we may have to change our minds. Not now. Darling, get in the drawer. I'm off to beard the Captain."

A moment and she'd stepped in the drawer and was lying down and he'd pushed her out of sight. Paul shoved the life preservers into the cabinet, locked her hat and coat in his bag. He took a last quick look around the cabin—his clothes hanging on the wall, his toilet articles, the basket of fruit on the berth. Nothing there to catch the eye of any casual visitor, no sign of Mary's presence.

Outside in the corridor he started toward Cabin 5, then turned in the opposite direction and moved toward the Captain's private quarters. By now the ship's doctor would probably be in charge, and Captain Schott would have left the scene of the tragedy. Strange he hadn't already come to Cabin 12, that Paul was obliged to seek him out. Strange …

Paul was so deeply preoccupied as he made the turn leading to the Captain's quarters that at first he overlooked the fact that someone else was also headed there. And then he raised his eyes and saw the hurrying figure ahead.

Even from the back he recognized Frau Van Anda's nurse. Lotte wore a dressing gown, black and dingy like her hair. She was moving quickly but stealthily on slippered feet. As she passed beneath one of the dim blue lights he saw the white flash of an envelope in her hand.

Paul dropped back. When the woman ahead reached the Captain's door and turned around to look quickly along the corridor, he was not in sight. She rapped softly, rapped again, hesitated, unlocked the door and disappeared inside. Captain Schott wasn't in, but Lotte had a key.

In much less than a minute she was coming out again. And now her hand was empty. The door swung shut behind her. It was then that Paul knocked his knuckles against the rack of life preservers concealing him. Lotte didn't pause to try the door. She gasped and fled.

The Captain's door had barely missed the latch. A hairbreadth let Paul in. The envelope was lying on a little table beside the Captain's bed.

It was an ordinary ship's envelope stamped with the name of the *Shalimar*. A little British flag was printed in the corner. The envelope was fat and bulky and it wasn't sealed.

When Paul picked it up the envelope flap fell loosely open and the snapshots came tumbling. out, fluttering to rest upon the Captain's bed. One of them slid off on the floor. There were a dozen of the snapshots. They were all alike.

Paul had never seen the picture before, and now he gazed at it incredulously.

He was looking at a picture of himself and Mary, clear, distinct and very good—but entirely new to him. A picture of himself and Mary photographed on a blazing July day with the lovely familiar arch of Washington Square behind them. Mary wore a hat that was new that day, and she was smiling. He was frowning in the sun, bathed in sweat, calling out to Max to hurry. It was the picture Max had taken seven months ago just before he started on his final journey. The first shot with his brand-new camera.

Paul knew then how wise had been his decision not to give Mary over to Captain Lucky Schott. As he stooped to gather up the snapshots and return them to the envelope, he knew.

The film from which the prints were made wasn't in the envelope. But that particular film had been in Max's possession at Reykjavik. Max's camera and films had not been discovered among his effects. They had accompanied him aboard the fishing boat, as they accompanied him everywhere he went. The film had been in Max's possession on the day the *Irma* was sunk by a German submarine.

The Captain's cabin was very still. To Paul the sound of his own breath seemed loud. The film that showed himself and Mary on that long-ago summer day had survived the destruction of the *Irma*. These prints had been developed from that film. If Max had gone down with the fishing boat, how could the pictures exist? What was the answer?

Paul thought of one. Suppose that all along they had been mistaken and deceived about what had happened outside the harbor at Reykjavik, just as the Icelandic authorities had been deceived? Or had the authorities up there been truly deceived? The reports from Iceland had been curiously inconclusive.

The *Irma* had been shelled and sunk, but the bodies of the four men aboard—Max, the Thorgsens and the other lodger—had never been recovered. There had been no witnesses to the tragedy. Suppose the vessel had been fired on *after* her passengers had been taken off. More than one torpedoed seaman had seen the inside of a German submarine. Suppose that somewhere in the world Max was still alive.

With steady hands Paul thrust the envelope into his pocket and stole out of the Captain's cabin.

NINE

When Paul returned to Cabin 12, Captain Schott was waiting there. He opened the door, and there the Captain was. His stout body was settled in the only comfortable chair, he had turned on the lights and made himself at home, but he hadn't searched the cabin. In that first sinking glance, the instant he spied Captain Schott in calm possession, Paul's eyes had gone to the berth. It had not been touched. The basket of fruit was just the same, the blanket folded at the foot. The drawer underneath the berth was undisturbed, pulled out the tiniest crack to allow for air just as he had left it. And then perched on the Captain's knee Paul saw the single shoe—a little high-heeled shoe, size four, russet alligator leather bought in a Fifth Avenue store.

"Good evening, Mr. Strong," said Captain Schott with a smile of gentle welcome, as though this were a social occasion and Cabin 12 belonged to him. "I was wondering where you were. Sit down, if you please. I daresay you've heard the news and know why I'm here."

Yes, Paul knew. But there were a lot of things he didn't know. He resisted a foolish impulse to walk across the room and sit on the berth, as though his nearness to her would offer Mary protection. He took the other chair.

"You want to talk to me about Adelbert Griggs," he said.

"It's not that I *want* to," said Captain Schott in placid correction. "I have no choice. Unfortunately, the Royal Mounted, awaiting the arrival of Adelbert Griggs in Halifax, will expect from me a report on what has happened aboard my ship. I've known Major Thomson who's in charge at the port there for a good many years. A sound man, Mr. Strong, an astute police official. The Major will hold me responsible for a full and accurate report on this—unhappy affair."

Paul wondered what Major Thomson would make of those snapshots in his pocket when he got an opportunity to show them. And then it flickered through his mind that aboard the *Shalimar* the man who sat opposite him was judge and jury too. How was it going to be on shore? With shock it struck Paul that the snapshots proved nothing in themselves; it was the story that went with them, their presence in the Captain's cabin. He should have left them there. No, that would have made no difference. Captain Schott's possession of the snapshots could be explained in a dozen innocent ways; because the pictures *were* of him and Mary, Paul himself would be presumed to have brought them on board. How was he to show the Royal Mounted that Max Ferris had snapped that picture, that the film must have been taken from Max at the time of the "disaster" off Iceland? There was no definite way of showing that. It might boil down to which one of them Major Thomson chose to believe—Paul Strong or his old friend, Captain Lucky Schott.

"Exactly what do you want to ask me?" Paul said evenly, and turned steady eyes on his guest. He, too, could play that this meeting was purely social.

"I do wish," said Captain Schott, and his gentle voice was faintly querulous, "that you'd keep in mind I'm acting for Major Thomson. Personally I find this most distasteful. But I feel sure when we reach Halifax on Wednesday the Royal Mounted will want an account of your relations with Adelbert Griggs."

"Relations is hardly the word," Paul said. "The man was a stranger to me. I barely met him."

"Unfortunately it would seem that you met him at a rather awkward time. Mr. Strong, I know you talked to this man very shortly before he died with a bullet in his head. There was a packet of matches...."

"I lent him matches," Paul said. "Major Thomson can hardly consider that of interest, no matter what his concern with Adelbert Griggs."

Captain Schott shifted position. He maintained his firm grip on the little shoe, holding it as though it were a treasure, something of special and peculiar import to him. Paul didn't look at the shoe. Not once, after that first glance.

"Mr. Strong, you may have heard that this man Griggs was dismissed from the Canadian Army some months ago, charged with carelessness in the escape of a German prisoner of war from Sedwedge prison camp. Griggs was a camp guard. It appears that the Royal Mounted now believe this carelessness of his to have been deliberate."

"I know nothing about an escaped prisoner of war," Paul said, surprised at this turn. "I have told you that my encounter with Adelbert Griggs was very brief."

He was looking at the Captain. It seemed to him that there was a flicker of relief in the bright blue eyes. It seemed to Paul that the smile which had never left the soft full mouth deepened as though Captain Schott was pleased.

"Had Griggs no friends or acquaintances aboard?" Paul asked suddenly.

"So far as I have been able to discover, *you* are the only one who so much as spoke to him."

"Have you examined his luggage?"

"Naturally. The man had no personal papers of interest. That type seldom does."

"Did you examine his trunk?"

"His trunk, Mr. Strong?"

"Yes, his trunk."

"Adelbert Griggs came aboard with a single Gladstone bag. A small amount of clothing, nothing else. He had no trunk."

Paul opened his mouth in astonished protest, and closed it just in time. Mary had seen in the suicide's cabin a large black trunk that had once belonged to Elise Van Anda. Now, it seemed quite clear, the trunk was no longer there. Was Captain Schott protecting Frau Van Anda, or had the heavy awkward trunk been spirited away before the Captain reached Cabin 5? Under the circumstances Paul was hardly in a position to press into the mystery of the vanished trunk or to wonder about its possible contents. It was too late now to change his story, and place himself in Cabin 5.

"There was no trunk," Captain Schott repeated placidly. "Now we've settled that, suppose we get back to you and your conversation with Griggs. You've said that you talked to him."

"Briefly, yes."

"What did you talk about?"

"The convoy," Paul said suddenly and yet very deliberately. He kept his eyes on the Captain's face. "We talked about the convoy that will be leaving Halifax for the north sometime this weekend. Your convoy, Captain Schott. Griggs was drunk, but he had an idea something might *happen* to the convoy."

Captain Schott had a highly disciplined face. But he hadn't hidden relief and now he couldn't hide its opposite. His fixed smile wavered. His square hands closed still more tightly on the shoe. There was a tautening of the muscles in his jaw and deep down in his eyes flashed something cold and hard. The expression, rage and fury and menace and perhaps a touch of fear, was there and then was gone. Captain Schott began to laugh.

"My dear Mr. Strong," he said, "I must give you credit for a lively, journalistic imagination. But I am afraid you underestimate Major Thomson if you expect him to take you seriously. Frankly, I don't believe you."

So Captain Schott was going to try and laugh him out of court. Captain Schott didn't propose to take seriously any suggestion of danger to the convoy. Captain Schott wasn't interested. Why?

And then Paul recalled the Captain's cheery nickname. Lucky Schott, the torpedoes always struck fore or aft him. Lucky Schott, who'd seen many other vessels perish on catastrophic voyages in the past and himself had passed unscathed through submarine-infested waters. Captain Lucky Schott. Half a convoy was lost, and he and the *Shalimar* miraculously escaped.

Sometimes miracles had strange answers. A sailor man, a trusted, unsuspected captain, could be that lucky if he knew when an attack was planned and how and where it would come and dropped out of convoy and left the other brave ships there to die. A captain could be that lucky if he himself provided the information that resulted in the attack.

Paul looked at Captain Schott and felt the rise of the coldest anger he had ever known. His own purpose took shape. Captain Schott wasn't going to get away with this. Something was set for Saturday. Something that he had to stop—must stop. On Wednesday they would arrive in Halifax. On Wednesday he would talk to Major Thomson, he would …

Captain Schott was doing the talking now. "You see, Mr. Strong, I understand your motive. You see, I have guessed the subject of your conversation with Adelbert Griggs."

"Have you?" said Paul, and even in his anger wondered how Captain Schott could sound so positive about a conversation which had not occurred.

"You talked to Adelbert Griggs about the woman who wore this shoe," said Captain Schott abruptly. He held up the little shoe and the light from the lamp shone on the high, stilt heel. "Naturally. I don't know precisely what the two of you said. I do know that the stowaway I was pursuing earlier tonight was this woman. I don't know whether you or Griggs or both of you together assisted in smuggling her aboard, I don't know what caused the quarrel …"

"Quarrel? There was no quarrel. Griggs and I didn't talk about a woman," said Paul quite truthfully. No such woman existed. There was only Mary.

For a moment Captain Schott was silent. In the quiet of the cabin Paul could hear the faraway throbbing of the motors. Imperceptibly the motion of the boat had become less steady. Crouched in hiding in the airless drawer, Mary would probably be sick in earnest soon. He felt ill himself, spiritually and physically. With sick eyes he looked over at the berth, at the folded blanket, at the pattern of the light falling on

Frau Van Anda's stupid, unwanted fruit. He couldn't look at the Captain anymore.

"Captain Schott," he said, "I can't tell you why Adelbert Griggs killed himself. I can assure you that a woman had nothing to do with his suicide."

"Suicide!" exclaimed Captain Schott in much the same tone that Frau Van Anda had used. Perhaps his voice was even more astonished. Open-eyed, he stared at Paul. "Suicide! Are you joking, Mr. Strong?"

"Surely you mentioned a gunshot wound," stammered Paul. He had turned away. Now suddenly he felt his whole body stiffen, grow tense and still.

"Come, come, Mr. Strong. Are you pretending now you don't know that Adelbert Griggs was murdered?"

"Murdered!" echoed Paul. At first he couldn't believe he'd heard the word correctly. Mary had seen the gun in the suicide's hand, she had seen the newspapers he'd spread to protect the floor, she had met Griggs in the waterfront restaurant when he was drinking to build up his courage.

"I'm surprised at you, Mr. Strong." Gleaming in the Captain's smile, a broad smile that split his face and almost warmed his eyes, was real amusement. "You're a clever, intelligent American journalist. I'm amazed you didn't realize that when we reach Halifax you'll find yourself involved in a murder inquiry. Adelbert Griggs was certainly murdered."

"Murdered," Paul repeated mechanically, as though it were the only word he knew.

"Luckily *I* found the body," said the Captain in his gentle, musing way. He emphasized the pronoun very slightly. "In consequence, and this will be a great relief to my good friend Major Thomson, I can be sure of *my* facts. The facts are clear. Adelbert Griggs was shot at close range, caught unaware while he was reading his newspaper, caught off guard because he was befuddled by liquor or so the ship's doctor thinks. At any rate the doctor agrees with *me* that Griggs was murdered. The conclusion is inescapable. There was no weapon of any kind in Cabin 5."

"What became of the gun?" Paul asked aloud. Actually he was asking himself what had happened to the gun which Mary had seen in the suicide's hand. It couldn't just disappear any more than a big heavy trunk could disappear. "What became of the gun?"

"A sensible question. I cannot produce the gun for Major Thomson, but fortunately I can tell him where it is. The gun is lying at the bottom of the ocean. Flung there by the murderess. I nearly caught her, Mr. Strong."

"I don't understand," Paul said, and did not.

"You will, Mr. Strong. You will understand. I haven't told you how I first discovered the female stowaway and why I didn't catch her. Or have I?"

"No," said Paul. "No, you haven't told me."

"It happened this way," said Captain Schott. "Shortly after I left the bridge tonight, I heard a shot from Cabin 5. I rushed in that direction, and saw this woman—a small blond woman in a crimson coat—running down the corridor with a gun in her hand. You may ask, Mr. Strong, why I didn't pursue her. I can only answer that I was betrayed by too much—heart. I didn't know that Griggs was dead."

The Captain paused to shake his head at his own weakness. Unless perhaps he paused so that Paul could comment. But Paul was stricken dumb.

"While I stopped to make sure that Griggs was beyond my help, the woman got away. But her escape I can assure you is temporary. Mr. Strong," he said crisply, "let's have done with playacting. When you came in the cabin, you had returned from hiding this woman. I ask you to take me to her."

Once again Paul looked full into the Captain's face. The hard blue eyes with a little glint of mirth that didn't hide an expression of vengeful triumph deep down below, met his own unblinkingly. And now Paul understood a great deal.

Adelbert Griggs had killed himself. But a suicide wouldn't do for Captain Schott. He wanted a murder. So he had turned the suicide into a murder. It was as simple as that. It was Captain Schott who had discovered the body in Cabin 5. It was Captain Schott who had removed and thrown the gun into the sea, rearranged the newspapers in the cabin, and then called in and convinced a credulous doctor.

Captain Schott was going to permit no loose talk before the Halifax authorities about danger to the convoy, something set for Saturday. He and Mary were to appear before Major Thomson, accused of murder, fighting for their own lives, all irrelevancies ruled out, everything they said against other people disbelieved and discredited.

In the game of trading fictions, Captain Schott had come off the victor. He had set his scene. His case was almost watertight. Mary had come secretly aboard the *Shalimar*. She had left her shoe in Cabin 5. She had stayed there many minutes. Her fingerprints would be everywhere.

Captain Schott had turned a suicide into a murder. It would be difficult indeed to establish such charge against the Captain of the *Shalimar*; Major Thomson had known Captain Schott for years. With time, of course, Paul might establish it. Captain Schott must have a murky past, murkier associates. In any attempt to harm the convoy he would need outside assistance. Paul Strong was a reputable New York journalist with a powerful magazine behind him, and even in his first shock he wasn't really afraid that Mary would hang because Adelbert Griggs had killed himself. His fear was of a different sort.

Time was the factor. Saturday, next Saturday, was the day burning in his mind. The *Shalimar* would not arrive in Halifax until Wednesday. It was impossible that he could unmask and overturn Captain Schott by Saturday, convince Major Thomson that the Captain was criminally involved in some unknown plot against his own convoy. It was impossible that by Saturday he could interest Major Thomson in examining a theatre program and finding Lisa Tennevant, when the whole attention of the Royal Mounted would be focused upon Mary Strong. He couldn't use the addresses on the program and find Lisa Tennevant himself, he couldn't find out anything about the plot, locked up in jail. Locked up in jail, he and Mary could accomplish nothing. Not by Saturday.

In some distant portion of his brain, Paul realized that Captain Schott was also playing for time. The difference was that the Captain's gamble was going to be successful. Unless he could keep Mary hidden two more days, and, on Wednesday night, figure out some way to sweep both of them through the gauntlet of the Canadian Royal Mounted lined up and waiting at the dock in Halifax. In that bleak moment of his weariness and despair, such a project seemed remote beyond belief.

Captain Schott had won. He had done everything he could to ruin Mary, and yet the Captain didn't care personally whether she lived or died, whether she hung or in the end went free. It mattered little to him whether the murder charge stuck or not. It had only to stick through Saturday, and after Saturday Captain Lucky Schott would be seen no more in Halifax harbor. Sitting there, Paul knew all those things.

He got up on his feet, as the *Shalimar* plunged into the trough of a wave and righted herself. He was so torn to pieces inwardly, so worn out and exhausted, that he found it hard to stand. The cabin floor swayed. The chair he held trembled underneath his hand. Deliberately he steadied himself, controlled his nerves, waited for the motion to subside.

"Captain Schott," he said, "you have shocked me profoundly. I can't take you to this woman you describe, I don't know where she's hiding, I know nothing about her. That is all I have to say to you. Now, I should like you to excuse me. I want to go to bed."

He thought Captain Schott might start a stream of blustering objections, and braced himself to take it. But that wasn't the Captain's way. He rose obligingly. Again the floor rocked, more violently. A tumbler slid along the washbasin. On the berth the top-heavy basket of fruit teetered. Captain Schott put out his hand to steady it. He wasn't quick enough. Half a dozen apples and oranges rolled off on the floor, scurrying in all directions. A jar of jelly fell and smashed.

"Let it go," Paul started to say, but did not.

Captain Schott was staring into the basket. Nestled underneath a bunch of desiccated grapes, buried halfway down, was a small pair of sturdy walking shoes—undoubtedly the most serviceable in Frau Van Anda's collection. Paul understood at once. The Dutchwoman had killed him with kindness. Surmising for some reason of her own that he might have urgent need of a pair of size-four shoes, she had provided them from her own wardrobe. Captain Schott also understood. His triumphant laugh rang out.

"So, she's been here all the time! Mr. Strong, you are less intelligent than I imagined. I must ask permission to search your cabin again."

"It isn't necessary." On stiff, numb legs Paul walked over to the drawer underneath the berth. He leaned down and pulled it out. The sudden light was dazzling in Mary's eyes. She huddled in her cocoon, her face pale and scared. He stooped to unwrap the blanket. "Darling, don't be frightened, everything will be all right. You can come out now." Helping her to her feet, he locked his arm through hers. Together they turned around.

"Captain Schott," Paul said, "this is the woman you did not see running away from Cabin 5 with a gun in her hand. This is my wife."

TEN

It was half-past nine o'clock on Wednesday night, and a cold chill rain was falling, when the *Shalimar* docked in Halifax harbor. Ordinarily she would have sailed past the city and on into Bedford Basin to anchor with her convoy. Special circumstances had altered those arrangements.

Before they reached the gate ships which guarded the harbor entrance, Captain Schott had sent an urgent but carefully detailed message ashore. Adelbert Griggs was dead, murdered. He was holding Mary and Paul Strong, the guilty woman and her accomplice. At the gate ships instructions were awaiting him. The *Shalimar* had left the company there. Alone she had steamed past the lighthouse on Maugers Beach, past the gloomy ruins of the old Martello tower built in Napoleon's time when the English had first discovered that cannon balls glanced off rounded walls, past the clustered oil tanks of Imperoyal, past the Dartmouth airport from which the Hurricanes roared daily out to sea, and on toward Halifax. The stubby skyline of the town—the confusion of clocks and towers and smoke-stained chimney pots huddled about the steep rise of the Citadel—was obscured in rain and darkness. There were lights along the waterfront. From a shore, which was like a many-fingered hand, the docks and wharves stretched out.

The *Shalimar* ignored the beckoning fingers, and came in abreast the smoke-grimed bulk of the Immigration Building. It rose from the water edge like a Venetian structure. So close that from bow to stern her rail almost rubbed the landing stage, the *Shalimar* dropped anchor. The gangplank seemed hardly necessary, but it was flung across immediately. Two men who had stepped out of the building to the landing stage, watched with satisfaction. Both of them had anxiously awaited the arrival of the *Shalimar* since the receipt of Captain Schott's amazing message. One of them was an immigration official, the other was Major Kenneth Thomson, Superintendent of the Royal Canadian Mounted Police for the Province of Nova Scotia. Some of Major Thomson's men were scattered through the building. But no trouble was expected.

At nine-thirty-five Ordinary Seaman Brown knocked at the door of Cabin 12. His knock was a formality. He listened, however, until he heard an answering voice and then he took out a key, unlocked the cabin door, knocked again, and waited politely. The door was quickly opened.

"My wife will be ready in a moment," Paul said at once to make things easier for Ordinary Seaman Brown. He hesitated before he asked his question. A lot depended on the answer. "Where are they waiting—in the Captain's quarters?"

"Captain Schott prefers that the questioning take place ashore. In the immigration offices, I expect. He is talking to Major Thomson now. They will meet us at the gangplank shortly," said Seaman Brown, and coughed a little. It had crossed his mind that adjoining the immigration offices, although these people might not know it, was the prison where they would undoubtedly spend the night, and many other nights. From the waterside, by daytime, one could see the bars above, and, behind the bars, pale, staring faces. Not many women, however. Seaman Brown carefully did not look at Mary. "I can carry your bag, sir. It's raining like sixty."

"Funny, I thought I heard a train," Mary said. She had pulled on her crimson coat and stood at the mirror trying to make something of her battered hat.

Seaman Brown kept on looking at the floor.

"A whistle," Mary said. "I thought I heard a train whistle."

"The railroad station is close by, down the square, next the Haligonian Hotel," admitted Seaman Brown, after some deliberation. "A siding runs in at the Immigration Building. Sometimes you can hear the trains."

"I wish I was on one," Mary said.

Seaman Brown, who was used to English girls and decent reticence, found such frankness disconcerting. Almost shocking, like laughing at a funeral. He looked pained. But Paul thought to himself, "She's playing it exactly right. With luck, and if we move fast enough, maybe we can put it over."

During the two days they had remained behind a locked door in Cabin 12 with all their meals sent in and nothing said about air or exercise, Paul had had plenty of time to think. He had sat on the case of Paul and Mary Strong, and had ruled against his personal safety and— Mary's safety. He and Mary would be far safer locked up in prison fighting a fabricated murder charge than they'd be searching for Lisa Tennevant and the answer to the mysterious plot that endangered the convoy. But they weren't going straight from the *Shalimar* to prison if Paul could help it. If Paul could possibly arrange it, so he had decided two days ago, Major Thomson would be deprived of his prisoners until

Saturday. Or until Paul had definite and convincing information to offer the Royal Mounted.

Now, when he learned that the questioning was to take place in the immigration offices, that the men were waiting on shore, Paul saw a chance. He had a plan of sorts. A plan that might work because of its simplicity and boldness.

Everything depended on two things. Surprise—and how far they would need to walk on the deck outside to reach the gangplank. And of course a lot depended on what happened after they made that first important break. Thank God, Frau Van Anda's shoes fitted Mary. Cabin 12 was on the shore side. As the *Shalimar* nudged in alongside the long, narrow landing stage, Paul had stood at the porthole and engaged himself in feverish study of the Immigration Building. He didn't know where they'd dropped the gangplank. It was somewhere forward, out of his line of vision. But when across the rain-washed deck, almost resting against the ship's rail, he had glimpsed the landing stage—a kind of walkway that ran the length of the Immigration Building like a shelf, broken at intervals by squares of light marking the several openings that led within—Paul knew they had a chance.

"The Haligonian Hotel is quite a place, quite a place," said Seaman Brown. He coughed again and flushed. These people were hardly ordinary tourists.

"A friend of mine once stayed at the Haligonian Hotel," Paul said, and found himself distracted by the sharp and bitter thrust of memory. The friend was Max. When Max had come to Canada and failed to photograph the prison camps he had drifted on to Halifax. Eventually he had returned to *News Review* with that haunting series of the Cape Breton fisherfolk strewing flowers on the water for those drowned and lost at sea. Now Max himself had met with a mysterious fate on a colder sea. In far off Reykjavik Max had stumbled on some unknown portion of the plot that concerned them now. In Reykjavik, almost four weeks ago, Max had gone aboard a fishing boat that had been shelled and sunk by a German submarine, and thereafter her passengers had been seen no more. Strange, thought Paul, as strange and unreal as what had happened to him and Mary. Paul became aware that Ordinary Seaman Brown was looking restless. He turned toward Mary. "Darling, we mustn't keep them waiting."

"I'm ready now."

Seaman Brown picked up Paul's bag and led the way. The rain assaulted them the instant they stepped on deck. Lowering his head against it, Seaman Brown quickened his pace without noticing that the Strongs had slackened theirs.

"The gangplank is ahead."

The waiting men stood ashore a good ninety feet away. Taking shelter from the weather, the three of them had backed off the stage into a lighted doorway, from which they watched the gangplank.

"Come along, Mary," Paul said.

It all happened quickly. She felt his hand tighten on hers. He jerked her to a stop. They spun around. Together they went over the rail. The gap between the deck and the landing stage was narrow, but the stage was lower than the deck. She closed her eyes as they jumped, and opened them with the jar of their landing. She heard an astonished shout from the deck above. Seaman Brown ran to the rail. Over her shoulder, beneath lights farther down, she caught a glimpse of Captain Schott, the two other men. They looked stupefied with surprise. They started running. One of them ran up the gangplank. The other two had placed the heavy thud correctly, knew that someone had jumped from ship to shore. They started in the right direction, their feet thundering on the wooden walk.

She and Paul were also running. Hand in hand, they dived into the nearest opening of the building, ran down a flight of stairs. For a moment, in the sudden confusion of light and shadow, she was almost blind. The lights that burned overhead were very powerful but they were far apart and scattered, so that the ground-floor place was a patchwork of brilliant light and deep shadow—like an enormous checkerboard. The opening had led them into railroad sheds.

Men were working there. Someone yelled, just as Paul pulled Mary behind a stationary train. They ran around the train and leaped the track and were in another patch of light. Other workers spied them, yelled and set in pursuit of them. One man took aim and hurled his monkey wrench, as they whirled around again. It crashed against a freight car. Somewhere in the rear, Major Thomson was shouting vainly, "Halt, or I'll shoot!" But in the noise and uproar that rocked the railroad sheds, his voice was almost lost.

They ducked behind several coupled cars, and Mary's crimson coat was mercifully hidden. On one side was a concrete wall, on the other the darkened trains. It was black as a tunnel. They couldn't see, but from both directions they could hear pursuit closing in. Advance and retreat seemed equally impossible. The linked trains were tightly sealed, their platforms closed. Paul crawled over a coupling and dragged her over, and they dropped breathless to the other side. Again they ran. Almost immediately they found themselves outside the building and in the open. She felt the dash of rain. Escape seemed closer than it was.

Distant lights ahead glowed through the downpour—the lights of the tall hotel which turned its back on the waterfront, and, farther left, the lights of the railroad station. But there was a complicated spur of tracks to cross, and beyond, between them and the distant lights, lost in driving rain, an unknown stretch of darkness which must be hotel property. The shouts were directly behind them.

Paul turned left. In the gloom some yards away a kind of ramp led to a covered bridge which crossed the street, angled off sharply and ran along above a waste of marshy ground to enter the railroad station. The railroad station, like the hotel, faced on another street nearly two blocks away. If they could get on that bridge … They ran. And then Paul thought, "God, the ramp takes us straight into the Immigration Building."

He stopped just in time. The Security Guards, three of them, were posted in a small wooden shelter a short distance from the ramp and bridge. Nearby a street lamp shone murkily. Beneath it he saw a glistening tangle of posts and wire. Barbed wire fenced in the shelter, as barbed wire fenced in the block, and stretched for miles along the waterfront. They were caught on the wrong side of it. There had to be a gap, Paul told himself, back there at the point where the railroad spur swelled out into the many tracks edging the hotel property. His mistake had been to run for the station; they should have crossed the tracks and made straight for the hotel, gambling on the darkness that lay in between.

The Security Guards had heard the row break out in the railroad sheds, and had stuck grimly to their post. But they sensed that something had gone wrong. What? As Paul and Mary turned to double back, one of the guards glimpsed the running figures through the rain. "Halt, or I'll shoot!" Paul jerked Mary back against an air vent in the wall. Splinters of wood flew out from a spot a few feet away as the bullet struck.

By now the other searchers were pouring in increasing numbers from the sheds. In the confusion, in the rain and in the darkness, lay their chance. The guards wouldn't risk shooting their own. Several men ran by. They waited, hidden by the vent. Too soon, thought Mary despairingly, they started running again. Flashlights were blossoming all around them.

Dodging around obstructions, hugging the wall, racing past windows and doorways, they reached the spot Paul had decided on. Together, with him pulling her, they left the safety of the wall. They were stumbling across the network of railroad tracks, leaping the ties, sinking ankle deep in mud and muck, and still he pulled her on. At last they were at the hotel grounds, on the outskirts of the stretch of darkness.

It was a winter-killed rose garden, laid out in paths and beds, now deep in frozen mud and ruts that gushed with water. The hotel was still yards away. Flashlights were flickering like fireflies along the garden paths, will-o'-the-wisps in the pouring rain, and excited men were calling one another.

She gave herself up for lost, just as Paul dragged her forcibly into the greenhouse. Absolutely dark, the small glassed-in structure sat withdrawn a little, not far from the perils of the garden and the perils of the harbor street, but on the right side of the barbed-wire fence. He pushed her down on some sort of stool. She couldn't see the stool, or see his face, but she could smell the roses. She bent her head, drew a long deep breath and rested. Presently she sighed and straightened up, and began to wring out her dripping coat. Her hat was long since gone. But through it all, she'd hung on to her purse. That pleased her so much that, sitting there in the darkness, she pulled out her lipstick and drew herself another mouth.

Paul was watching the flashlights. They would come together and separate. They wandered toward the hotel and went in and came out again, so that he located a door. The door—a rear door—probably led into the storerooms or kitchens. For five minutes, for ten, standing motionless at the greenhouse windows, he watched the gardens. One by one the flashlights withdrew. Most of them returned to the harbor street, where he lost them. The last one vanished. He looked at the luminous dial of his watch. Fifteen minutes crawled by.

"Let's move on, Mary."

This time they didn't run. They walked almost slowly toward the hotel, moving noiselessly across the sodden ground in the shadow of a soaked and leafless hedge. Caution was more important now than haste. The door unexpectedly led them into the hotel garage. Cars were clustered there, many of them canvas-covered, raised on blocks. Beyond the garage were the kitchens, the storerooms, the laundry.

There was activity in the kitchens, the clatter of pots and pans. Music drifted down from several floors above. The laundry was dark, deserted and silent. Paul struck a match. A row of washtubs marched around the walls. Bundles of laundry, hundreds of sheets and towels and pillow slips, overflowed the tubs and tables, spilled over on the floor.

"This is the place," said Paul, "to get rid of that damned coat. Wait here for me. I'm going to scout the situation."

"Where? In the bar?"

"God knows, darling, I need a drink. Give me fifteen minutes to look around, and find a safe way out of the hotel. I've got a hunch our best bet is to stick around these parts awhile."

He kissed her quickly in the darkness, pressed something in her hand. After he had gone, after she had pulled off her coat and pushed it deep into one of the laundry bundles, she laughed softly to herself. She didn't need to look at Paul's parting present. She could smell it in the dark. Back there in the greenhouse, he had picked for her a single rose.

ELEVEN

Not half of Paul's fifteen minutes were gone when two young men, wearing the handsome light-blue uniform of the R.C.M.P., opened the door of the basement laundry. The two young men were a very small part of a large group, in and out of uniform, which had mysteriously descended upon the Hotel Haligonian to conduct a room-to-room search—much to the dismay of the management.

"I say," one of them called, "are you there, Mr. Strong? You may as well come out, and save everybody trouble."

There was no answer. The lights flashed on. The two young men were thorough. They moved quickly around the basement room, lifting the tops of washtubs, peering underneath, poking their leather-covered walking-out sticks—heavier than they looked, these—into overflowing laundry hampers. They opened up the cabinets that held the extra pails. They carefully investigated the closet where the soaps and cleansing fluids were kept. They examined the row of carts that rolled every morning through the halls collecting the soiled linens from seven rambling floors. Unfortunately for them, the young men were looking primarily for a six-foot man, clean-shaven, dark and in camel's hair, accompanied by his wife, who wore a crimson coat. They'd been told the wife was blonde, but they'd overlooked the fact that she was also very small.

"He is certainly not in here," said one to the other. "I think myself the old man is wrong for once. The pair of them are still on Water Street."

Suddenly a third young man appeared, and in some excitement called from the doorway.

"You two might step over to the kitchen. The vegetable cook heard someone running up the service stairs six or seven minutes ago."

They left in haste. Immediately, however, one of them returned to switch off the lights. He was the one who nearly caught her. A few minutes later Mary cautiously unwound herself from a pile of sheets, pulled a pillow slip off her head. She combed her hair again. She'd grown quite expert in the dark. Thank heavens, her simple smartly cut dress was of a material which didn't wrinkle badly and was black. Let them have a try at describing it!

She tiptoed to the door and listened. The kitchen was close by. The young policemen were apparently standing in the hall, still talking to the vegetable cook who had little more to offer except that the chef was waiting for the carrots. Very shortly the conversation was concluded, and the cook went back gratefully to his vegetables. The clatter in the kitchen was resumed. The crisp definite footsteps of the three young men retreated down the hall, and climbed the service stairs.

She followed them. The flight of stairs was short and led her up immediately into the hotel lobby, directly beside the elevators. She paused, astonished at the scene. New York had larger and more impressive lobbies, but only in Washington had she seen a lobby equally active and cosmopolitan. King George and Queen Elizabeth, who were to gaze at her so often from railway stations and shops and hotels, looked mildly disconcerted, too, as though they hadn't sufficiently realized that the small seaport city, which slept after every war, had wakened up again. The music floating down the grand stairway, where the twin portraits were displayed, was drowned in the babble of voices below. Every divan, every chair was filled, practically every inch of standing space was occupied. A small international convention was waiting patiently at the elevators. Men and women, too, in the uniforms of half a dozen scattered countries were flocking in and out of the dining room, crowded at the newsstand, leaning against the wall to scribble postcards, commiserating with one another on Halifax and on the weather. Piles of luggage hid the desk. Through it all, Mary heard the clear incisive voice of an English Squadron Leader demanding rooms.

"Arrangements, I can assure you, were made by wireless from London yesterday. Also, I wish you'd have someone explain to me why you colonials don't black out your harbors."

Mary missed the answer. She sympathized with them both, because she guessed that the youthful Squadron Leader, like herself, felt very far away from home. Behind a palm where a French girl was conducting a flirtation with a Pole who had recently acquired Canadian wings, she found a mirror. No need to be surreptitious. She surveyed herself boldly. Her lips and hair would pass, her dark frock was no more damp and wrinkled than several other frocks in the near vicinity. She had cleaned the mud from her shoes as best she could, but had been troubled about their appearance until she saw the lobby. It was tracked with mud, and a rivulet of water was actually running from the checkroom where scores of umbrellas were stored.

She rubbed a little rouge on her pale cheeks, and was satisfied. In this crowd, no one would give her a second glance. She looked around for the bar and failed to locate it. Working her way past the dining room traffic, past the newsstand, past the desk, she came abreast the revolving doors.

Some of her confidence oozed away. Two inconspicuous-looking men, wearing business suits, stood at each of the three revolving doors. They paid no attention to the people who came spinning in, but they were sharply interested in those who were going out. One young couple stopped, surprised at a polite touch on the arm. A low-voiced question was asked. The girl laughed, and the man reddened and pulled out papers. The girl's coat was plaid; crimson was the predominating color.

There were other exits, Mary told herself. At any rate her business was to find the bar. Drawn by the music, she wandered up the stairway to the mezzanine floor. On the left was a writing room doing service as a lounge, flanked by several darkened service rooms. She turned toward the ballroom on the right side, intending to move on past toward a smaller room beyond where she fancied Paul might be. A waltz was being played. The ballroom lights were romantically low. Glancing inside, Mary observed what she first supposed was a stag line, and then abruptly decided was not. The half a dozen young men who watched from the musicians' stand, and occasionally moved out quietly on the floor, were not dancing. They were asking courteous questions of certain of the couples, who, for one reason or another, had attracted their attention. Mary's heart thudded when someone stepped into her path. But it was only a middle-aged hotel attendant.

"I'm sorry, Miss, this floor is reserved for the dancers. We already have two hundred and twelve inside."

"Two hundred and twelve," she repeated, taken aback by his explicitness.

"Tonight, we were obliged to turn away several hundred more." He sighed at the loss to the management, which could not affect his own pocketbook in the least. "Regulations since that dreadful dancehall fire last year."

"The Boston nightclub fire?" she said before she thought.

"The St. John's Hostel fire," he replied, and looked at her with sudden interest. The Mounties were seeking a couple, of course. But this girl was unmistakably blonde. "Are you an American, Miss?"

Mary hesitated. It would be much safer to pass as a Canadian, but his remark had been less a question than a statement. She restrained an impulse to deny her nationality, and nodded affirmatively. This turned out to be fortunate. Because then she explained hurriedly that she was looking for the bar.

"The bar, Miss?"

His vague suspicion died in shock. "There is no public drinking in the Province of Nova Scotia! If you leave a request at the desk," he finished severely, "possibly Mr. Leatherstocking can arrange for you to obtain a permit to buy a stimulant tomorrow in our package store over town. But you must use it in your room!"

Properly rebuked, Mary hurriedly withdrew. As she went back down the stairs, she saw across the lobby a lighted alley which she had not noticed before. It seemed to be another exit. She made for it quickly.

The alley, banked in plateglass windows which showed a drugstore, a darkened barber shop, a crowded lunchroom, and a tiny club where visiting airmen lounged in easy chairs, gathered at a minute soda bar or collected eagerly at a correspondence rack seeking mail from home, debouched directly into the railroad station. The business of the policemen who stood vigil at this particular exit was evident at once. There was no need here to spare the sensibilities of the hotel patrons. These policemen wore the pale-blue uniform. Others in uniform wandered about the station waiting room beyond, were posted at every ticket window. The hotel, the railroad station and the Immigration Building, linked to the other two by the bridge, formed a kind of triangle. Mary realized that she and Paul were caught in a huge, three-sided trap; they had plenty of room to move around in and plenty of company, too, but they couldn't get out.

One of the policemen turned around and looked at her. Immediately she paused and began to study the variegated display in the shadow box window of the airmen's club. With great attentiveness she regarded a heap of fishnets, a rusty anchor, the twisted frame of a lantern which was not worth looking at, but which had miraculously survived the Halifax explosion a quarter of a century before. She gazed at a browned old chart of Sable Island, and read through the list of the known shipwrecks which had occurred there since 1801. Next to it a brightly colored modern placard announced that on Spring Garden Street the Superfluity Shop, which had already donated to the Atlantic War Fund sufficient money for fourteen mobile canteens, three wheel chairs, two beds in Queen Charlotte's Hospital in London, scores of radios and earphones for the men in the Merchant Navy, and many other things, was prepared to support the charity by selling back to the public what the public had given it—babies' woolies, superfluous clothes of all kinds neatly mended, cleaned and put in order, antique jewelry and furniture, etc. When the policeman seemed satisfied, Mary gave up her meditations on the Superfluity Shop. She shattered the watcher's last lingering doubt by strolling directly past him to enter the lunchroom.

The lunchroom was also thick with people. A sailor vacated a stool at the crowded counter, vigorously elbowed a path for her, and then turned suddenly shy and walked out before she could thank him. Mary sat down and ordered coffee.

"Two lumps, please."

"You are permitted only one," said a harried waitress. "And we've run out of cream."

"Take mine, Miss," said a familiar voice from the crowd behind her.

She turned on her stool. Without recognition, she and Paul looked briefly at each other. He held out a little pot of cream which he was balancing along with a cup of coffee, and turned around again to the group discussing the intricacies of modern shipbuilding as opposed to the grand old days on the Clyde.

Presently and separately they left the lunchroom. Still asking earnest questions, Paul accompanied his newfound friends back into the lobby, and parted with them, and didn't seem to be aware that a small blonde girl in black was lingering several yards away. He strolled over to the newsstand, being sure that she kept him in sight, and bought a paper, partly for the sake of behaving normally and partly because he wanted the satisfaction of seeing the name of the Princess Royal Theatre in print again. Earlier, stopping casually at the desk, he'd acquired a city map and had already located on the crisscrossed maze four important streets. Barrington Street where the theatre was, Marbury Lane where Mr. Alexander Campbell who'd printed *The Wild Duck* program had his shop, Archer Place for Frome & Frome who'd lent the furniture. Those three were centrally located. Madame des Brizac, the sempstress, apparently lived out some distance on the edge of town. He'd spotted Queen Street—her street—last.

On a sudden wild impulse he'd even looked up Lisa Tennevant's name in the local phone book, but of course it wasn't there. Not that he'd expected such an improbably lucky break, but long ago Paul had learned to check all the angles and never to ignore the obvious and the easy. As it was, he hoped he had more leads to Lisa Tennevant than he'd need. Any one of the four addresses lightly crossed on his map might yield up the present address of Lisa Tennevant—providing he struck the right person. After he found her, what happened was anybody's guess.

First of all, of course, he and Mary had to get themselves out of the

Hotel Haligonian. A careful tour had convinced Paul that they weren't to leave that night.

When he walked to the elevator and rang the bell, Mary was in the crowd. Five people got off at the fourth floor. Paul and Mary were among them. They didn't speak until they were safely on the fire stairs, and walking down again.

"Where?" asked Mary.

"I've found a place for us to sleep," he told her, and didn't find it necessary to add that by now he could have drawn an architect's blueprint of the Haligonian. "Nothing to recommend it except that those ubiquitous young men in blue spent easily an hour there, and certainly won't be back tonight."

"Tomorrow?"

"Sometime tomorrow," he announced with more confidence than he felt, "once we're safely out of here, we'll start off our inquiry as though we were a couple of regular reporters working on an ordinary assignment."

She looked at him in silence.

"First," he said, "I'll phone the office in New York from a booth far away from here. It won't be safe to tell them much, but I've got to tell them something. After that, we'll make a call at the Princess Royal Theatre."

"Darling, you sound awfully sure."

"Shucks, Mary. Better to be sure than sunk. They do seem to have us pretty well surrounded, but they don't know what we look like—which evens up the chances."

"Captain Schott knows."

"Captain Schott isn't doing the hunting, and won't be—with all he has to hide himself. If I'm right, his role will be to shrink modestly into the background, waiting for Saturday. Thank God, the Mounties have no photographs of us. Have you forgotten that I sensibly took away the Captain's pictures?"

She couldn't quite smile. Except for her, Mary realized dismally, Paul could march past the watching policemen through any door to freedom. She was the stumbling block. She could not, in midwinter, walk out of the hotel in a thin black dress—without a hat or coat.

They turned into the cluttered space where the Hotel Haligonian stored its damaged furniture in the optimistic hope that someday, when the war was over, the boss carpenter and his staff of three might come back to work. They crawled behind a barricade of broken bureaus, and lay down together on some sagging springs that Paul had covered with a length of moldy tapestry to simulate a mattress.

Mary went to sleep immediately. For a while, propped on an elbow beside her, Paul looked through his newspaper, squinting in the pallid rays of a lamp he'd rigged up on the floor and muffled with his handkerchief, trying to get the feel of Halifax from its press. War news mostly, wire stuff from Ottawa, Montreal, Toronto, not many local stories. Paul read stubbornly on. If he and Mary were to escape and tour the town, a strange town in a country that bordered the United States and yet still was strange and unfamiliar and foreign to them, searching for Lisa Tennevant, asking questions of strangers, they would need every scrap of knowledge they could get. Finally he let the newspaper slip from his hands. For several minutes he lay there staring into space.

He had the unreal, helpless feeling of a man faced with a grave and terrible emergency and cut off completely from his home, his business, his associates and friends, all his ordinary sources of information, all his ordinary ways of doing things. Major Thomson would find it simple to get in touch with *News Review* and tell his story. But it wasn't going to be easy for Paul to telephone New York. He'd been pretending to Mary, talking big. A few short hours had taught him that Halifax wasn't New York, his own careless, wonderful bailiwick, where millions of people made a certain kind of efficiency impossible and allowed a man elbow room.

Halifax was a seaport town, an important but a small seaport town, wholly geared to war. It was highly probable that *all* long-distance calls, *all* telegrams, with particular emphasis on those going outside the country, would be censored. The truth was that he and Mary were strictly on their own. They were wanted for the murder of a suicide who had been in serious trouble with the Royal Mounted; arrayed against them were all the forces of that powerful organization.

Suddenly the whole situation became bitterly discouraging to Paul. He saw no light anywhere, and little hope. Frau Van Anda, the redheaded Dutchwoman who had tried to befriend them, was herself involved in the plot. Frau Van Anda had given Mary a pair of shoes, but a trunk that had once belonged to her had certainly been in Cabin 5 before it was spirited away. Lotte, her bosom companion, was an ally of Captain Schott's. And where was Hans Van Anda? Adelbert Griggs, the former Security Guard who'd told Mary that the convoy was endangered, had told painfully little and he would never tell them more. For that matter, thought Paul staring into darkness, in his own self-appointed search for Lisa Tennevant he had little to work with—a theatre program, the addresses of strangers.

In that moment Paul Strong was very close to giving up. It seemed to him that the only sensible course was to go downstairs and surrender to the nearest policeman. He rose from bed and walked as far as the door before he knew he couldn't do it. But he could do something else. Something that would put him right with himself, and make him know that he was doing what he had to do.

He snapped on the light again and pulled out a pad and pencil. He wrote a note to Major Thomson of the Royal Mounted. It was marked "Urgent." Paul signed his own name, and promised to appear with his wife at headquarters on Sunday morning at the latest. It was an odd and encyclopedic message to be written to the authorities by a suspected murderer, a fugitive from justice.

Because Paul told everything, or almost. He told the story of Captain Schott, he told of Mary's meeting with Adelbert Griggs, he told of his own belief that some unknown danger menaced the convoy on Saturday. He told about Frau Van Anda and her son; he warned the Royal Mounted against the black-haired, flat-chested Lotte.

One thing only he omitted from his note. He didn't mention Lisa Tennevant. He held back that bit of information deliberately. The search for Lisa Tennevant was to be his and Mary's personal line of inquiry.

He addressed and stamped his message—using U. S. stamps and hoping U. S. stamps would do—and stepped out into the hall again. He was obliged to return to the elevators before he located a mail slot. In the ballroom across the way the dance was over. The dancers were gone. The dinner-jacketed musicians carrying their instruments were heading toward the elevators.

Paul was of no mind to be caught up in that exuberant crowd. The fewer people who noticed him the better. He dropped his envelope, moved quickly back around the corner and, to his dismay, found himself among a group of waiters who had just left the ballroom. The service hall was filled with them. He saw one of the waiters eye him curiously, and forced himself to pause and light a cigarette.

But as he went on and around the final corner, he thought the man was still looking indecisively after him. Patrons of the hotel should not be wandering around the service wing. Paul darted down the hall and turned hurriedly into the storage room before the waiter should decide to follow. He realized at once that he had turned in one door too soon.

This door was ajar; he had carefully closed the door upon the crowded, jumbled place where Mary slept. And he hadn't left a light on.

A swinging electric bulb, enclosed in a nest of wire, was burning here. It shone down upon rows and rows of trunks, arranged with aisles between them. He was in the trunk room of the hotel. Odd that a light was burning here, odd that he'd found the door ajar. But Paul's thoughts were still upon the waiter. He leaned back against the door and listened. Did he hear approaching footsteps? He looked quickly for a hiding place.

And then he saw a trunk that was out of line with its fellows, a trunk placed very near the door. It was a large black trunk, an elderly, travel-worn trunk with time-darkened brass mountings. Paul set down his cigarette and leaned closer. The light was poor, but beside the scrolled elaborate lock he saw a spot where the paint was new and glossy. When he touched the spot he felt the outline of the vanished initials. E.V.A.

Elise Van Anda's trunk that had mysteriously disappeared from Adelbert Griggs' cabin had as mysteriously reappeared in the trunk room of the Haligonian. What was in it? Something obviously that the authorities had not been meant to see.

Paul stooped to examine the lock. Opening someone else's trunk was undoubtedly a felony, and a few short days ago, when he was a law-abiding citizen in New York, not even journalistic enterprise would have induced him to do it. He had changed since then. The lock was good stout brass but of an old-fashioned design, and with age the trunk had shrunk away from it. If he had any decent sort of pry, he could probably conquer that lock but hardly without breaking it. Once he had seen Mary open a similar lock with a hairpin. He might try his pocket knife.

Paul was reaching for his knife when he heard the doorknob turn from the hall. He was learning fast. He even remembered to snatch up his cigarette before he vanished behind the row of trunks ahead. Fortunately he had picked his spot in advance. Squatted on his haunches, he was well concealed, and a crack between two trunks offered him a fair view of the door.

A pair of trousered legs came in. They weren't the waiter's legs. The stealth, the tiptoed steps, told Paul that before he raised his eyes. If he had no business in the trunk room neither had the man who had just come in. Peeping up, Paul examined the stocky legs, the thick neck and thicker shoulders and last of all the newcomer's hairless head, his hairless face. The man was shockingly bald. Some illness had robbed him of every trace of hair. He had neither brows nor lashes. There was no suggestion of beard on his cheeks or chin. On that naked, infantile face the highly adult expression had an unnatural, almost obscene quality. The whining, fretful voice matched the face. It addressed someone who had slipped in behind him.

"I can handle the trunk myself. Easy. Just show me where it goes."

"We're going to wait for him," a woman's voice said sharply.

The woman was Lotte. Her voice was sharp but she sounded nervous. Paul watched her close the door. Lotte was dressed for the street in the same dingy hat and coat she had worn aboard the *Shalimar*. She gazed at her watch.

"He should be here any minute."

As she spoke, the door was swiftly opened. Hans Van Anda came in on quick, light feet. Unlike his two companions, he wasn't nervous in the least. Preoccupied perhaps, hurried, but even in his haste, thought Paul, the young Dutchman seemed as casual and effortless as he had been that night when he strolled over to their table in the New York restaurant.

"We thought you'd never come," Lotte cried in relief. "Where have you been? Did you see Schott?"

"Schott is occupied with the Mounties. The stupid idiot should never have let that pair get away."

"Then they are—dangerous?"

"Dangerous, my good woman! If they're left to run at large, they may ruin everything."

"What do you mean to do then?"

"Never mind that now. We've got to get that trunk out of here," he said, with a curt nod at the hairless man.

Obediently the other struggled with the heavy trunk, heaved it on his back and staggered through the door. The scene was brief, the personalities and their relationships clearly defined. Hans Van Anda was by many years the junior of the three, but he didn't do the fetching and the carrying. It was Lotte who turned out the light and closed the door.

The door closed softly, and everything was quiet. Paul rose gratefully from his cramped position. A moment later he let himself out of the trunk room and slipped back into the room next door. He lay down beside Mary, put his arms around her and drew her close. At once he fell asleep. Tomorrow was another day.

TWELVE

Mary woke before seven o'clock in the morning, ravenously hungry and frozen to the bone. There was no heat in the storage room. The temperature had fallen sharply. Outside, the rain had turned into sleety snow. Paul had generously wrapped her in his overcoat, but during the night had evidently repented, and now, rolled up in it himself, lay beside her sleeping soundly. He mumbled but didn't wake when she pressed a note in his hand:

"Out to breakfast!"

On the mezzanine floor several yawning maids were sweeping out the ballroom, and waiters were setting up tables apparently in preparation for the annual breakfast of the Maple Leaf Club. Others were draping flags and seeding the speaker's table with various patriotic motifs. Mary descended confidently enough to the lobby, and then she paused. The divans and chairs were empty, the piles of luggage had vanished from the desk, the dining room was like a barn. In the early morning emptiness, the police were very much in evidence. In the lunchroom off the alley, five people occupied stools. Two of them were Mounties.

Mary's appetite deserted her. She beat a hasty retreat to the drugstore, went in and bought a toothbrush. She would go back upstairs, brush her teeth and make a leisurely toilet and then come down again. By eight o'clock the lunchroom should fill up.

While she was busy with her purchases, two middle-aged men came into the lobby from the street. One of them looked very tired. The young men at the revolving doors saluted smartly, as they strode past them and over to the desk.

Emerging from the drugstore, Mary nervously decided against the elevators and walked back up the stairs on the mezzanine floor. It was a fortunate decision. Simultaneously with her arrival the elevator arrived from the lobby. The brass doors slid back. Three men got out. The first to step out was Mr. Leatherstocking, the troubled and distressed manager of the Haligonian Hotel. His voice floated across the stairwell.

"I prefer, gentlemen, that we confine our conversations to my office. The staff is sufficiently disorganized as it is. Personally, I am quite satisfied that these people are not in my hotel."

"They spent the night in your laundry, sir," said a voice Mary did not recognize.

But she recognized the man, although she had seen him only once, very briefly, under the dim light of the landing stage. He was Major Thomson, Superintendent of the Mounted Police. His companion—the third man in the party—was Captain Schott.

Mary was standing on the other side of the curving flight of marble stairs. She turned immediately toward the nearest door and started in. Just in time she saw the sign: Manager's Office. The next door was locked. She opened the third door and disappeared, as the three men turned around.

The scrubwomen's dressing room was bare and small and—occupied. A stout, thickset woman, who evidently visualized herself as size 40, was struggling to pull over her head a dress that should have been size 44. She heard the door close, and mumbled something from the folds that sounded like:

"Washed only once, and will you look how it's shrunk."

Mary had a panic stricken second to decide. The instant the thickset woman won the battle and freed herself, she would be politely directed elsewhere. Elsewhere meant the hall outside, and two doors down the hall was Captain Schott. A row of scrubbing pails lined the floor. Above them hung a row of brown-gingham uniforms. When the thickset woman, red-faced and panting, emerged to the light of day, Mary was swallowed from neck to ankles in a brown gingham uniform and starting on the buttons.

"Can't you find a better fit, dear?" asked the other. "I expect you can't, you being so scrawny like." She gazed in modest admiration at her own sweating girth. "New?" she asked, mildly inquiring.

"Since yesterday," Mary said.

"I'm quitting soon myself," the thick-set woman confided. She seemed gloomily glad of company, as she examined the splitting, seams of her dress and complained again of shrinkage. Her feet hurt, she said. And no wonder.

"They work you here like you wasn't human; the help is always changing, you won't stay long yourself. As bad as them war factories, this place is. Smaller pay, too. You ought to try for chambermaid, dear. Lighter work."

"I'm strong," Mary said.

"Sometimes the puny ones surprise you." The stout woman heaved herself to reluctant feet. "I expect we'd best get started before the super comes snooping by; that woman's got an eye like an owl and a tongue like an adder. Here's your pail; you'd better take the bigger one, dear; I'm not as young as I used to be. The rags and soap are over here."

With a sinking heart Mary accepted a large pail of soapy water, a brush, a rag, a bar of soap. She hadn't bargained for this. It would be fatal to venture outside with her head uncovered, even in uniform. Looking around in a kind of quiet frenzy, she snatched up a clean white cloth and bound it tightly around her long blonde hair. Her companion cried out in objection.

"Your hair's your best point, dear. Maybe you've got no figure, but that real blonde hair is right pretty. The super don't insist on caps."

An argument was averted as the door opened again. Mary stepped instinctively closer to her large protector, prepared for the super and immediate discovery. But the hatchet-faced excited girl who came bursting in was another char.

"When did you check in, Christy? Late as usual, I bet. I been on duty myself since midnight, and I heard the news almost the first. Not much gets past Bess McDonal, if I do say so. Do you know why the super isn't on the floor?"

"She's gone and broke her neck," suggested Christy hopefully.

"They're in conference, all the floor supers is," announced the hatchet-faced girl impressively. "We've got German spies in the hotel—two of them."

"Well, I never! Where, Bess? I'd like a look at a German spy myself."

Mary said nothing at all. Perhaps it was her silence that caught the attention of the newcomer. Bess McDonal's eyes hadn't closed in sleep for twenty-four hours, but were as sharp as her needle-chinned face.

"Who are you?"

"Mary," said Mary faintly.

Bess sighed in disappointment. It had been too much to expect, of course. The woman sought by the Mounties was one Mary Strong. Any fool would have known enough to give a different name. Lana say, or Veronica or Madeleine. She hesitated.

"Mary Harris," Mary said.

"Don't scare the child to death, or you'll have her quitting before she rightly starts," snapped stout Christy, suddenly alarmed that she might lose her helper. "She's new this morning. Where is it you say they got these spies?"

"They haven't got them," said Bess, again triumphant. "The Mounties are looking everywhere. They were in the laundry last night."

"Go on! Next you'll be telling us they left their calling cards."

"They found the woman's coat wrapped up in some soiled sheets—a red cloth coat. I saw it with my own eyes. Red cloth and with a beaver collar. She won't get very far, I guess, without a coat!"

With a last sharp glance at the small pale girl in the unbecoming, ill-fitting uniform, Bess withdrew. She meditated going home, and spreading the wonderful news. On second thought she concluded she'd best step upstairs and look for the super. No harm in checking. She knew her duty, did Bess McDonal.

A few minutes later, Mary and Christy were on their hands and knees in the hall, scrubbing their way toward the stairs. No sensation could cheer Christy for long. She commenced a mournful initiation of the new help.

"The stairway's the worst, dear. All of them marble steps! It seems a shame, I always say, to scrub them off just so people can muck them up again. You'd think them dancers might sometimes remember there was such a thing as mats to use on muddy feet, but I do believe they hop them over."

Mary kept sedulous eyes on her work. Swabbing the marble floor before them, they had inched abreast the manager's office. The door was open. She distinctly heard the soft gentle voice of Captain Schott, the rumble of Major Thomson, the unhappy murmur of Mr. Leatherstocking. The three of them were discussing a girl at large in the hotel, a small blonde girl without a coat. At this point Christy showed a certain natural inclination to slow up, but as Mary hurried by her better nature asserted itself and she hurried, too.

"We're not going to a fire, dear. Push yourself too hard on your first day, and you'll blister up. You're panting now, like a little horse. Look out close for chewing gum. Folks will drop it anywhere. That's one good of the war I tell my old man, they can buy less to chew!"

By the time they reached the stairs one of her predictions had been fulfilled. Already Mary was beginning to blister up. Talking steadily the while, Christy had nicely saved her strength. All at once, as she looked down those awful stairs, her eyes brightened.

"Well," she breathed, "the super was jawing about it yesterday, but I forgot them buzzards was coming. We'll have to skip the stairs. What a pity!"

Promptly on the dot of eight, the members of the Maple Leaf Club had arrived at the Haligonian Hotel to eat their annual breakfast. In chattering dozens they spun through the revolving doors, went thronging toward the elevators, came streaming toward the grand stairway. Christy could hardly believe her luck.

"I'll look after the pails, dear. You run quick to the ladies' retiring room, and see if that girl Melba has tidied the bath. Directly they check their wraps, they'll be going in to muck it up. You'd better take your mop."

Mary got creakily to her knees. As it turned out, the bath off the ladies' retiring room could have done with a thorough cleaning, but there wasn't time. A group of six women, five of them gray-haired and middle-aged and talking of nothing briskly, and one sulky depressed young girl who was present against her will, walked in as she finished a mechanical mopping of the tiles. The older women had the grace to hesitate, but the girl made straight across the wet floor to the mirror, leaving fresh tracks as she went. Taking out her tools, she managed almost simultaneously to get a lipstick smear on the mirror, to spill powder in the washbowl, and to knock her purse off on the floor.

"Pick it up, why don't you?" she said crossly to Mary, and turned back to the mirror.

Mary stared at the scattered contents of the purse. And then she carefully gathered up the change, the handkerchief, the aspirin, the little address book, and snapped the catch. She returned the purse intact—with one exception. She kept the coatroom check. Five minutes later, she had a coat. Because she was in uniform it was a simple matter for her to convince the checkroom attendant that the owner of the coat had found the ballroom chilly and had sent her to fetch it.

"They're already starting the speeches," Mary said, which was quite true. The voice of the lady president was clearly audible in the lobby. "Be quick, please, I was told to hurry."

Locked in one of the toilets off the ladies' retiring room, Mary shucked her uniform and put on the coat. It was a soft gray squirrel. Tucked in the sleeve was a gray-silk scarf which made an adequate closely fitting turban. The uniform, bundled up, went swiftly into the towel hamper. Mary took a last quick look at herself. She walked out boldly, pretending she wasn't frightened.

There were four people now it would be disastrous to meet—Captain Schott, who knew her as Mary Strong, Christy, and the suspicious Bess who had accepted her as the newest of the transitory scrubwomen, the sulky nameless girl who owned the gray squirrel coat. Mary fully intended to return the wrap and very soon. What she had in mind was the quickest shopping trip of her career. She fervently hoped that Paul would sleep till she got back.

She was lucky at the revolving doors. A bellboy loaded with a bundle of magazines for the newsstand was coming in. One of the two policemen frowned at him, gave Mary an admiring glance, and then gallantly spun the door for her. As easily as that, she left the Haligonian Hotel.

The taxi stand had been empty since the war began. In a barren, ice-glazed park across the street, Lord Cornwallis, the founder of the city, hugged his bronze cloak around him, held a bronze cocked hat full of snow, and gazed remotely upon a little red trolley car that came clattering impertinently around him. In the thin gray distance, on much higher ground, she could see huddled buildings that must mark the shopping section. Mary caught the trolley, as the bewhiskered conductor, muttering to himself, was changing the seats around for the trip back over town. With surprising speed the trolley climbed away from the waterfront, gathering passengers as it went along. Up the rise that led toward the Citadel, which once had defended Halifax, lay the scattered, half-modern, half-pre-Victorian center of the town.

Gambrel roofs and peaked chimney pots nudged the flat unimaginative roofs of the practical present. Today and yesterday met like neighbors; history in the making and history made and done with. A crowd of swaggering, fresh-cheeked middies, who wore stripes for Nelson's wounds, gazed solemnly at a group of flyers as they passed them by. An old blind Negro climbed aboard his oxcart, as Mary alighted from the street car. She watched in wonder until the oxen passed. One of the Preston Negroes, whose great-great-granddaddy had fled with his Loyalist master during the American rebellion, was on his way to market with his catch of cod.

Quaint wasn't exactly the word, thought Mary. Embracing cemeteries and churches and monuments, overlooked by the lonely star-shaped fort on the hill above, and yet filled with strident clamor below, its narrow crooked bumpy streets and bumpier sidewalks thick with uniforms passing in double streams, Halifax clung to its past in no wistful way, but was sturdy, brawling, masculine—a man's town made for sailor men. A woman would have softened and cleaned it up, straightened out the higgledly-piggledy skyline, and stolen away its character.

On a noisy, dirty side street, Mary found the Superfluity Shop. She was almost surprised to discover how much like any other ladies' exchange it was.

Inside, a sweet-faced volunteer worker bent over the salesbook with knotted forehead, trying to balance the receipts of the day before. More money had come in the shop than goods had gone out, and how could that be? Possibly someone had been overcharged. Still if all the proceeds went to charity, pondered the lady, too deeply concentrated to hear the opening door, should one consider an overcharge as cheating the customer. How was one to decide which customer had been overcharged, and wouldn't even a discreet inquiry start talk of inefficiency. She wasn't inefficient, thought the lady indignantly. Didn't she volunteer her time? Mary cleared her throat. The lady dropped the puzzle with relief, rose at once and welcomed her with a gush of salesmanship.

"A fine Georgian inkwell was contributed last week, if you're looking for a wedding present. Oh, dear, I remember now the inkwell was sold. Such a shame! I'm sure you'd have loved it; a perfect gift these days when we must choose tiny things. I daresay the groom is in the service, so you wouldn't care for china, I suppose. Now, we must have something.... A hat and coat! Dear me, I'm afraid we have nothing that would suit you." Surprised into actually looking at the customer, the woman's vague eyes fastened on the expensive squirrel coat. "You understand our things are used."

"For my mother's maid," said Mary, glad of the opportunity to get in a word herself. "A good warm coat, inconspicuous. Tilda is about my size, and she won't mind if it looks a little worn."

"I should think not," said the other warmly.

Mary chose a black coat, not too well cut but of fine English tweed, and a small black hat somewhat the worse for wear. She'd chosen the right shop, thought Mary. She much preferred to brave the hotel a second time, and then leave it forever, in clothes that were not brand new.

Down the block, at an oculist's shop, Mary bought a pair of steel-rimmed spectacles that added five years to her age and worsened her vision considerably. Another stop produced mascara and a different, darker shade of face powder. She had her last inspiration outside the shop where she had paused to catch the trolley again. It was accurately called the Variety Store.

The grimy show window was filled with everything that people didn't want—corncob pipes and coat racks made from antlers, beaded lamps and velvet pincushions, gilded sea shells and seaweed fans, satin pillow tops hand painted handsomely with likenesses of the King and Queen, Mr. Churchill and Mr. Eden, and even one pink-cheeked view of President Roosevelt that must have given a lot of trouble to the artist. Fenced off from the merchandise, cold noses pressed against the glass, three melancholy Scotties sat upon a bed of straw. Apparently they had moved as slowly as the dusty pipes and pillow tops. Their babyhood was long behind them.

Two minutes later Mary owned a Scotty. His mournful air touched her heart and her imagination. A couple with a dog would never be suspected by the Mounties. The proprietor almost wept when he took her money.

"I hate to see the little fellow go, Miss, that I do. A sweeter, better-tempered animal you and I will never see," he declared, thus proving, as Mary was soon to discover, that liars are international.

THIRTEEN

Paul's worries began when he woke up and found Mary missing. Descending quickly to the lobby, he discovered with quiet fury that the lunchroom was overflowing but that she wasn't in it. It was half-past eight o'clock—the breakfast hour was in full swing. Velvet ropes barred him from the dining room, but he had a sufficient view to make sure she wasn't there. Casting an automatic eye toward the exits, he observed that the watching men in plainclothes were still in place. His alarm lessened. Then, Mary hadn't been arrested. She was still somewhere in the hotel. But where? No use searching; they'd never get together that way. The thing for him to do was settle in some fixed position in the lobby. Again he inspected the policemen.

Even for a pair of suspected murderers, it struck him that the Strongs had rated a rather extraordinary turnout. It was because of the importance of their "victim" of course—the wretched Griggs. But how was Griggs' importance to the Royal Mounted to be explained? His crime—if indeed he had connived at the escape of a German prisoner of war—had been committed many months ago. Something that had happened recently must have revived the interest of the Royal Mounted in the man they had cashiered from the service and then turned loose. They had been waiting at the dock for Adelbert Griggs. They had radioed Schott to put him under guard. Why? Was it possible the Mounties had heard some rumor of the plot that was engaging Paul's own attention, and that they believed Griggs had been involved in it?

No, that could hardly be. It seemed all too clear that Major Thomson trusted Captain Schott, who was certainly a member of the conspiracy. Furthermore Paul could think of no possible connection between the escape of a German prisoner of war five months ago and some unknown danger to the convoy on Saturday. He would have liked to learn more about the incident at Sedwedge prison camp, but at the moment he saw no way of doing it.

His mind returned to the problems of the present. He bought a morning paper at the newsstand, and among the hungry group waiting outside the dining room, found an inconspicuous place where he could keep an eye on the lobby. He braced himself for an inspection of the front page of the *Halifax Journal*. It was a surprise. Not a word was printed about the escape of Paul and Mary Strong from the *Shalimar*.

The Strongs weren't mentioned. Eventually on the third page he came across a name he recognized. Adelbert Griggs had achieved eight brief lines. The item read:

> There passed away on Monday, aboard a vessel incoming from the South, Adelbert Griggs, one-time resident of this city, veteran of World War I, more lately of the Security Service. Following the escape of Baron Ludwig Hartz from a Canadian prison camp some months ago, Mr. Griggs retired to private life. Burial will be in Halifax under the direction of the R.C.M.P. Services private.

"The papers here don't print the news," remarked a confidential voice beside him. "Read the *Journal* from cover to cover and you'll know hardly more than when you started."

This was so exactly what Paul was thinking that he jumped a little. The stranger who shared the bench with him was fifty or so, a small bearded man in a naval uniform. The scarlet stripes between the gold bands on his sleeve announced his calling.

"Dr. MacGregor," the bearded man said quietly. "Over from Edinburgh studying the effects of long exposure and subsequent shock in the merchant marine. Shock is my particular specialty. For a moment there, you resembled one of my less serious cases. Don't be annoyed, young man. Snap diagnosis is a habit I acquired during the blitz, when I was on the look-out for signs of crack-up among the civilian population."

Paul wished that Dr. MacGregor would take himself and his habit elsewhere.

"The slightly dilated eye," said the Scotsman, still thoughtfully regarding the patient. "The vaguely hunted look. The haste with which you are folding up that newspaper, the jerky, uncoordinated gestures. They all add up. Your nerves are in a bad way this morning, young man."

"I am waiting for my sister," Paul said.

"Ah!" said the other ruminatively. "Well, possibly that may explain it. Strain and irritation … I daresay you want your breakfast. But, on second thought, I believe that's only the surface explanation." He looked at Paul intently. "If you'll forgive me, I fancy you are suffering from what I call Halifax fever. Most transients, myself included when I first arrived, experience the same symptoms—a touch of claustrophobia, the sense of being pushed and crowded by forces greater than we are and whose workings we do not fully comprehend, pointed up, of course, by the insecurity that comes of finding no news in the paper when big news is always in the air. Do you follow me?"

"Precisely," said Paul, hoping to close the conversation.

Dr. MacGregor was relentless. "Some of the secrecy, I will grant you, is necessary; the greater part, in my humble opinion, serves only to work mischief with civilian morale. Breeds rumors, jumpiness like yours, general uneasiness.

"Several weeks ago"—his voice dropped lower—"you may be interested to hear, there was a robbery in the artillery school over town. Some small arms disappeared, half a dozen of these Aldis lamps that are standard equipment in lifeboats also went; a young Canadian flyer who'd stopped in to take a shower-bath lost his money and all his clothes. It would have made an interesting little item, and might have assisted in capturing the thieves, who I understand are still at large, but it wasn't printed. Now, sir, how do you justify the omission of that item?"

"I don't," Paul said nervously. Even in a crowded place, the doctor's intensely confidential manner was bound to attract attention. Already a stout man across the way was beginning to be interested.

"Take the convoys as an example of a different kind," said the doctor, moving closer. "These, I will admit, are necessarily kept as secret as possible. The harbor is always closed when a convoy is going out. A month ago, however, one of the smaller ships caught fire in the channel some miles out. It was promptly scuttled, but within an hour half the population had the jitters, was sure Halifax would blow sky high in a second explosion. No public alarm was sounded. Not a line was printed about that unimportant fire. None was necessary; these things travel in the air. For instance, almost everyone in the hotel could tell you that a large convoy will soon be gathering in the harbor. Why? Because last night a small convoy arrived to join it. My own impression, also gathered from the air, is that something peculiar happened aboard one of those ships."

As Paul edged away, Dr. MacGregor edged more firmly forward.

"Your nerves are no shame to you, sir. Just relax, is my suggestion. Where was I? Oh, yes, about something peculiar happening in the harbor last night. You've guessed that too, I can see."

Paul started to shake his head. The doctor chuckled. His finger stabbed the newspaper.

"The only story that interested you was the only one which caught my own attention. This Adelbert Griggs who passed away. Passed away of what? And why is his retirement following the escape of Baron Ludwig Hartz mentioned unless it has significance? No doubt you recall the Baron's flight."

"I can't say I do."

"You surprise me, sir. The real truth, of course, the inside story of Sedwedge, has been deliberately withheld from the public. However, the Baron's escape was featured prominently in the press. It could not be hidden. Think back, and I'm certain you'll recall."

Anxious as Paul was to hear the story of Sedwedge, he was still more anxious to conclude the conversation. The fat man across the way was now watching them with sharp attention.

"I was out of the country last September," Paul said. Dr. MacGregor glanced thoughtfully at the newspaper on his lap. The month in which Baron Ludwig Hartz had escaped from Sedwedge prison camp was not mentioned there. Nor had the doctor mentioned it. The bearded man was plainly awaiting an explanation. Paul moistened his lips.

"Now that you've reminded me, I believe I do recall the case indistinctly."

"Indistinctly! Strange, your memory should be indistinct about such a dramatic affair! My own is crystal clear, though until you mentioned it," whispered Dr. MacGregor, "I didn't recall that the escape had occurred in September. Remarkable, how differently the human mind will work. Yours, for instance, clings to an inconsequential date and forgets the main event. Baron Hartz, of course, was the young Nazi ace who broke prison camp and flew out of Canada in one of our own planes."

"Damn careless of the authorities," muttered Paul.

"It would seem that way at first glance, wouldn't it? But I've always wondered myself if that particular escape couldn't be interpreted in another way."

"How else?"

"The Sedwedge airfield—I daresay you know it's now one of our important antisubmarine bases—is a good ten miles from the prison camp. Nevertheless Ludwig Hartz reached the field, stole one of the patrol planes and headed out to sea. Tell me how he managed."

"Suppose you tell me."

"Inside help," whispered the doctor. "Inside help. The fact cries itself aloud. Can you, as a sensible man, deny it?"

Paul entered no denial. The doctor's face was now only inches from his own. The doctor's breath stirred against his ear.

"Six months ago, in September, as you reminded me, Hartz fled

Canada. He hasn't been seen or heard of since. Most people think he crashed into the sea. At any rate, there seems to be no question that Hartz is either dead or safely out of the country. But what interests me is this. Apparently they haven't closed the case."

"Haven't they?"

Dr. MacGregor leaned still closer.

"My dear sir, are you aware that at this moment the lobby is bulging with secret police?"

"No!" said Paul.

"Yes! Now that's nothing to improve our appetite for breakfast, is it?"

At that moment Paul saw a girl in a shabby black hat and coat lead a Scotty in from the railroad station. Thick ugly glasses screened her eyes, her brows were penciled black, the hat pulled low hid every scrap of hair. He looked a second time, and got quickly to his feet.

"There's my sister now."

"If you're in the mood for company," said Dr. MacGregor, rising too, "I'll eat my bite of breakfast with you. I have a bit of idle time before I catch the ferry back to Dartmouth."

"Have you?" said Paul, deciding to leave the situation up to Mary. If she could walk out of the hotel and acquire a wardrobe and a dog in something under an hour, she could handle the good doctor. He mumbled the introduction.

"Unfortunately, my brother and I aren't breakfasting here," Mary said at once, and very definitely. Her face was clear of worry; her mind churned with it. She and Paul must disembarrass themselves and leave immediately, in advance of a messenger who would soon arrive at the checkroom with a gray squirrel coat. Even now Captain Schott was somewhere around the hotel. She smiled at Paul. "So sorry, dear, if you've made an arrangement with Dr.—MacGregor, is it? I should have phoned about the change of plans. At the very last moment I decided I'd better bring Bosco in to the vet."

"His old trouble?" asked Paul, and tried to look sympathetic as he eyed the dog. There was something about the slant of Bosco's head, the way he curled his black-gummed lips that was not particularly appealing.

Mary nodded. She turned her smile on the doctor. "I know you're thinking it's silly to be such a fool about a dog as to rob my brother and myself of your company. But Bosco's almost a member of the family."

As she leaned to pat the Scotty on the head, he growled and showed his teeth. She straightened hurriedly.

"Afraid of crowds," Paul said. "Always was. You're not afraid of me, are you, boy?"

This time Bosco didn't growl. He missed Paul's hand, because Paul was quick. His teeth sank into his ankle. Paul managed a grin.

"A game we play. Not so rough, boy, you'll tear my trousers. You'd better let me have the lead, sis." Fortunately his socks were dark, and would hide the blood. As Mary gladly surrendered the lead, Paul hoped to God he wouldn't limp.

"Well, goodbye, Doctor. Some other time I'd like to hear more about your work."

"Who's your vet?" asked Dr. MacGregor abruptly. "Old Timbucks?"

"Why, yes," said Mary, very thankful that he had provided a name.

"Right on my way to the ferry," Dr. MacGregor said happily. "I'll just trot along with you. You won't mind a longish walk, I hope."

"I'm afraid …"

Paul glanced over at the desk. A group of British engineers, stipulating with courteous British firmness better service than they were likely to receive, had suddenly dissolved. Directly behind them stood a small fat woman, red hair blanched with gray; she was encircled by a mound of luggage starred with the labels of the world's great hotels.

Frau Van Anda had also spent the night at the Haligonian and on a softer bed. She had just checked out, and was waiting for her bill. The largest of her diamonds, held in an old-fashioned claw of yellow gold, glittered like a little sun as she rapped it sharply against the counter.

"Please make haste."

"Boy! Madam requires assistance." No boy was in sight. The clerk gave every evidence of surprise and furiously struck his bell. "Now don't you worry, madam. It will be several minutes before your account is ready."

"I have exactly ten," said Frau Van Anda, and turned around.

Paul moved fast. He and Frau Van Anda met like two colliding trains, with mutual exclamations of joy. They spoke simultaneously.

"My dear Mr. Str—," she began.

"I wonder if you remember my sister Mary," he said.

Mary stepped forward. It was the longest second of Paul's life. He watched Frau Van Anda take in Mary's clothes and glasses; she looked at her own shoes on Mary's feet; she looked at Bosco. She met the doctor's interested stare with a stare of her own. Her small bejeweled hands fluttered at him.

"Such sweet children, these two are. I'd hardly have known Mary, she's grown so much." She turned back to Paul. "How pleasant and unexpected to meet this way! Years, hasn't it been? And now no time to have a real talk. I can't even ask you to our rooms. I had hoped to be here several days, but Lotte …"

"Lotte?"

"Lotte complains greatly of the confusion in the hotel and the noise. So now it seems my son—you will remember Hans—has found for us other more quiet—lodgings."

"Oh, is Hans in town?" said Mary, unpleasantly startled.

The Dutchwoman nodded and said with a certain quiet emphasis, "Unfortunately you will have no opportunity to see—Hans. But Lotte should be down any minute." Frau Van Anda glanced anxiously toward the elevators. "I'm sure, you both know how much Lotte would hate to miss you."

Her meaning was quite clear. Paul got again the sense of an exceedingly strange relationship. Frau Van Anda had no control over her nurse; the horse-faced Lotte would be delighted to betray them. Frau Van Anda was moving to other lodgings, her luggage was packed and waiting; Paul could have sworn that she didn't know where she was going. A light flashed as one of the elevators went up. With no air of haste Paul glanced at his watch, started, looked chagrined, began murmuring apologetically that Mary had an appointment.

"With old Timbucks," chimed in the doctor helpfully, "a mortal terror on tardiness. Though I suppose I could telephone …"

Paul let Frau Van Anda check that. She wouldn't dream of interfering with their plans. A hurried visit satisfied no one. Lotte must bear the disappointment. At any moment their taxi was expected. In wartime one must not keep a taxi waiting.

"Goodbye, my dears, till next time. No, I won't say goodbye. I hate the word."

She bent forward and kissed Mary's cheek. To Paul's embarrassment she kissed him, too. Her small fat hands clung to his lapels and dropped. He thought her eyes were wet. As they moved speedily away and on across the lobby, he felt in his overcoat pocket. Yes, she'd put something there. A square of smooth slick paper, small but thick, folded many times. It didn't feel like ordinary writing paper. He remembered she'd been standing beside a rack of hotel literature while she waited for her bill. This felt disappointingly like one of those illustrated folders.

Glancing back, he saw that the Dutchwoman had returned to the desk. For a moment, surrounded by her luggage—so all along she'd meant to stop in Halifax, or had her plans been changed for her like theirs?—she looked strangely lonely and lost, and then a crowd closed around her.

"A nice old lady," said Dr. MacGregor, hustling to keep up with Mary. He looked reflective. "What's wrong with Lotte?"

Mary didn't answer. She had just perceived that their troubles weren't over yet. A disturbance had broken out at the checkroom.

A sulky, dark-haired girl who had suddenly missed her checkroom ticket was demanding the immediate delivery of a gray squirrel coat. Beside the girl stood Bess, a Bess quivering with the triumph of her life, flanked by an iron-jawed woman who must be the super. They were all talking at once. One of the young men at the revolving doors sped over there.

Dr. MacGregor slowed down immediately. Annoyed by a sudden twitch on the leash, Bosco decided he too would linger. He sat down stubbornly on the floor, and continued the rest of the journey across the lobby on his seat. Breathless, and a shade reproachful, but not to be lost that easily, the doctor caught up.

"These little dramas interest me," he explained, with a last regretful glance toward the agitated knot of people collected at the checkroom. "Did you happen to notice that disagreeable young girl—the one with the dark hair and eyes—was very angry? The other two were egging her on."

"I didn't notice," Mary said.

Paul was too preoccupied to offer any comment. It was enough for the moment that he had got himself and the infuriated Scotty safely through the doors and out into the open. At that, except that they had yet to get rid of MacGregor, things hadn't worked out badly. Intent upon the checkroom disturbance, the Mounties hadn't been concerned with the disorganized departure of three people and a dog. Paul breathed more easily. The doctor wagged his little beard at Mary in reproof.

"You will find more satisfaction in life, my dear, if you take more pleasure in studying human nature as it shows itself in the small everyday events that occur around us. I, for instance, should have liked to see how that coat business worked out, just as I should have enjoyed meeting Lotte. Now, we'll never know. Watch out there for the curb!"

In her haste to get far away from the Haligonian Hotel in as short a time as possible, Mary had stumbled. The doctor took her arm.

"Spectacles new?" he inquired.

"I've worn them for years. Astigmatism."

"Hmm. Strange, I had an impression you were seeking to look under the lenses. A fairly common habit with a new pair of spectacles."

"I'm used to these," Mary said emphatically, and looked through the thick powerful lenses, and in the ensuing blur almost stumbled again.

"Astigmatism often goes with an inferior sense of balance," said the doctor kindly.

Occupied with Mary's troubles, Paul neglected his own and allowed the leash to go a little slack. Suddenly he felt the leather strap shoot from his hands. In a twinkling Bosco was free. With the leash flying like a banner after him, the Scotty headed back toward the Haligonian Hotel.

Paul went after him. Bosco sped like an arrow for the entrance, glimpsed Paul from the corner of his eye and changed his plans. Barking joyously, the Scotty scuttled out into the street with his master hot on his heels.

A trolley car, pressed by a ten-ton truck, was clattering along the tracks. But the orange taxi was moving fast, dangerously fast for such an icy narrow street. Bosco, yelping with fright and indignation, barely missed its flying wheels. The orange taxi shot around the truck and rushed on.

Paul had a flashing view of the interior through the window, before the windows were snatched away. Frau Van Anda was seated on the jump seat, clutching to hold her hat in place. Two people occupied the rear seat of the taxi.

Both of the other passengers were women. The woman who was closest to Paul was Lotte. She also was holding her hat. But the woman who sat farthest away from him indulged in no such graceless gesture. Perhaps her slender feet were braced firmly on the floor, perhaps long training in her early youth had taught her how to handle her body. The jolting and the speed did not discompose her.

She had leaned slightly forward to speak to Frau Van Anda. Her smile was warm and intimate, and, he imagined, tender. Paul saw her clearly, the black upward thrust of her hair beneath a small bright hat that clung closely to her head, the clean line of her profile, the soft warm smile. The third passenger was the woman of Max's seventeenth letter, the woman he had come so far and risked so much to find.

She was Lisa Tennevant.

FOURTEEN

Every thought vanished from Paul's head except pursuit. He had entirely forgotten Bosco. He had even forgotten, as he ran down the middle of the street, that his racing figure was in full view of the Haligonian Hotel.

He had no hope of overtaking the speeding car. But before it got away he meant to catch the number. He chased the orange taxi into the next block. He never saw the passengers again. By the time the taxi swept around the corner one of the women had pulled down a curtain.

Paul stopped then. He stood foolishly in the center of the busy street. His chase had been in vain. Strapped to the back of the taxi was a large black trunk. It rose halfway up the level of the rear window and sagged below the bumper. The license plate was neatly hidden.

Behind him the trolley car clanged indignantly. A passenger car blew its horn, a truck driver swore. Dr. MacGregor, breathless and winded, was calling from the sidewalk.

"My dear chap, didn't you hear me shouting? I've caught your dog for you."

Surely enough, the helpful little doctor had Bosco firmly in tow. Paul was muttering explanations and excuses that sounded thin even to their author, when Mary caught up with them. The doctor explained to her.

"The most extraordinary thing! I thought your husband was chasing a taxi, and all the time it seems he was after the dog. Didn't notice I had nailed the wicked fellow."

"No," Paul said. "No, I didn't notice."

"Your pet is a nervous type, isn't he?" remarked the doctor. As he turned over the leash and began to readjust his beard, he cocked a thoughtful eye at Bosco. "I hadn't realized the breed was so high-strung. Fortunately Timbucks is particularly fine with the—unusual dog. Shall we resume our interrupted journey?"

There seemed to be no other choice. Swinging along like a nimble gnome, Dr. MacGregor led them at a rapid trot through the oldest, most dilapidated part of town. The cobbled street, two short blocks from the harbor, lay parallel with it at an angle on the rising hill. Cheap boarding houses with scabrous mansard roofs eaten with salt and spray, frowned at them. Inhospitable signs that said "No Vacancies" loomed from unwashed windows. Grimy restaurants and long-vacant buildings that had suddenly bloomed into life as hostels and Y.M.C.A. huts and Salvation Army hotels had already spilled out their morning parade of boys in uniform and gone back to sleep again until evening. Sleety snow was spitting in the air; a cold damp wind blew up the side streets dropping to the harbor; the cracked broken sidewalk ran at a steep slant and was thick in almost jet-black ice.

"Stays for months on end," announced the doctor cheerfully. "Almost a Halifax trademark, gets its color from the villainous Sydney coal the way the buildings do. Not clean, the way I'm told your American cities are."

Paul didn't recall mentioning his nationality. With despair, he observed that Bosco was preparing to sit down again. In God's name what was Dr. MacGregor's definition of a longish walk? He could hardly ask how far they were from Timbucks, when he was presumed to know.

"Like me to handle your pet again?"

Paul grimly shook his head. Glancing furtively beneath the lenses of her spectacles, Mary saved herself from falling over an obstacle that rose abruptly from the sidewalk like a jolly-looking slot machine. It was plump and squat and painted bright red, but it was too low for a fire-alarm box. Besides it hadn't any handle.

"What in the world?"

"A mailbox," said the doctor quietly, and eyed her in a very speculative way. Something was trickling down her cheek. In the snow, her thick black brows had begun to run. Recalling in desperation that he worked with the merchant marine, Mary asked some question about the hospital that lay across the harbor in Dartmouth. At once the doctor's temper changed. His merry malicious face saddened; his step slowed. A moment passed before he spoke.

"Yes, my boys are over there. I call them mine, though they belong to all of us—the unsung heroes of this war." He sighed. "It's ridiculous, I suppose, to evaluate bravery, and weigh it like a pound of cheese. There is valor, and no denying it, in a quick clean death in the air. But my own boys are those who make the North Atlantic run too many times."

"Survivors of torpedoed ships?"

"For the most part, yes," said the doctor bitterly. "We've run the U-boats to cover in many parts of the Atlantic and cleared the convoy lanes. But still my boys come in. They bring them in with frozen hands and feet, they bring them in babbling and delirious; the surgeons cut away the gangrened flesh and tend their bodies. My own job is different.

It isn't always easy to persuade a lad who's lost both feet and seen his comrades freeze to death, that life holds much for him. His nervous system rejects the proposition, his mind chooses its own form of death."

Mary was reminded of the other lodger. Out of nothing, she said, "We had an acquaintance like that once, a young boy who drifted several weeks in an open boat in the North Atlantic in winter."

The doctor stopped and stared at her. "Several weeks in the North Atlantic in winter! Impossible! He'd never have survived. You must be thinking of Southern waters."

"He did survive."

"What's his name? It's the most remarkable case I ever heard of. The longest on record is five days."

Mary hadn't counted on starting a debate. She said, "We never learned this boy's name. When he was rescued off Iceland, he'd lost the power of speech and almost lost the power of motion. For weeks and months, after they picked him up, he lay absolutely quiet in bed."

"Quiet! Motionless! Extraordinary!" By now the doctor's professional interest was thoroughly aroused. "Apathy, my dear young lady, isn't typical of shock. In point of fact usually you find the exact opposite—enormously increased motor activity. My boys go into convulsions with an unexpected sound, tear the sheets to pieces, barricade themselves behind their beds as though they were at battle stations. Their poor scarred minds are always expecting another attack by sea or air. How'd this case react, for instance, when a plane flew overhead?"

"I don't know," said Mary, confused.

Dr. MacGregor had stopped dead on the curb. His astonishment was undoubtedly sincere. Paul felt confused himself.

"As it happens, Doctor, we never met this boy. However, we heard his story in detail in letters from a—friend. It is quite true that for months the boy never spoke and was seldom seen to move, except at mealtimes. His appetite was prodigious."

"Atypical again!" cried the doctor. "Complete loss of appetite is one of our chief problems. In their withdrawal from life, most of these shock cases are subconsciously protecting themselves from self-made charges of cowardice. In other words, they feel they aren't entitled to food, that they don't deserve it, laboring as they do under an intolerable burden of self-imposed guilt. It's a moral problem. Once you remove the guilt, once you convince these brave youngsters they aren't cowards, that they aren't morally responsible for their nervous systems, then they will improve and start eating normally."

"I see," said Paul, who didn't see at all how the case of the other lodger was to be interpreted now.

Dr. MacGregor's voice was brusque. "I wonder if you do see what is very clear to me. This acquaintance of yours didn't drift for weeks in an open boat in the North Atlantic, and lie abed for months in profound shock. He was shamming."

"Shamming!"

"Shamming," repeated the doctor, pleased with the word. His small bright eyes twinkled wickedly. "Just as I strongly suspect you two are."

"I'll be leaving you now." The doctor held out his hand and shook Paul's strongly. He took Mary's hand, and shook that too. "It's been a pleasant walk. Most enlightening. Give my regards to old Timbucks, if you can find him."

"What …?"

"I've never heard of a vet named Timbucks," said the doctor sunnily. "Come to think of it, I don't believe I've ever heard the name at all. Just popped into my head. Timbucks—rummy sounding, isn't it?" Cocking his head on one side, he gazed from one astonished face to the other. He chuckled. "You shouldn't try to pull an old man's leg, children. By the way, I suppose you'll be looking for a place to stay. It's rather chilly to be sleeping in the open."

"We …"

"Town's crowded. I suggest you try Canary Cage Lane. As we passed by, I saw that miracle in Halifax—someone hanging out a vacancy sign!"

With that the Scotsman turned on his heel, and went skipping down the icy side street to the ferry house. Dr. MacGregor enjoyed gathering little facts in and around Halifax, and he was vastly pleased with his latest collection. When he entered the ferry house, however, his smile had faded. He walked on past the ticket window to the telephone. He didn't look his number up; in fact it wasn't listed in the book. But the number that the doctor called was a number he knew very well.

FIFTEEN

In silence Paul and Mary looked at each other. A dirty little girl peeped around a corner and whistled at Bosco. The Scotty barked at her. The little girl promptly threw a stone. They began to walk again.

"Paul, I hate to tell you," Mary said presently, with an uncertain laugh, "but the truth is—I rather liked that man. Even though I don't trust him as far as I'd trust—trust …"

"A trust company," Paul supplied abstractedly. "Darling, please don't leave orphaned sentences hanging in the air that way." He had already got over his first amazement, adjusted himself to the disconcerting fact that they hadn't deceived the good doctor for a single minute. After all, thought Paul, glancing at his wife as they turned and walked on toward a less dreary neighborhood, it would have been surprising if they had deceived the fellow. Mary's ideas of disguise would make a blind man blink.

But if the doctor had wanted to betray them—and here was the important thing—he'd deliberately passed up his opportunity at the Hotel Haligonian. So far as that went, he had become a sort of accomplice. Dr. MacGregor could hardly go running to the Mounties, without explaining his previous silence. Well, the man was gone; they'd got rid of him. Paul shook himself.

"Let's find a restaurant. You must be starving. I can certainly eat."

She glanced at him sidewise.

"Aren't you going to tell me who was in the cab? Who besides Frau Van Anda and Lotte? You wouldn't have chased them that hard."

"She was."

"You mean …"

"Lisa Tennevant," Paul said.

"Oh," said Mary blankly. She missed a step on the sidewalk. "Then we won't be going to the theatre, after all. Or—will we?"

"I rather think we will."

"But if she's right here in town …"

"Halifax isn't exactly a village, darling. Possibly the theatre, or one of the others mentioned in the program, can give us a line on the lady's local address. The taxi certainly didn't. The license plate was covered up."

"But what was Lisa Tennevant doing with Frau Van Anda and Lotte?"

"That," said Paul, "is among the many mysteries. I could wish that Max had been a trifle more explicit."

"Paul, what do you think really happened to Max?"

"Darling, I don't know. And please don't ask me what Max could have found out in Reykjavik about a plot against a convoy here. Or where the other lodger figures. What we both need now is coffee."

"A gallon," agreed Mary.

"Here, take my handkerchief and scrub off your face. And for heaven's sake let me stow those spectacles."

Mary handed him the spectacles. She watched him reach automatically toward his pocket, and then drop the glasses in the gutter. "Paul, I'll burst if you don't tell me what you've got in your overcoat pocket."

Paul started. He had been so careful; he knew he hadn't touched the folded paper since they'd left the hotel lobby. He had barely touched it then. He had meant to keep back the news of Frau Van Anda's message until he had a chance to discover privately what it was. Mary smiled to herself.

"Darling, you almost always walk with your left hand in your pocket. This time you didn't."

"Well, I'll be damned...." Paul began to laugh.

They found a restaurant nearby, crowded, of course, and noisy, incongruously gay for the hour. At a battered upright piano an unself-conscious girl was banging away, delighting a group of sailors clustered around her with a song they'd brought over from Newfoundland the day before.

> "If your father's a Newfy—Then your mother's a goofy
> And you'll ride a tin fish till you die."

It might have been midnight, thought Mary, instead of half-past nine in the morning. Everywhere in Halifax was the feeling of restlessness and rush, overlaying the gnawing, subterranean strain of all-out war. Everywhere were people who were briefly there, pausing on their way to keep an appointment with victory or, perhaps, with death. The restaurant was filled with them. That man's ribbons had been won for bombing Berlin and soon he would be off again; his companion had won his ribbons and his appalling scars on a sea of flaming oil.

After Paul ordered and lighted his cigarette and hers, he brought out the folded paper. As he'd half expected, it was a piece of hotel literature which Frau Van Anda had picked up at the desk of the Haligonian and then folded in a neat tight square, scarcely an inch across. It felt hard to the touch, with a lump in the middle. He unfolded the paper quickly. There was no writing on the thick glossy sheet. But as the last crease opened, something dropped to the tablecloth, tinkled against a plate.

It was a small flat key—a trunk key. Instead of a written message Frau Van Anda had sent them the key to her trunk. They stared. Their faces fell.

"A trunk key," said Mary, disappointed, "is no good to us without the trunk."

"When we find Lisa, we'll find the trunk. It's somewhere here in Halifax."

"Unless they've taken it to Sedwedge," she suggested.

She spoke absently. She was thinking less about the eventual destination of the trunk than about its possible contents. And suddenly Paul's attention was elsewhere. A man at the next table sat half hidden by a newspaper, but he wasn't reading; he seemed to be staring covertly at the key. Paul tensed, relaxed when their neighbor laid aside his newspaper and began placidly spooning oatmeal. One of the hazards of the hunted, Paul reflected, was the psychology of the hunted. It was hard to fight against the idea that every casual stranger was an enemy, that secret unknown watchers ringed one in. He picked up the key and put it in his pocket.

"Let's hurry with our breakfast, darling. Before we find a room we'll have to collect some baggage. We should be settled in proper lodgings before the theatre opens."

Mary smiled. Paul had been disturbed about their neighbor, and now was not. He was himself again. He had taken calm control of the key, as though there was nothing unusual about its arrival, nothing baffling in its implications. Paul could make any situation seem businesslike and normal. He was acting as though they were on a regular out-of-town assignment. It was for reasons like that, thought Mary, that she loved her husband—very much.

When the Strongs left the restaurant the man at the next table was still eating oatmeal. He waited until they passed through the door before he stepped to the telephone.

An hour later, equipped with a secondhand suitcase filled with a few toilet articles but for the most part with secondhand books, Paul and Mary and the now dispirited Bosco turned weary feet into Canary Cage Lane. Number 36 was even grimier and shabbier than its neighbors. Number 36 was a disreputable, battle-scarred old house, an old rip of a house with a false front, peeling paint and sagging steps, and with lace curtains hung at its dirty windows. It was like an alley cat with a ribbon around its neck.

"It looks exactly like what the doctor would recommend," Mary said, interested at once in the sort of lodging house that made sensible people shudder. "Reminds me of him somehow, except he's cleaner."

"It seems to be this or nothing," said Paul, inspecting Number 36 with anything but pleasure. Apparently this was the only vacancy sign in all of Halifax. They'd walked blocks and seen no other. "This time, thank heavens, we can settle our story beforehand."

"I'd like to be promoted back to wife."

"You're jolly well right." The sign beside the door announced one room only, a top-floor room, at that. Paul considered a moment. "We'll be honeymooners, to explain our being here in town. Why honeymoon in Halifax? Well, you have an uncle you hope may be coming in by convoy. No need to be specific; it won't be expected."

"Honeymooners from Winnipeg?"

"God, no. We stick to the U.S.A. where we know the difference between the House and the Senate. You didn't recognize a mailbox when you saw one, and, to be strictly truthful, I didn't either. Can you tell me whether Parliament meets in Ottawa or Montreal?"

"Darling, I'm convinced."

"We're here from Portland, Maine. It's not impossibly far away. And I know Portland. You don't have to talk about it. The less either of us talks," said Paul, having particular reference to his wife, "the better."

With a good sharp jerk on the leash, he convinced Bosco that he was going up the steps. He thumped a rusty knocker. Nothing happened. He thumped again. There were rustlings inside. An untidy girl of fifteen or so opened the door and peeped out at them.

"Maw's away, death in the family, she don't like lady lodgers, because of lipstick on the pillow shams, she can't abide dogs, because they muck up everything," said the girl on one long breath. She drew another. "I'm supposed to be keeping idle hands from the devil's work, and be busy tidying up. You'd best come back later, and Maw will tell you you can't have the room no matter what you pay."

Paul thrust his foot into the crack. Mary, who wasn't fond of housework herself, guessed of disorder overhead. If Maw had been away all morning

...

"I'll tidy the room myself." A gleam of interest showed in the bright young eyes. Mary pressed her advantage. "I'll tell you a secret. This is our wedding trip. We've been walking hours, the town's so crowded. Where else are we to go?"

The fifteen-year-old's romantic heart was touched. By now Mary was inside a dank and odorous hall that smelled of ferns and coal gas.

"What's your name, dear?"

"Elsa, but Maw is sure to make a fuss. She's had a world of trouble with lady lodgers. Now's the time, Maw says, for landlords to take it easy; the good Lord knows they've had it hard enough."

Opening off the hall was a dreary parlor, with a floor littered with wire and fern and ribbon like the back room of a florist shop. Elsa was twisting in her hands a half-completed wreath of immortelles, black, leathery, repulsive-looking flowers stuck with bits of wire.

"For the deceased," she announced with mournful pride of workmanship. Laying down the wreath, she glanced toward the stairs and then dubiously at Bosco.

"We never had no dogs before."

"He's a wedding present, Elsa."

"Is he now? I was thinking he looked exactly like a dog I seen over town yesterday in the Variety Store window."

There was a strained pause. For all its cosmopolitan air, Halifax retained certain smalltown aspects.

"You're a bright girl, Elsa," Paul said, hating the heartiness of his voice. "That's where we bought him—with a wedding check. Shall we go on up? The little fellow won't give any trouble."

"Wait a bit! First, I better see your registration cards." Elsa's businesslike air was obviously borrowed from her mother. She folded her hands on her apron and waited expectantly.

Paul was momentarily at a loss. Then he vaguely recalled that Canada had registered her population, that every Canadian was obliged to carry an identification card. He gave Mary a look.

"We're from the States, Elsa. Our home is in Portland, Maine."

"Oh, Americans," said the girl, relaxing. "I expect you think I'm stupid not to guess right off by your voices. Maw says all you people from the States talk through your noses. Anyway, she says, you don't squeeze a penny till it's bent like some others she could mention!"

Blithely ignoring glimpses of unmade beds and rows of unpolished shoes and unemptied wastebaskets sitting in the cavernous halls, Elsa then galloped up the stairs. The house seemed to be deserted. When it appeared that she could climb no higher, she led them into a gloomy attic room that evidently had been unoccupied long enough to become a sort of hospital for invalid furniture from everywhere. Reminiscent of their accommodations at the Haligonian, it was even mustier. A bent spittoon twinkled from one corner; dust gathered on a crystal radio set in another. Dust lay thick on a naked mattress lying on a bed that looked as though generations had breathed their last on it—but some time ago. Mary was surprised to notice several drawers pulled from the bureau, and an empty chest with the lid lifted, as though a recent hurried attempt had been made to clear the place.

"You'll find sheets and pillow shams in the bottom drawer; it sticks," announced Elsa cheerfully. Mary turned resignedly in that direction.

"The dog can sleep on the floor. Maw will throw a fit if you take him in bed with you," began the fifteen-year-old, and suddenly turned crimson.

"We wouldn't think of it," Mary said gravely.

But Elsa, stumbling over her own feet in a misery of embarrassment, had run out of the room. The door banged behind her. Mary laughed and looked over at Paul.

"I'm glad I'm not as young as that. Mentioning a bed, and us a honeymooning couple!"

"I wonder." Paul was listening. He hadn't heard any feet going down the stairs. He listened a moment longer to make sure. Rising, he crossed to the door. He didn't want to catch the child red-handed. Before he turned the, knob, Paul took pains to rattle it. Elsa had time to scramble to her feet, but there was dust on her knees and a circle of dust around the eye which had been applied to the keyhole.

"I forgot to tell you that the water closet was down the hall," she gasped and again she fled. This time they heard her stumbling down the stairs.

"Youth," Paul said dryly. "If that child is suspicious, we're going to have to watch ourselves with Mother," he said, and stopped himself.

Mary had paused beside the window. He watched her standing there, and knew why she was gazing down with dreamy pleasure at an empty sidewalk. She was assimilating and savoring the fact that they were free at last. Free and with a room of their own with a water closet down the hall. Free to take a bath if they liked, or just to stand and stare. Across the way a child's white face was pressed against a window pane. The child waved, and Mary waved back. Somehow it seemed like a good omen. He went over and slipped his arm around her.

Across the stained discolored rooftops, through the sleety falling snow, a section of the harbor was visible. Already a part of Saturday's company was gathered and busy with preparations for the departure. Many blocks away and out of sight, the *Shalimar* had dropped anchor. The vessels that had sailed north with them had moved on into Bedford Basin. In the meantime others had arrived. Paul watched a clumsy tanker moving ponderously up and down; its degaussing device was being tested. A little tug scooted along beside it. Nearby a covey of slim corvettes, sleek and sinister, slid past an anchored battleship and went hurrying toward the gates and open water. The Dartmouth ferry hooted impudently and cut across their bows.

Somehow that small incident summed up the scene to Paul. Danger from the outside seemed incredibly remote. Gazing at a tiny section of one of the most closely guarded and geographically impregnable harbors in the world, Paul found the proposition almost impossible of belief. On Saturday the convoy would be forming in the harbor. *In the harbor.* That was just it. How could a handful of plotters hope to harm a mighty convoy while it lay inside Halifax Harbor?

There were sufficient guards scattered along the waterfront to hold off a small-sized army. Hidden gun emplacements commanded every inch of shore and water. To be sure a daring submarine had once slipped into Scapa Flow. But that was long ago in the early days of the war. No German submarine had ever got safely through the mine fields that protected Halifax. On occasion U-boats had been reported lurking near and even touching shore in other, less closely guarded regions of Canada's long and lonely coast. Never around Halifax. They were spotted first.

A formation of patrol planes floated lazily through the leaden air, heading out to sea. The laziness of their appearance was deceptive. Like the slim corvettes, the planes were armed to do battle with the U-boats, bomb and blow them from the water—far away from Halifax.

What was the plotters' plan of action?

Paul sighed, started to turn from the window, hesitated. On the sidewalk below a fat man went around the corner. The flirt of his disappearing coattails showed briefly. For a moment Paul dimly remembered that a fat man had been seated across from him and Dr. MacGregor in the lobby of the Haligonian. He frowned vaguely, then shrugged. Damned if he would jump at shadows. Paul might have been more concerned if he'd seen still another man who had glided into an alley not far from Number 36. The second man, pausing in the alley, had pulled a muffler around his face, although it wasn't that cold. Perhaps he was sensitive about his appearance. He was so extremely bald.

Thirty minutes later, leaving Bosco curled up comfortably on the floor, Paul and Mary left the bedroom and went quietly down the stairs. Elsa was in the parlor. She had completed her wreath. When they reached the hall, she was furiously hammering it into a place of honor upon the stained brown wall. They could have passed, unobserved. But suddenly—perhaps the girl's precarious position upon a chair, the hammer in her hand, was responsible—Paul thought of something.

"Elsa," he called, "when did you put up the vacancy sign outside?"

"Why, just before you came along," said Elsa, twisting around like a stork and speaking thickly of necessity. Her mouth was full of tacks. "It's down now. You and your wife were the very first to see it."

So Dr. MacGregor hadn't seen the sign go up. How had he known there would be a vacancy on Canary Cage Lane? Paul felt Mary's fingers tense on his arm.

The parlor was dim and dusky, all its curtains drawn. The wreath of immortelles clung to the wall like a fungus growth. The funereal blossoms twined around and embraced in leathery fingers an enlarged photograph of a small, weak-looking man with a small neat mustache. Adelbert Griggs had posed on the steps of Number 36 in uniform, but even in happier days he hadn't appeared to be a hero. Elsa began to blubber, and the tacks started spilling from her mouth.

"Paw wasn't much good, I expect. Everybody says so. But I was awful fond of him." The last of the tacks spattered mournfully upon the floor. She climbed off the chair. "You two have got his room. Maw had it cleared out right off, though I wasn't supposed to tell. Some folks is squeamish, she says. I hope you aren't."

SIXTEEN

Barrington Street, the main artery of Halifax, had caught the impromptu spirit of the town, the restlessness and rush, all the pulsing life and all the lack of order. It was packed with a jumble of public buildings and business establishments and private residences, mixed together like a cardboard street put up by a rather backward child. A fine jewelry store rubbed shoulders with a bootblack parlor, the windows of a modern department store nudged the windows of a junk shop. The Governor's house, a beautiful Georgian dwelling that might have jumped from a park in Surrey, except that its classic façade was deeply stained by smoke, looked across a double line of street cars upon the straggling expanse of St. Paul's cemetery. It was said that long ago the Governor's cows had grazed where the quiet dead now slept, undisturbed by the clamor and turmoil that swept about their final home.

The towering British lion surmounting the monument at the cemetery gates and dedicated to the heroes of Sebastopol, looked serenely back across the turbulent street upon the Princess Royal Theatre. The theatre was hardly a stone's throw from the Governor's noble Georgian home. Its architecture was pure Hollywood. A line of people, mostly men in uniform, had formed on the sidewalk outside it. Paul and Mary took their places at the end of the line.

As they moved along, Paul watched Mary from the corner of his eye. She'd been shaken by the incident at Canary Cage Lane; he'd been shaken himself. An uncomfortable friend Dr. MacGregor had turned out to be, Paul thought, and wondered irritably why his instincts told him the merry-eyed, malicious Scotsman was—a friend. Impulsive, individualistic, a natural show-off delighted with his own acumen—all those things described the doctor. He was as odd and unpredictable an ally in his own way as was Frau Van Anda. Suppose the doctor had imagined they were interested in Adelbert Griggs, and so had sent them to the best possible source of information—his home. Was that it? Well, it didn't matter. The hell with Griggs and Number 36 Canary Cage Lane.

Dr. MacGregor, for all his air of knowing everything, had no way of guessing their mission at the Princess Royal Theatre; that at least was their own secret, thought Paul, and looked sharply up and down the slowly moving line. There were no policemen in sight. There was no one who attracted his attention—in sight.

Ten minutes passed before the Strongs reached the cashier's cage. They bought tickets and stepped aside to wait until the rush in the lobby was over. At last the girl cashier was free. Paul gave her time to redo her lips and stretch and yawn. Then he stepped up again to her glassed-in cubicle.

"Were you working here last September?"

The pretty face behind the glass looked startled. The yawn stopped in the middle.

He said quickly, "That does sound odd, but I'm trying to locate a theatrical company who played here last September. A one-night stand. *The Wild Duck*. Can you tell me where the company is now?"

He detected a change in the girl's expression. She was going to ask him to explain himself. Well, that was natural. He'd asked an unusual question. Leaning forward, she spoke through the hole cut in the glass. To his surprise she didn't seem to be surprised at all, or even curious.

"You mean those amateurs, don't you? They weren't real actors, most of them. Just a social club that used to play around the provinces. I believe the group once had headquarters somewhere over Montreal way, though they were mostly on the road. But of course the clubhouse is closed now.

"The group has been broken up," she went on hurriedly. "Or so I've heard. Quite a long while ago. They gave their last show here, I know, and broke up right afterwards. Their club had a kind of funny name."

"The name would help," Paul said slowly, still watching her. She'd been surprisingly quick to remember the details about an amateur company that had appeared in the theatre for a single night some months ago; and why was she talking so fast? There was something about the girl's eyes.... "In point of fact," he said, "it's Lisa Tennevant I'm looking for. I've heard she's here in Halifax. If she has a local agent or, better still, if you happen to know where she might be stopping ..."

"Lisa Tennevant! Oh, she was a *real* actress! And so lovely looking. I don't know her local address, but ..."

Paul saw the girl's hands move. He didn't see her press a button concealed underneath the ticket shelf that sounded a buzzer in an upstairs office, but he saw her turn her head expectantly. Inside the cage, a telephone tinkled. Smiling in an apologetic but rather breathless way, the girl quickly swung around on her chair. She had turned to answer the house telephone a fraction of a second before it rang. Her words were inaudible and brief. Almost immediately she swung back to them.

"Funny, the manager just called. He'll be glad to tell you what you want to know about Lisa Tennevant. He's coming downstairs from his office."

"We'll go up to him," Paul said at once. The dismay on the pretty face confirmed his doubts. Maybe there were no policemen in the lobby, but something was seriously wrong. A reception had been prepared for them in the manager's office. He could not imagine why, and he didn't waste time wondering. At the moment the question was academic.

He grabbed Mary's hand, and they ran across the lobby. Dreaming at his post, the ticket taker awoke with a start. He saw the cashier dart out from her cage, heard the manager shout from the stairs. As Paul dropped tickets in the box, he grabbed for them. He almost had Mary's coat, when Paul's leg shot out and tripped him up. The youth went sprawling to the floor. Before he gained his feet, the pair had vanished into the darkened auditorium. Indeed before the ticket taker was upright again, two other suddenly impatient customers had sprung up from nowhere and brushed past the box. The first man had a ticket, the second simply dropped a bill. But neither one, the boy was to remember indignantly, paused to lend *him* the slightest assistance.

Machine gun fire was rattling from the screen. In the semi-gloom at the rear of the theatre, people were standing packed like matches. An usher was offering single seats.

"Take one quick," Paul whispered. "I'll meet you in an hour underneath the biggest clock in Halifax."

Immediately they separated. The other members of the party, of whom the Strongs were happily unaware, also melted away. Mary had slipped into a seat in the center of the house when ushers with flashlights began moving among the throng in the rear. They even came quietly down the aisles, but here the search was perfunctory. Balked by the packed rows of seats, the muttered annoyance of the patrons, the ushers and their flashlights soon withdrew. Mary was much too intent on settling herself to observe that a stout man had found a seat directly behind her. A well-padded elbow brushed her shoulder.

"What do you suppose the trouble is?" wheezed a voice from the obscurity behind her.

"I have no idea," said Mary in vague reply.

In a measure this was true. She knew whom the ushers were looking for, but she had no idea how the Mounties, who must be behind the management's interest in them, would know they were going to appear at the Princess Royal Theatre asking about Lisa Tennevant. It had not yet occurred to her that the Canadian Royal Mounted Police might be interested in *anybody* who was interested in the disbanded theatrical company. It had occurred to Paul.

A little later, when he strolled into the smoking lounge, intending to leave the theatre by a different exit, he found the first evidence that his surmise was true. Cozy and informal, the lounge was a kind of modern copy of an old-fashioned green room. It was brightly lighted and yet filled with soft laughter—a rendezvous for couples concentrated on the quick urgent business of love in wartime. On the walls hung photographs of acts that had appeared at an earlier and less baroque Princess Royal, vaudevillians and dancing dogs and acrobats, dignified legitimate stars, autographed pictures of motion picture actresses not half so pretty as the girls who were looking for secrets in their sweethearts' eyes. The alarums and excursions of courtship comfortably behind him, Paul was feeling warm and sorry and a little wistful about the kids, wishing them luck he'd had himself and knowing sadly that their generation wouldn't have it, when his eye was caught by a picture across the room. Even from the distance it struck an off-key note among the others. It was a view of the Canadian Rockies, and didn't quite cover a faded spot on the wall. Paul moved closer. Another and larger picture had hung there until quite recently. The wall was dusty.

He stepped aside, as two women—obviously attendants—approached and stopped directly in front of the Canadian Rockies. One of them straightened the frame. The other had a bottle of cleaning fluid in her hand. She was clucking over the faded wall.

"I can get off the dirt all right, but it's going to show."

"Better to look at an ugly spot," said the other sharply, "than at the faces of traitors!"

Traitors? Paul's nerves jumped. He stared at the wall. As though it was still before his eyes, he conjured up a vision of the picture that wasn't there. *The Wild Duck* Company, with Lisa Tennevant among them, had just been banished from the wall. He felt sure of it. If he'd come to the smoking lounge a little earlier, he'd have seen *The Wild Duck* Company go, the Canadian Rockies come. Traitors? The women said no more. While he lighted a cigarette, Paul sized them up. The cleaning fluid woman looked like a talker. Too bad, he couldn't get her by herself. Paul drew closer.

"My wife," began Paul casually, "cleans paper by making a kind of paste."

"Now does she? Salt or cornmeal? I've used cornmeal myself many a time, but some say …"

"This is paint," said her companion coldly. "Come on, Alice, let's try and find a bigger picture," and at once the two attendants were gone.

They disappeared through a door that let them back into the service quarters. Paul spent a moment in thought. Somewhere beyond that door, in the theatre's storeroom probably, the women would be hunting for a bigger picture, talking perhaps of a subject that must be paramount in both their minds. Traitors? Somewhere in there might be the discarded picture of *The Wild Duck* Company.

He had no idea he was attracting attention until he heard a sudden giggle behind him. Three schoolgirls, gathering up their things to leave, were watching him, whispering together. One of them nudged another.

"You ask him."

The girl who asked had a pert pretty face. "It's the funniest thing about that picture, the one that isn't there," she said to Paul, with another explosive little giggle that sent her companions into fresh convulsions of mirth. "Are you and your friends doing some kind of treasure hunt?"

"My friends?"

"Two of them already have been in here looking for the picture, though they both pretended they'd come in to smoke," she said. "The second man was the best-looking thing, or so Gracie seemed to think"—an indignant denial from Gracie, and then the clear young voice went on—"oh, I'll admit he *was* extremely attractive—a tall foreign man with his thick red hair. Because of your all wanting the picture," she said to Paul, "we were wondering if you were on a treasure hunt."

"A treasure hunt? Yes," Paul said, "I suppose you might call it that."

The short hall beyond the smoking lounge wasn't meant for public inspection. It was dingy and uncarpeted, with doors of frosted glass on both sides. Before Paul tiptoed very far, he located not the storeroom that he sought but the manager's office. A telephone was ringing in there, very shrill in the quiet hall. It rang on and on. Was no one in the office, after all? Again the phone rang. Paul opened the door a crack and looked in.

The office was empty. Tilted against the desk, turned away from him, was a large framed picture. All that he could see was the dusty back.

Abruptly the telephone stopped ringing. Everything became very still. Paul glanced up and down the hall. Then he stepped noiselessly into the manager's office. As he reached the desk, the telephone suddenly exploded into renewed and angry life as though unwilling to credit a businessman's absence in the middle of a business day. Paul cursed to himself. The continued clamor was sure to bring someone on the run. He cocked a wary eye on the door, then cautiously slid the receiver off the hook. He cupped his hand around the mouthpiece and muttered a low hello.

"Thomson of the Mounted," snapped a voice that wasn't used to dalliance and delay. "That you, Brown?"

Paul started. His fingers tightened on the receiver. Thomson of the Mounted, was it? Major Kenneth Thomson of the R.C.M.P. desiring most urgently to speak to the manager of the Princess Royal Theatre. Why? In half a second Paul swiftly and regretfully decided he couldn't simulate a voice he'd never heard and get away with it.

"Brown has stepped out a moment," he said, adding quickly, "If it's about *The Wild Duck* Company matter ..."

"It's about the escaped prisoner himself, Baron Hartz. We have received a report...." There was a sudden, cold pause on the wire. "Who are you?"

"Just a friend," Paul said in his most helpful tone. "I'm waiting for Brown myself. Any message you care to leave I'll gladly ..."

"Say I want to talk to him *privately*," and with a sharp, conclusive click, Major Thomson of the Mounted was gone.

Well, that was that. Paul frowned a moment, wondering about that report on Baron Hartz who'd escaped from Sedwedge Prison Camp by air five months back. In five months and with a powerful airplane it would certainly seem that the fugitive Baron had had ample time to remove himself from the reach of reports and find refuge far, far away from Canada or that long since he had crashed and died in the sea. And then Paul set down the telephone.

His business was with Lisa Tennevant and the amateur company. He reached for the picture, and cautiously, careful of unnecessary noise, pulled the heavy frame away from the desk, faced it out. The light was poor, so that at first the faces behind the glass looked blurred and ghostly. A crowd of people, not in theatrical costume as he'd expected, but wearing sports clothes, sweaters and ski jackets and heavy boots, as though they'd just come in from skating, grouped informally in an informal, hunting lodge kind of room. An oak-beamed room with a big stone fireplace and skis leaning against it and a big fire burning. The headquarters of the club, probably....

A caption was printed underneath. Paul's eye stopped abruptly at the name of the club.

Icarus.

That was the name of the amateur theatrical group, disbanded six months ago.

Icarus was the name Max had signed to his cable. The Icarus Club. Another link with the seventeenth letter.

Paul raised his eyes to study the photograph. There weren't so many in the group, at that; two dozen perhaps, strangers, people he'd never seen before. *The Wild Duck*, of course, is predominantly a man's play; three feminine roles as against twenty played by men. In the photograph the males of the Icarus Club swamped the sprinkling of women. Paul picked out Lisa Tennevant without difficulty, although she was seated in the background. Her slender figure was muffled in a thick sweater and clumsy skiing trousers, and still she looked poised and elegant. She held a pair of skates, and had chosen a pose that was charming and graceful. She sat on a leather sofa, dangling her skates, grave and unsmiling, wholly unaware of the camera. An actress, a professional, a pretty woman fresh from the outdoors, gazing with inscrutable eyes at an unprepossessing-looking man who sat uneasily beside her. She might almost have been thinking that her companion's appearance had little to recommend him as an actor.

He was the bald man—the bald man who had left the trunk room of the Haligonian Hotel the night before with the big black trunk on his back.

Paul gazed long and hard at the faces of the strangers surrounding the pair. The faces of those mediocre players who had toured Canada until their Club disbanded told him nothing. Traitors?

Carefully Paul replaced the frame against the desk. And then he heard approaching footsteps. A shadow fell across the frosted glass of the door. Someone rattled the knob. The manager?

Swift steps carried Paul across the office. He was behind the door when it opened, flattened against the wall, crouching low so his head wouldn't be silhouetted by the glass. When Brown turned around to close the door, he would bowl him over with a football tackle and be out and away down the hall. But the door didn't close. It was left standing open, with Paul crouched behind it in the angle against the wall. And it wasn't the manager who had entered the manager's office.

It was the bald man. He didn't pause to look around. He walked quickly to the desk and snatched the heavy frame from the floor.

Paul didn't hear the second man approach and stop abruptly in the hall. But suddenly, directly behind him, he heard Hans Van Anda's low and angry voice. It spoke very close to his ear, pitched to reach the desk. The redhaired man had paused at the threshold and was looking in from the hall.

"I thought I might find you here," he said. "Put down that picture and get back about your business."

It was obvious that the bald man was unpleasantly startled by the encounter. He whirled around from the desk. But he still clung to the heavy frame.

"I can put it underneath my coat."

"You can leave it where you found it. Sometimes I could wish the good God had given you brains," said the cool contemptuous young voice in the hall. "That picture has hung in the theatre for months. If it disappears now, don't you know the authorities will be bright enough to suspect where it's gone? No, my stupid friend, it's much too late to worry about your own skin now. Your job is to bring in that meddling pair, and without delay!"

Paul hardly breathed. That meddling pair meant him and Mary. Slowly, slowly he moved his head so that he could peep up through the crack in the door at Hans Van Anda, standing in the dusk of the hall. The redhaired man was young enough to be the son of the man whom he addressed with such frigid scorn; his pale, determined face was infinitely more frightening.

"I won't permit them to interfere," said Hans Van Anda. "I don't know what their friend Ferris may have told them in the letters I didn't get. I think it's likely Griggs told the girl what was in the trunk. Those people aren't fools, you know. Even now they may suspect what is set for Saturday."

"No one has ever told me exactly what is going to happen Saturday," said the other sullenly. "I'd like to know."

"I daresay you would. You know enough already. Suppose you keep your mind on your own job. You may safely leave the rest to me and—the Baron."

A moment later they were in the hall, and once again the picture of the Icarus Club was resting against the manager's desk. One of the men closed the door. Their footsteps died away in opposite directions.

For a long second Paul didn't stir. One thing was sure. Hans Van Anda had a more recent report on Ludwig Hartz, fugitive prisoner of war, than did Major Kenneth Thomson of the Canadian Royal Mounted Police. The bald man was acting under orders, working in the dark. But Frau Van Anda's redhaired son knew exactly where and how to locate

Baron Hartz, and why the fugitive had returned to Canada. Still crouched rigidly against the wall, with the retreating footsteps echoing in his ears, Paul decided that he himself could answer the why. Ludwig Hartz, vanished from Canada months ago, had returned to play some part—an important part—in the destruction of the convoy.

Paul straightened up. Simultaneously, the telephone rang again, a long shrill imperative blast. This time the footsteps hurrying down the hall outside were undoubtedly the manager's.

Paul got himself past the desk, past a bank of filing cabinets, and on into a smaller adjoining office. Fortunately the manager's secretary was out to lunch. The way to escape was clear. Paul tiptoed toward the door. And then, on the secretary's desk, beside a typewriter and a pile of unsigned letters, he spied a second telephone that must be an extension. He paused. Noiselessly he lifted the receiver. There were voices on the wire.

Breathless from his race along the hall Brown had already answered in the other office. The conversation was well begun. It was Major Thomson, again, and the Major was talking.

"Thank God, I've finally caught you. Who was your friend? About Hartz—there's been a surprising development. We have reason to believe that the fugitive was secretly landed on our shores some days ago by submarine."

"By submarine!"

"For God's sake, keep it quiet," snapped the Major. "We have no desire to alarm the public at this stage, or until we pick up the landing party. For your own information a report from Iceland indicates that Hartz hid out some months in the home of Nazi sympathizers named Thorgsen, posing as a mental case."

In the other office, Brown made exclamations of surprise. In the secretary's office, Paul almost dropped the receiver. With those few crisp unexcited words, the world turned upside down for him. The bluff, respectable Thorsgens of Max's letters disappeared and along with them the helpless, hopeless boy who was the other lodger. The Danish fishermen had rescued the boy from a drifting lifeboat that was swamping fast, but no one had ever seen the boat. It had not existed. Any more than the pathetic survivor of a torpedoed merchantman had existed. Ludwig Hartz, fugitive prisoner of war, had landed a stolen Canadian bombing plane on the far northern sea, and he had found friends.

Major Thomson was saying something to the effect that a shortwave sending set removed from the stolen plane had been discovered in the Thorgsens' cellar, was expressing his personal belief that the Danish fishermen had been returned to the Germany which had always possessed their secret loyalty. Brown was continuing his clucks of amazement. And then Paul was jerked back to attention by Max's name.

"We have evidence," said Major Thomson, "that Hartz was accompanied to Canada by an American photographer, a chap named Max Ferris. Apparently Ferris is a close friend of the Strongs."

"The Strongs?"

"Yes, the Strongs," repeated the Major impatiently. "That young American newspaperman and his wife. The two of them are in this affair up to their necks."

Paul opened his mouth and closed it. On the point of entering the conversation and making it three-sided, he checked himself just in time. His hands were sweating as he replaced the receiver. It was too late now to confide in Major Thomson. Much too late. That time was long past.

He knew that Max had never willingly accompanied Ludwig Hartz, that Max, who had discovered too much in Reykjavik, had been shanghaied, kidnapped, but proving it to the Royal Mounted was another matter. Proving his innocence and Mary's and their own good intentions was another matter, too.

They were in too deep for any possible retreat. There was nothing left for him and Mary now except to produce the whole truth—before Saturday. They must work quickly. On tiptoe he left the secretary's office.

SEVENTEEN

A stiff wind blew Mary up the flight of steps that led to the biggest clock in Halifax. The old town clock, as it should be, was in the center of the town. It perched on the shoulder of Citadel Hill, like a four-faced guardian of the earthen breastworks and frowning bastions above. The star-shaped fort sat in lonely isolation on top of the hill and looked across the crowded rooftops of the town upon the feverish activity of the harbor. Bristling with guns, strongly fortified, it had an oddly period air, like a suit of armor. It didn't seem quite real. Smoke was puffing from chimneys protruding from the earth banked around the outer walls. The humped-up earth, hollowed out and roofed in sod, was inhabited. The soldiers who were walking to and fro on guard, blown by the fiercer wind above, lived in there.

Mary wondered uneasily if she were encroaching on a military reservation. And then, with a start, she perceived that the clock was also inhabited. In the square base of the clock, below the tall four-faced turret, was a neat little door. Eight shining lace-curtained windows looked into the four tiny rooms that were the clock tender's house. Mary made the discovery, just as she reached a little wooden sidewalk that ran around this strange clock. She turned at once to retreat. But the door popped open, and like a cuckoo, the clock tender's rosy-cheeked, white-haired wife popped out.

"Are you waiting for your young man, dear?"

"Why, yes, I am," Mary said.

"You looked so cold and blown about, I thought you might like a dish of tea. I'm having mine. Every day at half-past two o'clock," said the cheerful voice, "I drink my tea. As punctual as the dear Duke himself, my husband says I am."

Mary felt somewhat baffled.

"He built the clock, dear," said the other in gentle reproof, "many long years ago. His Royal Highness, the Duke of Kent. Our dear Victoria's father. Now there was a man couldn't abide unpunctuality. In himself as in others. The Duke was fair."

Mary followed her through the neat little door, and looked curiously around at the cozy little kitchen with a tea kettle purring comfortably on a potbellied stove. She'd half expected to see weights and machinery peeping from the corners, or at least to hear the sound of loud ticking.

The clock tender's wife smiled.

"The works are all below, except, of course, that it's wound above. Up the stairs you go"—she gestured toward the minute hall—"and crank the handle for fifteen minutes, no more, no less, and you're done till Saturday again. Except for a bit of oiling now and then. 'Twas different in the old days, when the tender was obliged to climb outside the turret and cling there like a fly, cleaning the ice from the hands, with his good wife inside hanging onto him. We're all glassed in now, all four of our faces. A nice tidy job it is now, dear; satisfies the soul. As I tell my Andrew, not many people in this world live on such friendly terms with Time."

Mary felt at peace herself. Tea was poured, good strong tea, steeped until it was almost black. The clock tender's wife went on gossiping about the Duke of Kent, as though he'd dropped in yesterday. It hadn't ever occurred to Mary that Queen Victoria, who had always seemed so complete in herself, had required the services of a father. That the man existed, had actually led a long and independent life, lived many years in Canada as Commander-in-Chief of the British forces in North America, and all this before his famous dumpling daughter was sired, came as something of a surprise to her. She soon discovered that a good many Haligonians liked to remember that a Royal Prince had once lived among them. In certain quarters His Royal Highness, the Duke of Kent, was apparently still a controversial topic.

"Oh, I know the dear Duke has his critics. You'll hear talk, dear. But we owe so much to him." As Mary glanced through the window giving on the steps, her hostess glanced through another and up the hill. "'Twas His Highness built the Citadel for us, brought in shiploads of maroons from Jamaica to cut seventy feet off the hill and make it flat before he laid a single stone; that's the kind of style I fancy myself. Some may tell you that slicing off a hill is flying in the face of Providence, tampering with God's geography, but I consider that a narrowminded point of view. An orderly man, who wanted a fine flat hilltop for his Citadel was our Duke, exactly the sort you'd picture for the dear Queen's father. I've always been so sorry he couldn't be there when she got us India. My, how he'd have enjoyed the coronation!"

"When did he die?" asked Mary, wishing that Paul were here.

"Only a few years after he left us, dear. When the little Queen Victoria was in her cradle, long before she was a Queen. January 23, 1820—a nasty, rainy day. He'd got wet feet a few days before and manlike wouldn't change his boots. Pneumonia." She sighed. "The Prince's Lodge, out Bedford Basin way where he used to live, is rack and ruin now. The house burned down, the lovely gardens gone. He'd cut out paths in the woods around, all laid out like the letters of the alphabet, twenty-six of them, neat and orderly like himself. Even now if you look right close you can find the shapes of some of the letters, all overgrown. And of course you can still see the little heart-shaped lake that …"

Suddenly the chattering voice paused. Mary waited in intense interest. The clock tender's wife looked uncomfortable.

"Some will gossip about their betters," she then said firmly. "You've heard that scandal loves a shining mark. 'Tis true that when the Duke left Halifax he went back to England and married Victoria's own mother. 'Tis also true that the dear Duke didn't dwell alone in the Prince's Lodge. The heart-shaped lake was dug for another lady's eyes."

"Victoria's father!" cried Mary, shocked herself.

"We mustn't judge, dear." The little lady's cheeks were pink, her eyes were bright, but her voice was firm and unfaltering. "Kings and Queens and Royal Princes have different problems altogether. I say if the Duke lived with this lady thirty years, and he did, dear, thirty years, 'twas a proper marriage and lasted longer than many a one does nowadays!"

They were drinking their third cup of tea when Paul arrived. Mary knew at once that something important had happened, that Paul wasn't going to be interested in any recital of the Duke of Kent's adventures.

As they walked down the steps out of the early nineteenth century and back into the twentieth, she saw him staring across the town at the distant harbor. His face was grim. A moment earlier she had missed his one quick glance at the row of dusty store fronts that squatted on the street looking up the hill. In consequence she didn't notice an unobtrusive loiterer, moving slowly along the block, whose step had suddenly quickened. But Paul perceived that the bald man had made the appointment at the clock and with time to spare. Obviously, he and Mary had been overheard at the theatre.

The words of Hans Van Anda came back to him: "Your job is to bring in that meddling pair." Their own job, Paul reflected bleakly, was different. Their job was to discover the nature of the plot against the convoy and track down the plotters before Saturday. They were to do this singlehanded, while simultaneously they avoided capture by either the Royal Mounted or those others. Well, one thing at a time. Obviously the first thing necessary was to shake the bald man.

Mary tucked her arm through her husband's and decided not to pester him with questions. She was thinking of the theatre program. Three addresses remained of the original four that might lead them to Lisa Tennevant—Alexander Campbell, the printer, Madame des Brizac, the sempstress, Frome & Frome, the furniture store. Which would Paul choose first?

For the next few minutes one would have thought that Paul was headed nowhere in particular, that the search for Lisa Tennevant had vanished from his mind. At the bottom of the hill he swung his wife quickly past the dusty store fronts and across the street into the City Market—a big square building, crowded with farmers and fishermen, standing at denuded booths that had been picked almost bare by early-morning shoppers. At a stand where salted herring and pickled clams hadn't caught the public fancy, Paul paused abruptly. To Mary's surprise and the unconcealed astonishment of the proprietor, an elderly Scot, he acquired two bottles of the pickled clams.

"Sure you want two? My wife puts them up. Speaking for myself, pickling spoils the flavor of the finest clam."

As the elderly Scot reluctantly wrapped the quart-sized bottles in a newspaper, Paul leaned across the booth and engaged in a whispered conference. Mary caught something about a boat. It seemed that Paul was asking where he could go and hire a boat. Why in the world? Before she could inquire Paul had swept her the length of the great bare market and through the back door. They were among the oxcarts and the battered trucks, among lounging farmers who had sold their wares and were comparing profits while they waited for their wives to come back from shopping trips in town. Here Paul disposed of the pickled clams. A dozing Negro awoke with a start as the bulky parcel, accompanied by a bill, was dropped into his lap.

"Take it home," Paul said, and his voice rose clearly. "Jonathan will get you on the phone tonight."

Jonathan? wondered the confounded Mary, and then managed to hold her tongue.

There was a gleam in Paul's eye. He knew what he was doing and he was enjoying himself. Not once did he look behind.

The bald man was suffering agonies of indecision. To be sure he was keeping the pair in sight, but at what cost to himself! Under his very eyes, his victims were plainly making future plans, engaging in baffling and entirely unanticipated activities, and without allowing him a second to investigate. What was the meaning of the scene Paul had played with the elderly Scotch fisherman? By returning to the market later, the bald man had decided wretchedly, he might find out. If he could only reach a telephone now, call in assistance, receive further instructions …

What was the pair doing now? What were they saying to the Negro? Money changed hands. Lurking near the rear doors of the market, the bald man heard very clearly the mystifying words he had been meant to hear. One thing was certain—with five dollars in hand the Negro wouldn't be long available. Already the fellow was shambling to his feet. Nearby Paul and Mary seemed to be examining one of the oxcarts, exclaiming to each other like two pleased, unhurried tourists. The bald man paused only a moment to request an explanation of the gratified but wholly bewildered Negro, and that moment was enough.

Immediately he paused, Paul and Mary darted around the corner. They went into the market again, and out another door. As was usual with Halifax sidewalks, this walk swam with people. They threaded swiftly through the crowd down the descending slope toward the Grand Parade below and thicker crowds. Unfortunately, the nearest streetcar stop was blocks away; even with a good head start, they would never make it. Damn the lack of rapid transportation; Paul had a flashing homesick vision of New York's subways.

Flanking the sidewalk were dreary warehouses, locked and bolted. On the other side, however, were shop windows that suggested at least temporary concealment. When the descending traffic halted, they ran across the street. Caught in traffic, wheels almost to the curb, was a jaunty roadster. It blew its horn at them. Paul glanced around from the corner of his eye, stopped abruptly.

"Well, bless my soul," cried Dr. MacGregor from the wheel, "you two *are* in a hurry! Can I drop you anywhere?"

Mary hesitated. Paul did not. He pushed her into the car, got in himself, slammed the door. He glanced back toward the crowded sidewalk. The bald man was not in sight. Dr. MacGregor promptly cut off the ignition.

"Were you expecting someone else?"

"No," Paul said emphatically. "No, indeed. If you'll just drop us at the nearest streetcar stop … We are rather in a hurry...."

To their joint relief, the doctor started the engine again. The roadster jerked back into traffic, went jolting down the hill at a fast erratic clip. The doctor seemed to be paying more attention to his guests than to his driving. He had, of course, observed that Mary had removed her spectacles and washed the black from her brows and lashes. So much was implicit in his quiet remark that she was looking very well.

"I'll gladly take you where you're going," the doctor offered. "In point of fact I have a call to make over town at the Halifax Artillery School. You'll remember my mentioning the school this morning."

Paul did remember vaguely. Something about an unsolved robbery of small arms and ammunition. Under the present circumstances he didn't care to be reminded of the morning, or to become involved in a lengthy conversation. Already the doctor had crashed across a trolley car junction, spun around a corner and was now sailing blithely along a street that had no trolley tracks. Paul became increasingly anxious to get out.

"Are your affairs progressing satisfactorily?" inquired the doctor, negotiating another turn.

"Well enough," Paul said unencouragingly. His eyes were on the street ahead. When he spied tracks again, he would call a halt.

"Did the lodging at Number 36 work out?"

"The room suits us perfectly," Paul replied politely, and ten called out, "If you don't mind, I think I see a trolley stop."

"I saw it myself," said the doctor, and sounded a little hurt. He pulled at once to the curb. Murmuring thanks, the Strongs alighted. The doctor leaned out the window for a last remark.

"Goodbye, children, for the present. Remember Halifax is a small town. In one way or another, we will probably meet again."

With that the jaunty roadster flashed around the corner and was gone. Mary looked at Paul.

"Darling, I feel haunted."

To tell the truth, Paul felt haunted himself. Halifax might be a small town, but there had been something a little too fortuitous about the doctor's sudden appearance in his jaunty roadster, welcome though it had been. It heightened a feeling that Paul had had from time to time since morning—an uneasy feeling that he and Mary were walking through a jungle with secret watchers everywhere; that they were being led and controlled; that their freedom was illusory. The psychology of the hunted again. Paul looked sharply at a woman who had paused to buckle her flapping galoshes. She looked back at him in surprise. Paul shook himself. If they were to be deflected by every tiny inexplicable circumstance, if they lost their nerve because of the continual feeling of threat that hung over them, they would get nowhere. Time was pressing. He took Mary's arm and they joined the crowd that climbed aboard the trolley.

"Where now?" asked Mary.

"I thought," said Paul, "we might tackle Alexander Campbell, who printed *The Wild Duck* programs. One hundred and twenty-two Marbury Lane. Only where is Marbury Lane?"

Happily, after examination of the city map, it developed that the trolley was going the right way. During the ride Paul dismissed the doctor from his mind and devoted himself to the problem represented by the unknown quantity who was Alexander Campbell. The programs had been printed long ago. It was possible that Campbell might not recall very much about the theatrical company after the lapse of so many months, but another problem occupied him more acutely—the hazard of the Royal Mounted.

Back there at the Princess Royal Theater, his own personal line of investigation and the line of the Royal Mounted had disconcertingly crossed. The Royal Mounted was interested in *The Wild Duck* Company; so was he. If the disbanded theatrical company was suspect, it was more than likely that the Mounties themselves had questioned Alexander Campbell. Caution was indicated.

They alighted from the trolley two blocks short of Marbury Lane and walked. A swinging sign—Job Printing: Best in Halifax—announced the premises of Alexander Campbell before they reached it.

A skinny, high-waisted private house had been converted into a business establishment. There were plateglass windows on the ground floor, and the press was operating in the cellar. Its rhythmic thunder mingled with the complex noises of the street. Marbury Lane wasn't quiet. In a vacant lot across the way a group of boys were engaged in a snowball battle. Their happy shrieks mingled with the pound of traffic and the press. The inevitable crowds surged along the sidewalk, concealing the windows ahead. Paul and Mary struggled forward, reached the shop.

Abruptly Paul's step slowed.

At the plateglass windows stood a lone young man. He was staring at the display of printed calling cards and business announcements, printed posters and paper bags. He seemed to be absorbed in a collection of brightly colored valentines. His gloved hands were clasped behind his back; his walking-out stick hung at his side. The young man wore the familiar azure blue of the Royal Mounted.

Accident?

Paul and Mary walked quickly by. A crowd of soldiers, charging forward four abreast, swept them around the corner into an even noisier street. The Halifax Artillery School, a square brick building converted from a paper mill, announced itself with gunfire. In a basement gymnasium target practice was progressing. The sidewalk shook underneath their feet with every volley. This, scarcely a hundred yards away from Alexander Campbell's shop, was the military establishment that had so interested Dr. Angus MacGregor. The doctor was undoubtedly in the square brick building now; he might appear at any moment.

Paul and Mary exchanged a long look. Silently they decided that the Mountie was the lesser evil. With one accord they went back around the corner and returned to the printing shop. The Mountie was gone; the show windows were now deserted. So it had been an accident. A hurried glance through the windows satisfied Paul that the uniform wasn't on the premises. No one seemed to be in the shop except a dull-faced girl speaking on a telephone. They walked firmly up the steps and inside.

They entered a large cluttered room, poorly lighted, with a splintery floor vibrating to the press underneath. Sample books overflowed everywhere, the walls were hung with examples of the printer's art. Remember Hong Kong, said a sign; Sporting and Fancy Pheasants, said another. The dull-faced girl was languidly chalking an order on a blackboard near the telephone. She came over reluctantly to the counter that divided the room.

"We would like to see Mr. Campbell," Paul began. "A special job."

"Wedding announcements," confided Mary, with her most charming smile.

The dull-faced girl was not romantic.

"The boss hasn't been around today."

"When do you expect him?"

"He had his car washed," she offered unhelpfully. "The garage phoned to ask when he was picking it up. I told them I didn't know."

"In that case," Paul said pleasantly, "we'll wait."

She looked at him suspiciously, and voiced immediate objections when he started through the gate that split the separating counter. There were chairs on her side, but she had her work to do and she hated anything that might put her to the slightest trouble.

"I suppose you can wait in the boss's office, though I can't see it's any use."

"We can be looking through your sample books," said Mary heartlessly. 'The wedding announcements, you know. Please find us all you have."

The dull-faced girl gave in. She gathered up a pile of the heavy books— Paul hardheartedly allowed her to carry them herself—led them along a narrow hall, past a boxed-in staircase that descended to the thundering cellar, and installed them in her employer's office. She closed the door, and washed her hands of them. In the office the vibration of the press was less pronounced; the busy traffic of the street now seemed far away. The small room was stiflingly hot; a coal stove in the corner threw out fierce waves of heat.

Mary amused herself by leafing through the sample books and wondering about other people's weddings, and Paul strolled over to the windows. The windows looked out on the alley. An adjacent door gave on a flight of outside steps that dropped to the cobblestones below. Across the way he could see the rear of the Halifax Artillery School. They had stopped firing over there. The target practice must be over now; the only sound was the mutter of the press. Was it a coincidence that the printer's private office should be so close to a place where an unexplained robbery had occurred? In wartime the theft of arms and ammunition wasn't a light offense.

A truck rattled down the alley, and then the cobblestones were quiet. Mary took out a scrubby handkerchief and mopped her sweating brow.

"Paul, can't you do something about that stove?" In the distance that marked the front of the establishment they heard the thin whine of a telephone. "I hope the order is good and complicated," Mary said unkindly. "How long are we going to wait?"

"A few minutes more."

"What do you intend to say to Mr. Campbell? Will my feminine wiles be needed?"

Paul shook his head.

"I'm going to ask Campbell straight out about *The Wild Duck* Company. I hope to God he does remember Lisa Tennevant. Mary, I'm not quite sure ..."

"Well?"

"I'm not quite sure we want to locate Lisa—just yet."

"But, darling, that's the whole point ..."

"Is it? I don't think so, Mary. Don't you see that our focus has shifted? Our business is to locate the plotters, without their locating us, and learn the story behind them. Max's seventeenth letter, the arrow pointing to Lisa, doesn't necessarily mean the lady will help us—willingly."

Mary was silent.

"Lisa keeps such strange company, darling. I've been wondering whether in the end we won't decide to talk to her with the Royal Mounted along!"

Paul went to the stove and attacked the damper vigorously. His efforts served merely to increase the heat. Mary watched him with amusement and then walked over to the door. She opened it to let in a breath of air.

She glanced idly down the flight of steps into the alley.

A dark-green car, freshly washed and polished and shining even in the dullness of the winter afternoon, turned in from the street. So Campbell had arrived.

Mary started to call to Paul, and then did not. She quietly closed the door.

Paul looked up and saw her eyes. He reached her side. Wordless, she nodded toward the windows.

The green car was now parked. Alexander Campbell had alighted in the alley and was approaching the steps, walking fast. Alexander Campbell was the bald man they had eluded back there at the city market.

EIGHTEEN

As Alexander Campbell opened one door they were out the other and in the hall. But the dull-faced girl was coming from the front of the shop; they heard her footsteps. The telephone call became clear; she had talked to her employer at the garage and he knew—if she did not—how important these particular customers were. Escape was cut off from that direction as it was cut off from the alley. The girl was coming closer. Another turn and she would be upon them.

A door opened on the boxed-in staircase to the cellar. They vanished through it. Campbell and his employee met in the hall. Below the press thundered, but the furious anger in his voice was carrying.

"Gone! You stupid fool, you let them get away!" There was the sound of a blow, a cry of pain. The bald man might take orders from Hans Van Anda, but on his own home grounds he was master. The girl was sobbing.

"I swear they didn't pass me."

"Where are they then?"

"They must be in the alley. They were in your office a minute ago. One of them was fixing the stove."

"The alley! Get Bill to block the other end!"

Bill? They had seen no Bill. Obviously he must be at the presses. Paul anticipated the next move barely in time; he saw exactly what would happen unless they moved fast; the staircase door would open, they would be trapped there on the steps. There was a coat closet at the bottom of the precipitous flight. They got themselves into it, and closed another door.

Simultaneously the girl was screaming down the stairs. At once the presses were stilled. Someone ran by them, and then not quite by. There were hot water pipes in the closet; it was, if possible, hotter than the office, but Mary went icy cold.

Suddenly the running footsteps had stopped. Someone had paused at the closet. Bill was reaching for the doorknob on the other side.

Paul grabbed the knob on his side. It was a gentle, noiseless grab. He held the knob firmly, evenly with strength precisely balanced. He felt and resisted a jerk from the other side, a shift to slower, stronger pressure. The knob mustn't move the fraction of an inch. Nothing must suggest a tug-of-war. There was a second try. The knob didn't budge.

"Locked, by God," a voice muttered.

Again the girl screamed from above. This time the footsteps ran on up the stairs. The door up there banged, and then all was still. Mary sagged against her husband.

"Darling, hold my hand."

"Maybe you'd better hold mine."

He kissed her, laid his wobbly fingers briefly on her face. And then for a moment his hands were otherwise occupied. In the stifling darkness of the closet he went quickly, methodically, through several coats, eventually found what he sought. Mary heard his sigh of satisfaction as he slipped the gun into his pocket.

"I thought that was what our friend stopped for."

"You don't know much about shooting one."

"They don't know I don't."

Unmolested, they walked past the silenced presses and out again to the blessed busyness of the sidewalk.

Not quite fifteen minutes later they were standing at a streetcar stop, blocks away, and Paul was calmly studying his city map. Madame des Brizac, 27 Queen Street—a long way out. Madame des Brizac—a sempstress. She hadn't described herself as a *couturière* even on the theatre program.

Earlier in the day it had been possible to picture a motherly middle-aged French woman, a fat comfortable soul with bastings on her dress and pins in her mouth, kneeling on the floor, chattering away with her customers. "We'll just take a tuck in here…. You have such a pretty waist…. And shall we show a little more at the neck?" It had been easy to picture Madame des Brizac warming at once to Mary, sharing the things she knew about Lisa Tennevant, the other members of the company. It was less easy now.

"Paul, suppose she's in it, too. Like the printer."

"We'll have to chance it. There's nothing else for us, except to follow through. We have no other way to get the story, no sources left except the sempstress and the furniture store."

"Do you think the Royal Mounted might be watching her? They were at the theatre."

"I'm afraid we've got to chance that, too." Paul stared unseeingly across the street at the Provincial Building, a structure as serenely Georgian as was the Governor's noble house; the exquisite timeworn lamps at its doors once had lighted London's Waterloo Bridge. On its icy, winter-killed grounds, among the frock-coated statues of Halifax's great man, a, bronze mustachioed private soldier raised his unsheathed sword to the memory of those who had died for the Empire long ago in Africa. Warfare must have been simpler in those days. Paul suppressed a sigh. "Damned if I can understand why the Mounties weren't watching Campbell, why they let him run loose. I've got a strong hunch Campbell was behind the robbery of the Artillery School."

"Do you think the doctor suspects it?"

"I wouldn't be surprised."

Mary looked at him in silence. Paul couldn't answer the question in her eyes. Where did the robbery fit in? Where indeed? The theft was important; no doubt of that. But surely the robbery of the Halifax Artillery School was on too small a scale to affect, in any serious way, the safety of the convoy. Supposing sufficient small arms and ammunition had been stolen to equip fifty desperate men; supposing the main body of the plotters, those men and women who had once belonged to the Icarus Club and had since gone underground, lay in hiding somewhere in Halifax—although he and Mary had no evidence of that. Even allowing those two things, even assuming the plotters to be fanatics who set no value on their own lives, they could not hope to make a surprise attack upon the harbor with any expectation of getting at the assembled ships; they would die in the street without ever passing through the gates. It would be like attacking the Springfield Arsenal with a popgun.

So far as any such attempt was concerned, the Royal Mounted was warned and on guard. He himself had warned them that the convoy was endangered. They would take extraordinary precautions to protect it. The Mounties and the harbor guards would be ready to hold off any danger they could postulate or imagine, prepared to handle anything that had ever happened in the past. What Paul feared, remembering the contemptuous confidence of Hans Van Anda, was danger of an unimagined kind, something that had never happened before.

Alexander Campbell himself didn't know the nature of the plot; he hadn't been trusted with that vital information. The secret was locked in the head of Hans Van Anda. And of course Baron Ludwig Hartz knew what was planned for Saturday; he had returned to Canada to see it through. Suddenly Paul wondered if the plot might not be the creation of Ludwig Hartz. It seemed very likely.

During those tedious months while the young German had lain in bed at Reykjavik, posing as a mental case, he must have been pondering the future. Patiently, stubbornly he must have turned over in his mind all the ways he could return to Canada and pay the Canadians back. Pay them back for God knows what; imprisoning a German officer, perhaps, interfering with the liberty of action of one of the Master Race. Vengefulness was a German trait. Germany was always paying somebody back for something. At last, or so it seemed to Paul, young Baron Hartz, fugitive prisoner of war, must have hit upon the one plan. He had found his plan and come back to Canada.

Was Lisa Tennevant in the Baron's confidence? Where were the other members of the disbanded Icarus Club? Where was the Baron himself? Where was Max who had discovered too much in Reykjavik? Thick and fast, the questions multiplied.

"I wish to God," Paul said to Mary, "this was New York and we could hail a taxi. It's going to be a long ride."

Paul and Mary rode out of town to the last stop on a trolley car packed with soldiers. They arrived at real country, rolling, hilly, with lonely fields deep in drifted snow and leafless trees that stuck up from them like grotesque, twisted candles on a frosted cake. It was nearly four o'clock, a steel-gray winter afternoon. The wind that blew in from the harbor was damp and cold.

Queen Street, ambitiously named, was a country road ignored by almost everybody except its scattered residents in times of peace. Thirty soldiers alighted with Paul and Mary, fell into rank and marched up the lonely road four abreast. As they marched, they sang. It was, thought Mary—pleased by the incongruity, the marching men, the strong young voices flying out across the vacant fields—wonderfully tonic and reassuring, as festive as tagging along behind a parade.

Twenty-seven Queen Street—number arrived at by some mysterious system best known to the postal authorities—was a good half-mile from the streetcar stop. The soldiers set a brisk pace, but Paul and Mary kept them well in sight. Twenty-seven Queen Street leaped up from the midst of snowy trees and white encroaching fields, one of those isolated farmhouses whose loneliness was only emphasized by another farmhouse directly across the road. At the other farmhouse there was activity and life; a pleasant plume of smoke rose from the chimney, a cat scampered for the kitchen door.

The singing men passed on by. The Royal Mounted was not watching number 27 Queen Street. No one lived there anymore.

It was a pretty little house, white and clean and plain, dwarfed by a tremendous barn some distance behind it. The barn was boarded up; the windows of the house were boarded up. A sign was fastened to the door. Underneath a solitary apple tree, buried in the drifted snow, rose a forgotten swing. Their footsteps made a clean new path as they walked to the porch. The sign said only: For Sale.

Down the road the voices of the soldiers grew fainter, died away. The gray afternoon had a felty stillness. Mary looked back at the double line of their own footprints, and shivered in the raw cold air. A long-distance moving truck, turning patiently from every rut and slippery spot, came slowly along the road. It went by, and then disappeared as abruptly as though the earth had swallowed it.

Paul stepped to the edge of the porch and surveyed the empty road. A copse of evergreen and leafless elms blurred the nearby field. A short cut through the woods perhaps? Obviously the truck had turned in there. He fingered the gun in his pocket. They had better get started back to town. Why were they lingering here?

As he was turning toward Mary, it happened that he glanced out back, behind the cottage. The barn was set on lower ground than the house. Fruit trees and ragged pines, the pathetic arms of cornstalks, cut the view. But through a little opening, something caught his eye. He leaned across the railing, looked again. He frowned. In front of the cottage the snow was virgin, untouched. Out back was a patch that was chopped and marred; several planks lay scattered on the ground. It was then that Mary said:

"Neighbors, darling. Just look across the road!"

An aproned woman had emerged from the other house to feed her chickens. A smile of delighted surprise spread on the woman's broad face as she spied them, and immediately she was across the road and with them on the porch. She hadn't even waited to put down her pan of scraps. Madame des Brizac's nearest neighbor had the friendly motherly qualities that Paul had once pictured in the sempstress, and directness to a high degree.

"Are you folks thinking of buying?"

"Yes," said Mary, suddenly cheerful and light-hearted. She was about to add that they'd just been married when she saw Paul frown. This woman needed no urging.

"I hope to goodness some nice folks move in," she announced at once. "This place used to belong to my sister. Anybody at all," she said frankly, "would be an improvement on the last. Lotte des Brizac ..."

"Lotte?" said Mary, startled. Lotte was an uncommon name. She knew of only one. She and Paul had never heard the surname of Frau Van Anda's companion. "I wonder if we haven't met her. Is she a tall dark woman, very thin and …"

The other nodded emphatically. "You've met her, all right. Looks like a mean old horse." With her own words, the farm woman showed her first reserve. Her overpowering friendliness dwindled. She looked studiously at the scraps in her pan, as though from across the road she could hear hungry chickens calling. "Where did you meet Lotte des Brizac?"

Paul sighed to himself and went to the rescue. Mary's unguarded tongue was always getting both of them into difficulties.

"My wife," he said, "has a bad habit of confusing people. Our Lotte—we met her several years ago—was thin and dark, but her name was Dubois and she had a badly scarred face. Burned as a child," he added as an afterthought.

The farm woman relaxed.

"I hardly *thought* you knew Lotte des Brizac. There's been—well—unpleasant talk about her. I try to be charitable; it's true she's been gone a long time now, but she certainly left town in an awful hurry."

"Yes," said Paul.

"Maybe I *shouldn't* talk—my husband says so—but Lotte des Brizac did pack up and clear out right after the trouble over that escaped prisoner of war. You know—Baron Hartz."

The Baron again! So Lotte des Brizac had seen fit to leave Halifax and seek employment with Frau Van Anda in Milwaukee directly after Ludwig Hartz had flown out of Canada in one of Canada's own planes. Why? Sedwedge prison camp was easily a hundred miles to the west of Halifax. Camps for prisoners of war were closely guarded; the public was barred; Max had been refused permission to take even formal photographs. The fugitive had been assisted in his escape by Adelbert Griggs, a camp guard, but how could Lotte des Brizac, Halifax sempstress, have been involved? Unfortunately Lotte des Brizac's suspicious neighbor seemed unable to tell them.

"All I know," she admitted reluctantly, "is what I saw in the papers. The Lord knows they didn't print much. But I heard the Mounties questioned Lotte des Brizac last September, and then had to let her go. I expect they couldn't prove anything. I always wondered myself …" The farm woman hesitated. In the crystal hush they heard again the faint tremble of singing voices. Another group of soldiers, hidden by a bend in the road far away, must be approaching. The woman smiled.

"There's a camp over the way a few miles," she said. "These must be going into town. Daytimes I can tell," she said, "when there's a trolley by their voices passing, going the two ways. They're still a long way off," she said. "Listen. Their voices will fade as they go down the valley."

Even as she spoke the voices were heard no more. She smiled again a little mistily, as though every one of those boys she couldn't see was her son. Paul was not smiling.

"Tell me, what did you think about Madame des Brizac?"

She awoke from her dream. Her broad face hardened. "Ludwig Hartz walked on the field at Sedwedge last September, wearing the uniform of the Royal Canadian Air Forces. I always wondered if Lotte des Brizac hadn't made that uniform for him."

The Strongs were silent. The farm woman hadn't done with talking.

"Afterwards they say, after the escape, the young Baron crashed in the sea. You know, I'm glad. Sometimes lying in bed at night I think of him coming down on the water, sinking fast, trapped and frightened the way any boy would be, and I feel no pity."

She sounded startled, perhaps a little shocked to discover the bitter feeling in herself. But the good nature and kindliness had vanished from her face.

"I suppose you might say that's what the Germans have done for us, taught us to hate them all, even their boys. Boys like Ludwig Hartz— wicked dangerous boys whose hearts and minds and bodies are trained for nothing but to destroy and kill. Yes, I'm glad the Baron is dead."

The wicked dangerous young boy, who had escaped from Sedwedge prison camp and become the other lodger of Reykjavik, wasn't dead. He was back in Canada again, in hiding somewhere, his heart and mind and body consecrated to the destruction of the convoy. Yes, Paul felt very sure now that Ludwig Hartz was the author of the plot.

Across the road the farmer came up from milking, and saw them standing on the porch. He shouted angrily at his wife. At once, as though relieved to be done with them, she was gone. Paul and Mary watched husband and wife go in the house.

NINETEEN

The barn was set back farther from the clean white cottage than Paul had thought. If they made a direct approach from the porch, they might be noticed by the neighbors across the road. It seemed to Paul that he could detect a quivering curtain. Prospective purchasers would hardly be expected to prowl around the barn; the farmer might step over and start asking awkward questions—he certainly seemed to be a less agreeable type than his wife.

But before they returned to town, Paul meant to investigate that area of churned-up snow behind the house, those scattered planks. With its windows boarded up, with the neat "For Sale" sign on the door, it was true that the cottage looked as though it had been unoccupied for months. But Paul was wondering whether Lotte des Brizac, the owner, might not have seen fit to stop in with her guests after she left the Haligonian Hotel. He recalled his glimpse of the three women in the speeding taxi—Lotte, stiff and rigid and looking straight ahead, and beside her Lisa Tennevant leaning slightly forward to smile at Frau Van Anda, who hadn't known where she was going. Her son, she said, had found other more quiet lodgings. Someone had certainly been in the vicinity of the barn since morning, since noon, in fact. The snowfall had stopped at noon.

Paul took Mary's arm and they walked briskly along the road toward the trolley line, and then turned around and cut back across the fields. Circling the cottage, working their way under the cover of trees and bushes, they approached the barn.

The churned-up snow showed the marks of tires. The scattered planks lay near the barn. They had been hurriedly and recently pried loose from the wide double doors. Cautiously, with Mary breathing nervously down his neck, Paul pushed through the doors. Mingled with the stale cold odor of straw and mildew, was the sudden acrid smell of gasoline. Several tins sat inside the doors. In the dusk ahead, peeping from a stall, was the shine of headlights, a metal bumper.

Hand in hand, they stole forward. The orange taxi that had sped away from the Haligonian Hotel that morning with a heavy trunk strapped on behind had come to rest in the deserted barn. A twist of rope lay beside it on the straw-strewn floor. The trunk that had been tied on the back of this strange taxi was gone. Paul moved quickly back to the doors. Standing in the shadows, he spied out the land ahead.

Through denuded fruit trees and a sprinkling of the inevitable evergreens the back face of the small white cottage presented itself. He could see the roof, a portion of the second floor. Shuttered windows peered through the tangled branches like sightless eyes. There was no smoke from the chimney. The place appeared to be deserted. But confused footprints trampled the snow beneath the nearer trees, and other marks where some heavy object had been dragged along. As the trees thickened, the trail was lost. Sprawling firs cut off his view of the lower story and back door of the cottage.

"They've taken the trunk to the house. Mary, I could swear the three of them are in there now."

"Four," Mary said. "You've forgotten to count the driver."

"I'd like to know what they are doing. If we could only find out what is in the trunk … You wait here a minute."

"Paul …"

"Please don't argue, darling. Now we're here, I mean to look around a bit. It won't take long."

"Why can't I go too?"

"Because it will be easier if I go alone. I promise I won't ask for trouble. Don't forget I've got a gun myself."

Paul reached for the gun in his pocket. He snapped the safety catch, and at once made a discovery. The gun he had borrowed back there at the printing establishment wasn't loaded. Well, an unloaded gun would serve, in case a bluff was necessary. He didn't expect to need a gun. Mary looked at him sharply.

"Is something wrong?"

"Not a thing. Light yourself a cigarette; I'll be back to light your second."

He stepped quickly from the barn before she could press her inquiries. The trees offered the only cover; he dodged rapidly from one to the other, traveling fast across the open places. It didn't seem feasible to follow the previous tracks; he went more circuitously. Unlikely as it was that anyone in the house would be posted at windows that were boarded over, he took no chances. As he advanced, his confidence grew. There was no sign of life ahead. That meant the women and their companion must be nervous too. In midwinter they hadn't dared to light a fire. Lotte des Brizac hadn't dared to enter her own home from the front; she and her companions had slipped in by the back way, lest they attract the attention of the neighbors.

At length he reached the last sprawling fir that stood between him and the house. He pressed aside the heavy branches. At the back door of the cottage the trampled footprints showed up again, and, at that point, stopped abruptly. He could make out the definite outline of the trunk where it had been set down a moment at the flat stone step.

Kitchen, thought Paul, and located a window near the door. The moment of greatest danger remained. He forced his tense muscles to relax, ran lightly across ten feet of open space, and was at the house. He came to a halt directly outside the window he had marked down as his own. He had hoped the boards wouldn't fit too tightly.

Disappointment awaited him. The boards that covered the glass were stout and wide and they fitted together closely, with no cracks worth mentioning. He laid his ear against the wooden barrier, listened, heard nothing. The air space would swallow sound of course. It wasn't possible he had been mistaken. In every nerve he could sense the hidden life and hidden activities within.

He examined the wide planks with scrupulous care. Eventually, a few inches above his head, he located a knothole that had begun to rot. When he reached up and gently scratched it with his thumbnail, powdery dust came away. Underneath the wood was spongy, then irritatingly solid. He hesitated a moment, felt through his pockets. He found his pocket knife and attacked the knot hole, swiftly, but cautiously. Several minutes passed before the bit of wood dropped into his outstretched palm.

At once a ray of yellow light gleamed through the hole. Unfortunately the little opening turned out to be a maddening inch or so above the level of his eye, even when he stretched to his full height and stood on tiptoe. He took off his overcoat, doubled it up, laid it carefully on the ground and stood on it. The coat made just the difference. He saw only a section of the large, candlelighted kitchen, but it was a vital section. Lotte, Frau Van Anda, the taxi driver, were not in sight. It was Lisa Tennevant whom he saw very clearly.

In the background of the kitchen was a large, typically French fireplace with copper pots and kettles hanging, and a row of pottery figurines marching along the mantel. The fire was unlit. The hearth was bare and cold, and seemed barer and colder perhaps because of the candles that burned overhead among the pottery figurines.

Lisa Tennevant was standing near the fireplace, with her back to the window. She was leaning over an open trunk, as though checking the contents. In Paul's pocket was the key to that trunk, but he wasn't going to need it. The candlelight shone down on Lisa, threw the shadow of her bending figure, the shadow of the lifted trunk lid upon the floor. Paul looked straight into the open trunk. He had been prepared to see guns and ammunition, small arms innocently transported, and now, incredulous, he couldn't believe he was seeing correctly. At that moment Mary touched his arm.

"Paul! They're at the door. I just heard someone pull the bolt."

He snatched his coat from the ground and spun around. Simultaneously the kitchen door opened. Framed in the gush of candlelight, bright in the gray afternoon, stood Frau Van Anda with Lotte beside her.

"Won't you come in?" Frau Van Anda said.

Paul continued to pull on his coat. He brushed the snow from his sleeve and his eyes were calm.

"How extraordinary to find you two here," he said. "Mary and I were hoping to rouse someone. In town we heard about the house."

"A real-estate agent," added Mary.

Of course Lotte didn't believe a word of it. People running from the police are seldom in the market for houses. But Paul had a fairly clear idea that Lotte des Brizac wouldn't summon the Royal Mounted, even though her telephone might be connected. From inside a gay voice called, "Do bring them in, and do, in the name of heaven, shut that door."

When they entered the kitchen the trunk was closed. Indeed, Lisa Tennevant, wrapped in furs like the others, was sitting on it. She rose at once and came forward with outstretched hands.

"At last we meet! I must apologize for the house. We've only just arrived and aren't staying. It hardly seemed worthwhile to bother with the heat," she said, as though she were a hostess greeting welcome and expected guests. "Anyway, you're here! Of course you know we share a mutual friend."

Paul looked merely puzzled.

"Max Ferris," she said.

The Strongs were silent. She paused expectantly, and still they said nothing. A flicker of disappointment showed in her dark eyes. Her lips kept on smiling. She had been quick to release Mary's hand, but her slender chilly fingers clung to Paul's.

"Surely I'm not speaking out of turn—with *you*. I know you realize that our dear Max isn't dead. Of course we are among the few who do."

"Are we?"

She refused to be discouraged. Her glance, warm and intimate, searched his eyes.

"You are wise to be cautious. But somehow"—she hesitated—"I fancied Max had been able to get through a message to you."

There was another meaningful pause and again the Strongs were politely silent. The actress lowered her voice. "It's a complicated story, difficult to explain. In wartime one must be so careful and, after all, the secret isn't really mine. It's his, it's Max's."

They still waited courteously for her to go on. It was now clear to Paul that the actress had no idea how much they knew, what they had found out; that she was fishing. Their arrival had been completely unexpected; at the moment she didn't really know what to do with them. Like Alexander Campbell before her, she was without instructions to cover the situation. But her wit was quicker. In a moment, he thought, she would begin hinting that she and Max and perhaps the others were engaged in some mysterious piece of counterespionage. Well, he was prepared for that. Since he had glimpsed the contents of the trunk, Paul had been in no doubt as to which side Lisa was on. In his mind the outlines of the plot were emerging from the haze; soon he and Mary would go to the Royal Mounted; nothing could stop them now.

Even in defeat there was a little air of confidence about the actress that was vaguely disturbing, that made Paul remember his gun wasn't loaded. Releasing his hand with a last lingering pressure; Lisa walked over to the mantel and gazed absently at the barren hearth. Paul was watching closely; in the downward glance her swift dark eyes had flickered to her watch. So she was concerned with the passing minutes.

Suddenly it struck him that the other two—Frau Van Anda, pale and quiet, and Lotte crowded on a narrow couch beside her—were also concerned. In the frigid kitchen was an air of waiting. Why? The answer came at once. The women were expecting someone. Who? That answer was easy too. They were expecting someone who would know what to do with Paul and Mary Strong.

Lisa had drawn them far into the kitchen. Slowly, arm in arm, Paul and Mary started backing toward the door.

Overhead there were footsteps. Frau Van Anda's eyes flashed up. Lisa smiled to herself. So the taxi driver had been there on the second floor all the time. Paul and Mary heard the footsteps and then, in the distance far away, outside on the road, a more welcome sound. It was the distant rhythm of young, singing voices, heard before the marching feet of the soldiers were audible. Lisa frowned a little, this time glanced openly at her watch. Paul and Mary were almost at the door now. No one had objected—yet. One of Paul's hands was in his pocket, closed firmly around the gun. The other reached behind him, touched the doorframe, clasped the doorknob.

"Oh, you mustn't go. Not yet."

Instantly Lisa had flashed across the kitchen. She caught him by the wrist. The feet were coming down the stairs. Outside, commingled strangely, were the marching feet of the soldiers, the surge of the oncoming voices.

"We cannot stay."

"You must stay. In a moment now we will go to Max, we will take you there. You must see him without delay."

"We have other plans."

"I'm afraid you must change those plans."

A car drove up in the back yard. Lisa smiled triumphantly. As the smile formed, it faded. The car had not yet stopped when there came a thundering knock at the front door. Someone was determined to be admitted. Above the knock, was the swelling roar of the soldiers' voices. It sounded almost as though they might be on the snowy lawn, so loud and joyous were their voices. On the kitchen stairs the footsteps had come to a dead halt. Whoever had driven up in the car had prudently remained outside in the backyard.

There was another thunderous knock at the front door, accompanied by shouted song. Lisa ran.

Lotte sprang up from the fireside bench. She made a gesture as though to halt the Strongs and hold them in the kitchen, and then changed her mind at the flash of a gun in Paul's hand. By the time they reached the front door in Lisa's wake, running along a narrow hall, the gun was in Paul's pocket again. The farmer from across the road stood on the front porch, hammering with a hand that was like a ham. Gathered in the road behind him, spilling over on the lawn, clustered beneath the solitary apple tree, the soldiers had paused to watch and finish off their song. There was a last jubilant roar with the opening of the door. Across Lisa's shoulder, the farmer spied Paul and Mary clinging to him. He smiled broadly.

"My wife thought you two was over here, and I see she wasn't mistaken. She thought maybe you might like a lift to the trolley line."

"How kind of you! We were just this minute leaving." Paul turned to Lisa. "Tell Frau Van Anda goodbye for us. You might tell Max we will see him—later."

They rode back to the trolley line in a shabby car that was packed with soldiers, with other soldiers thick upon the running board. It wasn't until they were started back toward town that Mary had any chance to speak to Paul.

"What was in that trunk?"

"Uniforms."

"Uniforms!"

"Uniforms of the Royal Canadian Air Forces; I don't know how many. The trunk was jammed with them."

"But what does it mean?"

"After one more stop," Paul said, "after we call on Frome & Frome, I hope we will be able to tell the Royal Mounted what it means."

TWENTY

It was almost dark when they reached Archer Street and Frome & Frome. The store shared the quiet block—one of those little lost blocks tucked in between the noisy harbor and the brawling center of town—with a closed and shuttered warehouse. Modern furniture was displayed in its still unlit windows along with a sprinkling of antiques. For so large a shop there wasn't very much. Hard hit by wartime shortages, thought Paul. Frome & Frome didn't look like a busy place. Well, so much the better.

This was the end of the trail for them, the last of their personal investigation. This one more stop, and they were done. Gazing into the dusky store, Paul felt that sure knowledge in his veins. So far the theatre program had guided them well. At every step of the way they had learned something; at the Princess Royal Theatre, at Alexander Campbell's printing establishment, at Lotte des Brizac's cottage in the country.

"This time, Mary," he began, "we'll be ourselves, or as close to that as possible. Which means I'll do the interviewing. You, my darling, are inclined to oversell. Most people like to talk," said Paul to Mary. "Look at the Gallup polls!"

As he spoke Paul was dimly aware that behind them a truck had passed on the street. The wan light of the dying day was shining upon the plateglass windows, and for an instant he'd seen a dark moving reflection twist across the glass and then go by. He turned sharply, as the truck disappeared into the nearby alley. It wasn't the long-distance truck that had vanished in the woods back there in the country. It was an ordinary coal truck. Paul relaxed. He opened the door of Frome & Frome.

Inside, solitary among rows of chairs and sofas and bureaus and dressing tables, sitting at a desk in the back, was one clerk, a middle-aged, clean-shaven man who rose quickly to greet his customers. Bored, thought Paul, in satisfaction. Watching the door, this chap was, while he leafed through a pile of catalogs and pretended to himself he was busy. Before he reached them the clerk commenced apologizing for the stock, explaining as though it hurt him in his furniture-selling soul, that almost everything they saw was sold.

Paul granted with a sympathetic smile that the furniture business was shot to hell, that it wasn't a buyers' market, that a salesman with nothing to sell had lost something of himself as a human being.

"In point of fact," Paul began, "the only thing we need is a bedside lamp. Any sort will do. At present we're staying at a rooming house, Number 36 Canary Cage Lane ..."

Mary started in surprise, and then suddenly understood. The clerk had undoubtedly read the morning paper, had heard talk about Adelbert Griggs. This was going to be Paul's show. She settled back to enjoy it.

Magically, with the mention of that address, the clerk's boredom had vanished. Alive and interested, eyes sparkling behind his rimless spectacles, he awaited developments. Quite truthfully, Paul explained that he and his wife were strangers in the city, that they'd stayed at the rooming house only a short time; and then, less truthfully, he added that 36 Canary Cage Lane was in an uproar over the passing of Adelbert Griggs. It was all extremely mysterious. Naturally he and his wife were interested.

"I've been curious," Paul announced, again very frankly, "about the exact position of *The Wild Duck* Company. We've heard considerable talk in the house, of course, but nothing concrete. I understand that you people lent the company their furniture when they played here last September."

"Yes, it's true we did," said the clerk a trifle defensively. "It was explained to us," continued the clerk in the tone of one who'd told the tale a good many times before, "that the proceeds of all the performances given by the Icarus Club were to go to our various wartime charities. Under those circumstances, Mr. Frome was happy to do his bit to help. There is certainly no denying the group was clever! They were playing here in Halifax," he then said indignantly, "the very night that German baron got away from Sedwedge Camp."

At that point the clerk turned hesitant. After all, the inside story of Sedwedge had never become a public matter. One of those unfortunate affairs that in the public interest should best be kept private. Paul realized that perfectly, with an even more understanding nod. He himself had heard the wildest rumors concerning Sedwedge. Rumors so wild that he'd be ashamed to pass them on. It was a great relief to talk with an intelligent man who really had the facts. With that, the clerk's last hesitation melted.

"It was a miracle," he began, with a conspiratorial look around the empty store as though a hidden listener might be crouched anywhere, "nothing short of a miracle, that only one prisoner got away from

Sedwedge last September. The plan was for a general break."

Now he had begun to talk, the clerk was apparently eager to continue. He leaned closer toward them.

"The big break failed," he repeated, "but it wasn't for lack of care and preparation. The prisoners, mostly flyers shot down over London, the hardest type to keep behind bars, had guns and ammunition. They tried to shoot their way out. A lot of blood was shed before the thing was done with. Obviously"—the clerk's voice sank lower—"they had assistance from the outside. Someone smuggled those guns inside the prison."

"Someone?"

"A week before they came to Halifax, one week exactly, Lisa Tennevant and that amateur theatrical company, complete with props and costumes, entered the prison grounds."

Mary stared incredulously. "Why in the world …"

"They gave a Saturday night show before the Security Guards at Sedwedge Camp!"

Mary sat down abruptly in the nearest chair, and caught Paul's warning eye in time. Paul's face was calm, hiding both excitement and triumph. At last everything was falling into place.

Adelbert Griggs had been a guard at Sedwedge Camp. He, too, had been suspected of complicity in the escape of Baron Ludwig Hartz, and had been cashiered from the service. Lotte des Brizac had been questioned and she had left town. What had happened to the Icarus Club in September? Well, admitted the clerk, there had been no positive evidence against the group.

Canada was a democratic country with democratic institutions. Sadly enough, sometimes democratic institutions were of assistance to those who sought to destroy them. Downright Nazis, spies, traitors. In a democratic country, strong suspicion was not enough. Democracies had notoriously allowed themselves the luxury of being sentimental. Most of the members of the Icarus Club were refugees, the majority had fled from Europe after the fall of France, which meant they had attracted sympathy and in the beginning had found friends and backing.

Less sentimental people, and the Royal Mounted was not a sentimental organization, had realized that refugees, however pitiable their circumstances, were a peculiar and rather special class of folk. Every sensible person was aware that Hitler and his Gestapo had made use of the wretched who escaped from Europe through families and relatives who had not escaped. Every sensible person was aware that Nazi spies and saboteurs had sometimes been planted among them. Obviously a theatrical company that was largely male, barnstorming through Canada, had enjoyed many opportunities to gather information that would be useful to Canada's enemies. Following the Sedwedge incident, the R.C.M.P. had made a thorough investigation of the Icarus Club. Nothing tangible had come of it. After an exhaustive inquiry—the clerk knew as a positive fact that Lisa Tennevant and other members of the group had been held incommunicado and questioned for several days— the Royal Mounted had been reluctantly obliged to turn the company loose. Immediately, the Icarus Club had disbanded.

Now, five months afterwards, now when the members were scattered God knows where, the Mounted was attempting to round them up again. With no luck apparently. The twenty-five people, more than twenty of whom were men, had seemingly vanished. Strange, wasn't it?

Paul didn't think it strange. Nor did he need to ask why, at this particular date, a case five months old had suddenly sprung to life again. He knew. The truth had rushed upon him. His brain was on fire with knowledge. In the failure of the general prison break at Sedwedge five months ago, was the key to the present plot against the convoy. The inception of the second plot was there. Its roots were in Sedwedge, just as he had suspected since he glimpsed the contents of the trunk. The plot against the convoy, more complicated, more ambitious and more deadly, was an elaboration of the plot which had failed. The German mind was stubborn and thorough. The German mind was also curiously unoriginal.

But how was the sudden interest of the Royal Mounted in the Sedwedge case to be explained? Again Paul knew. Adelbert Griggs was the explanation. Adelbert Griggs who had left Canada in disgrace had been returning to Halifax on the *Shalimar*. But that wasn't the important thing. The important thing was that the Mounties had been awaiting him at the dock, expecting him. Why? How, five months afterwards, had they known Griggs would be aboard?

In a single bound, Paul arrived at the conclusion that he realized he should have reached at once, from the very first.

Adelbert Griggs wasn't traveling under guard or under arrest; he was coming home voluntarily, of his own free will. The Mounties were expecting him, because he'd sent them word. The one-time Security Guard had decided to clear his conscience, and then he'd lost courage and killed himself. There was the missing motive for his suicide. In the last extremity, the man who had sold out his own country could not face himself.

It all fitted together.

Before Adelbert Griggs left the world he was too cowardly to live in, just before he went on board the *Shalimar*, he had sent a telegram. That telegram had been addressed to his old superiors. Before he shot himself, Adelbert Griggs had disclosed enough of his own shameful past, his shameful present, to make the Royal Mounted extremely eager to collect the scattered members of the disbanded Icarus Club.

The official line of investigation and his own line had crossed, Paul perceived with shock and surprise, because the original source of information had been precisely the same. Adelbert Griggs had talked to Mary, had warned her of a projected plot against the convoy. Adelbert Griggs must have telegraphed the Royal Mounted to the same effect. But if the Royal Mounted was engaged in tracking down the members of the Icarus Club, why hadn't they located Lisa Tennevant? He—the amateur—had been able to do it. Why didn't the Royal Mounted pick up Alexander Campbell, the bald printer whose shop was directly around the corner from the Halifax Artillery School?

Paul pulled his thoughts back to the clerk. The clerk was looking restive, as though asking himself whether he'd talked too much or as though suddenly reminded that, after all, these customers had come in to buy a lamp. Murmuring that their modern lamps were to be seen on the second floor, the man turned toward the elevator.

But Mary had arisen from her chair and seized the first lamp at hand—a lamp that managed to be neither modern nor antique but possibly something in between. It had a lot of gold leaf and bronze on it, particularly the base which seemed to be the figure of an excessively stout and repulsive little girl holding up a perforated bronze umbrella that formed the shade. Mary looked mildly surprised at her inadvertent choice, as she said hurriedly:

"This will suit us nicely. I like a *solid* lamp myself." She handed the solid lamp to the clerk, and sweetly, inexorably, held him to the subject. "About Adelbert Griggs, there's something that puzzles me. Why a man who fought in the last war would help the Nazis just for—for money. Did he know Baron Hartz?"

"That I can't say, Miss. Seems hardly likely. The guards and the prisoners don't mix much." The clerk slowly turned back to theme "Most people here in Halifax," he said abruptly, "believe it was the woman got Griggs in all his troubles."

The woman? Mary looked at Paul. He was remembering how Lisa's hands had clung to him, the softness of her gaze. Mary was remembering a drunken ex-Security Guard weeping in a waterfront restaurant, and lying on the dirty floor trampled beneath his feet a theatre program torn to bits, with Lisa Tennevant's pictured face in a dozen pieces.

"You mean Lisa Tennevant?"

"Her, of course." The pattern was classic. All the tedious, dreary, conventional properties were there. An unscrupulous woman, a beautiful woman, a weak man, soft words, flattery …

"He met her on leave in Montreal, saw her in a show, I guess, and she smiled at him and Griggs was a gone goose. They say he was daft over Lisa Tennevant, out of his head, and him a married man, and her married, too. Disgraceful, any way you look at it, I suppose, but say what they may, I feel kind of sorry for him."

"Oh," said Mary, and yet for some curious reason neither she nor Paul was surprised. It was as though all along they had been prepared for this. It didn't occur to either one of them to question the fact that Lisa Tennevant had a husband who hadn't figured in her press notices. They knew instinctively it was true. "Oh, I hadn't heard," Mary said, "that Lisa Tennevant was married."

"She wasn't working at it," said the clerk grimly. "When she got out of Europe—this would be a couple of years back—she left her husband behind. She saved her own skin and left her husband, poor devil, rotting in a German concentration camp. Some think it was she who sent him there."

"What was his name?" Paul asked suddenly.

The clerk was afraid he couldn't say. Oh, yes, he'd heard but he'd forgotten. His brow wrinkled in the effort of concentration. Lisa Tennevant had come to Canada from France, but it didn't seem like the husband was French. Belgian, could it be? No, it wasn't Belgian.

"Dutch! He was a Dutchman. Yes, yes, that's it. The Germans grabbed him when they invaded Holland. An influential man, a rich man, I expect. He was arrested the day the Nazis came. But they didn't arrest Lisa Tennevant. She got out of Europe, so they say, with a pot of her husband's money."

"Dutch," Paul said insistently. "Dutch. Do try to remember. What was his name?"

Slowly the clerk's face brightened.

"Van Anda was the name," the clerk said, "Hans Van Anda."

TWENTY-ONE

Lisa Tennevant had put her husband in a Nazi concentration camp, and the Germans had kept him there. She had been allowed to leave Europe, because she was a Nazi herself. Hans Van Anda was still in a concentration camp or—dead. There had been no escape for him.

Then who was Frau Van Anda's redhaired son?

He was no son at all. Once you knew, Paul thought, you accepted instantly. The Dutchwoman and the redhaired youth had never behaved like mother and son. There had been no easy give and take in their relationship, always the pretense had been thin. At their first meeting with the pair, long ago in the New York restaurant, when first Frau Van Anda sought to help them, the masquerade had been implicit.

No, Frau Van Anda had not been reunited with her son. Elise Van Anda was among those wretched of the earth who had loved ones—an only son—trapped in Europe. She had acted under duress to protect the Hans Van Anda who was far away—under Hitler's power. Everything about her hesitations, her indecisions, her evasions and contradictions was thus explained.

Frau Van Anda had been drawn into the plot by a person who knew her well, knew her circumstances, the pitiful helplessness of her position, and how to play upon the knowledge. Lisa Tennevant had known where to locate her mother-in-law. Frau Van Anda had been used by the woman who had betrayed her son. For months she must have been a helpless pawn in the Icarus Club's sinister game.

But who was the redhaired stranger masquerading as Hans Van Anda?

Suddenly the last link slipped into place. Paul knew. The false Hans Van Anda was Ludwig Hartz himself.

Frau Van Anda had been useful indeed. She had provided the fugitive prisoner of war not only with her enforced protection but with an identity. The youth who had had no name in Iceland had found a name in New York. He had never been in Milwaukee. He had joined his "mother" in New York very probably on the day they first met him.

Ludwig Hartz had been smuggled down from Iceland to Canada by submarine, after the fishing boat had been shelled and sunk. Why hadn't the Baron remained in Canada? Why was it necessary for him to show up in the Washington Square apartment house occupied by

Paul and Mary Strong?

It was because of Max. Max and his letters. Max had discovered something of the plot during the period when he stayed at the Danish lodging house, with "the helpless mental case" across the hall from him. Max had been taken prisoner, had been put out of action on his own, but Max had written letters to his friends in New York and Ludwig Hartz had desperately feared the contents of those letters. Equipped with the name and identity of Hans Van Anda, he had gone to New York to find and steal the letters, and the theft had failed. He had no idea how very little the Strongs had known about him and all the rest of it—at first.

To be sure, Ludwig Hartz, who was the other lodger of Max's letters, was described as fair. A dye pot had taken care of the blond hair. Henna, so that the fraudulent son should bear a specious resemblance to his mother.

Young Baron Hartz, fugitive prisoner of war, returned to Canada after strange adventures, expected to lead in the destruction of the convoy. Lisa Tennevant was his good right hand, the resurgent members of the Icarus Club functioning again, in hiding somewhere, were his followers. Ludwig Hartz had planned with consummate care, with the stubbornness of the German mind, overlooking no detail, hurrying nothing.

Outside, night had fallen. Shadows crowded the unlit portions of the store, creeping from the corners. Only where they stood was a pool of light. Paul was lost to his surroundings.

"Paul!"

"Here's your lamp," said the clerk abruptly, and thrust out the parcel in his hands as though anxious to sever all connection between them at once.

He pushed out the lamp and backed away. Mary stood rigid beside her chair. Her face was very pale. She and the clerk were staring through the dusk toward the street. Paul turned his head. His heart lurched in his chest.

The door from the street had opened without a sound, and without a sound had closed again. Baron Hartz had not forgotten them, nor had Alexander Campbell. They had escaped from the bald printer once that day, and now again he had come for them. Moving on quick sure feet through the forest of beds and bureaus and dressing tables, the bald man was almost upon them. He'd pushed a handkerchief up underneath his cap with some idea of disguise but his browless forehead showed, his lashless eyes. In his hand Alexander Campbell held a gun.

"Out the back way, both of you," he said in a fretful, whining voice. "Never mind reaching for your gun. I know it isn't loaded. My car is waiting in the alley."

The clerk shrank farther away from Mary. Perhaps Alexander Campbell, misinterpreting the sudden motion, thought the middle-aged clerk was making toward his desk and the telephone. Or perhaps the quondam printer didn't think at all, but merely responded out of habit, welcoming any opportunity for an act of cruelty, necessary or otherwise. His motions were neat, quick, efficient—a kind of all-in-one operation, over in a second. He hit the clerk on the head with the butt of the gun, and the middle-aged man sagged unconscious to the floor. With his free arm, he reached out toward Mary.

"Get moving. You and the boyfriend, too."

Somewhere in there, somewhere within those thirty seconds, Paul too had stopped thinking. His gun might be useless, but there was something in his hand, something solid and heavy—the lamp. He hurled it straight into the face of Alexander Campbell, with never a thought that the proposition was hopeless. Now with the end so near, with success so close, now that he knew the truth, he refused to lose. It was as simple as that.

The base of the lamp caught Campbell on the side of the head where the skull is thin. Ten pounds of solid metal, thrown with the force of a pitched ball. He reeled under the impact, staggered against a canvas-covered glider that rolled with his weight so that his feet were jerked from under him and he fell over it backward. Tangled with the canopy, he crashed to the floor. Campbell could take a blow that would knock an ordinary man unconscious, and almost at once he bobbed up again. He hadn't loosed his grip on the gun.

By then Paul and Mary were at the back door of Frome & Frome.

The green car was parked in the alley almost at the service exit. Its motor was running. The mouth of the alley was blocked by one of Frome & Frome's trucks, which had apparently stalled. There seemed to be no one in it. No one was in sight on the dark and quiet street beyond.

Paul and Mary turned and ran the other way. The alley was black before them, slippery underfoot. But a long block ahead was another street—a busier street, moving traffic, lights, people.

Before they covered half the distance, Alexander Campbell was also through the door and in the alley. He made no attempt to use his gun. Nor did he try to overtake them on foot. He leaped into his car.

Headlights flooded the alley, bathed their flying figures in merciless glare. Actually they were aware of the rushing light, before they heard the rushing wheels behind them. It was Alexander Campbell's plain intention to run them down in the narrow alley.

Paul jerked Mary to the side against a wall. Snow and slush dashed into their faces as the speeding car was carried by. The bald man by inches had missed crushing them against the building. Possibly he prepared to turn around and try again. They never learned. In the wall was a door—closed but unlocked.

They stumbled through the door into the dark desertion of the building. Somehow Paul found and shot the bolt, and with almost shocking suddenness the pursuit was over. When Mary heard the bolt drop, she sank to the floor, too spent for speech, too spent for feeling. There was no further sound from the alley. No one was clamoring at the door. They had got away.

For several minutes Paul stood tense and motionless beside her. At last he realized that Alexander Campbell and his green car must be gone. There was no immediate hope of capturing him. Paul inspected the gloom around them. They had entered the rear of a wholesale fish house, as was attested by the sharp, prevailing smell. Nearby the dim shapes of clustered barrels, the recognizable square of a large refrigerator, chilly to the touch, sawdust scattered on the floor. And then ahead ...

"Mary, I think I see a light. Over to the left."

"Yes," she said.

"I expect it's the retail shop. Dear, I wish you'd try and stand up. We've got to start moving again and fast—get to a phone, get to the Royal Mounted."

"The Royal Mounted, Paul?"

"I know everything, darling," Paul said, and in the strange darkness his voice was very tired. "Maybe the Mounties will have to prove it, but I know. They're planning another general prison break, that's what they stole the guns and ammunition for. Most of the plotters aren't even here in Halifax; that's why we've seen so few of them; they're probably in Sedwedge now."

"Sedwedge!"

"In Sedwedge or somewhere close, hiding out, waiting a signal to shoot their way into the prison. Their job is to deliver the prisoners, turn loose fifty, a hundred, maybe two hundred Nazi flyers like the Baron. You can see yourself what the job of the Nazi flyers is."

The picture was clear now. Close to Sedwedge prison was the Canadian army airfield that Ludwig Hartz had visited last September, dressed in a Canadian pilot's uniform. That field was crowded with Canadian planes; stationed at Sedwedge were giant bombers that crisscrossed the gray wastes of the Atlantic on the endless search for U-boats. The bombers were loaded at night, ready for the dawn patrol. There would be guards, of course, but guards caught by surprise could be overpowered even if they weren't convinced by the unexpected descent of a hundred strange "Canadian" flyers in Canadian uniforms.

Halifax was more than a hundred miles away from the Army airport and the camp for German prisoners of war. The miles didn't matter. The crux of the plot against the convoy lay in the juxtaposition of a prison camp and an airport a hundred miles to the west. If you could bring together experienced German pilots and Canadian bombers, you could annihilate distance. You could destroy a convoy and a harbor, too. You could do what the Germans best loved to do—amaze the world by striking in a wholly unexpected way at an unexpected place. A hundred miles is very close—by air.

Young Ludwig Hartz had indeed been ambitious. He had put to advantage those months in Reykjavik and had laid out and planned in every detail a small war. A general prison break at Sedwedge, a descent en masse upon the airport, the capture of many bombing planes instead of one plane. These flyers, of course, had no hope of escape. They hoped only to live long enough to destroy the convoy and perhaps Halifax Harbor itself from the air—and with Canadian weapons of war.

"The rest of it is up to the Royal Mounted," said Paul to Mary. "It's up to them to find the hiding place of the plotters, and prevent the prison break. You and I are done."

His arms closed around her and briefly they clung together. And Mary knew she was desperately glad it was all over; glad that she and Paul, their own mission completed, could lay down responsibility and tell their story to the Royal Mounted. She had no idea how difficult that might turn out to be.

TWENTY-TWO

The light glimmering ahead was a faint almost invisible gleam, leaking underneath some distant door.

As they approached, groping past barrels of pickled cod and herring, past chunks of salted fish baled like cotton, their footsteps deadened in sawdust, they could hear muted voices. And, curiously, because it was so commonplace and blessedly normal, the chatter of a radio.

When they opened the door, they were led into a little back hall lit by a wall bracket and with a length of shabby carpet on the floor. The carpet ran up a short flight of stairs. The radio was playing up there, and they smelled something cooking in living quarters overhead. They turned on into the shop.

The fishmonger was a comfortable, well-fed man leaning over his counter and confidentially pointing out the merits of a fine freshly caught mackerel to a comfortable well-fed female customer. His mouth opened so wide that Mary saw his fillings. The mackerel slipped from his fingers.

"Where'd you two come from?"

"From the back, from the alley," said Paul, tired, hurried and impatient. "If you will let me use your telephone ..."

"From the alley, you say! From the back of my premises, you mean! Did that boy Joe leave that door unlocked again? I've told him, and told him ..."

"I've got to reach the phone," Paul said, "at once. An attempted holdup. A thug in a green closed car ..."

"A holdup!" exclaimed the other, spurred at once to action. "I'll pop right out and find Sydney Jones, the policeman on the beat. Sydney's an old friend of mine...."

"I want to call the Royal Mounted. If you'll just take me to your telephone ..."

"The Mounties? No, young fellow, Sydney is the man for us. I could be picked clean of the last herring on my premises and much the Mounties would care! Now, whereabouts in the alley did this holdup happen?"

"It didn't happen in the alley," cried Paul, maddened by the other's loquacity. "It happened at least fifteen minutes ago around the corner at Frome & Frome. I've got to get in touch with the nearest hospital. The clerk was knocked unconscious and ..."

To his amazement the excessive friendliness faded from the fishmonger's expressive face, disappeared altogether. The man had been taking off his apron and reaching for his hat. Slowly he retied the apron strings.

"Surely you know where Frome & Frome is," Paul said, baffled at the sudden change.

"Yes, I know," said the fishmonger. "I ought to know. I've got keys to the store upstairs."

"You've got keys!"

"Mister, I don't know what kind of a game you're trying to play on me, but I don't like it," said the fishmonger coldly. "I know you wasn't held up at Frome & Frome's fifteen minutes ago. Why? Because you wasn't in the store, that's why!"

"Of course we were in the store! We were buying a lamp when ..."

"Mister, you weren't buying a lamp from Frome & Frome this evening. Frome & Frome went bankrupt last week."

"Bankrupt! I tell you the store was open three-quarters of an hour ago."

"Frome & Frome closed its doors to business last Saturday night," said the fishmonger implacably. "Such furniture as remains on the premises, and this means everything, lamps included, was sold last week at auction. Sold the stock is and waiting to be called for; that's why I've got the keys. Frome & Frome made its last sale Saturday afternoon. The store ain't been open since half-past nine last Saturday night."

"The clerk ..."

"Suppose," the fishmonger said suddenly, "you show me this clerk you say is lying over there on the floor. I'd like to have a look at him."

What followed had the peculiar unreality of that twilit, uneasy state between sleep and waking. The fishmonger went upstairs and got his keys and a flashlight, and the three of them walked back through the redolent rear of the fish house. They passed through the door and, along the alley.

The green car was long since gone. That was to be expected. But Paul felt ridiculously unnerved when he saw that the furniture truck which had blocked the alley mouth had also driven off. Not that in itself the fact was particularly significant. But somehow in the steady beam of the flashlight the narrow twisted alley had become quite different, ugly still but—ordinary.

Its perils had shrunk away.

They walked past the service entrance of the store and on around, entering Frome & Frome through the front door. Again Paul felt curiously unnerved. There had been one light burning, near the back. It was not burning now. The fishmonger paused and pressed a master switch. Overhead lights bloomed all along the shop.

Paul stared.

The whole of the street floor of Frome & Frome, from front to back, had flashed into view. The rows of beds and bureaus and dressing tables, sold at auction last week, were ordered and undisturbed. The glider was overturned no longer; its canvas canopy flaunted a green-and-yellow banner beside the chair where Mary had sat. Nearby, correctly and neatly placed upon a table, was the bronze, heavy-based lamp, the stout little girl holding up her perforated bronze umbrella. Someone had picked up the lamp from the floor and removed the paper wrappings. Nothing remained to show that Paul and Mary Strong had ever been in the store before.

"Now where is your clerk?"

Paul walked on back into the store, walked as far back as the telephone, on the slim chance that the injured man might have crawled off somewhere into concealment. All the time he knew it was useless. The clerk was gone. There was no sign of him.

"Now," said the fishmonger triumphantly, "I hope you're satisfied. You'd better take your wife on home and ..."

"With your permission, I still intend to call the Royal Mounted."

Paul reached toward the telephone directory. The other man looked fleetingly disconcerted by such lunatic persistence, then shrugged indifferently.

"You won't find the number of the Royal Mounted listed in the book. They try and keep away the—cranks."

"Then I'd like to call a taxi."

"Mister, I guess it's your own funeral. But I ought to tell you the Mounties won't take a joke as well as I do."

Ten minutes later Paul and Mary left the store that had ceased to be a store a week ago and stepped into the second taxi they had seen in Halifax. The headquarters of the Royal Mounted—the Mounties had taken over the old Post Office Building—was only eleven blocks away. For eleven blocks Paul held Mary's hand, and they did not speak.

Once again they were on Barrington Street, driving directly through the crowded noisy center of town. The old Post Office Building was a dominating feature on the skyline to the east, its squatty, pointed tower visible across crowded rooftops. The driver didn't need to point it out. To Mary the building in the distance was like a mirage, an illusion. The whole town had become unreal to her, the episode in Frome & Frome was a dream. Only the silent pressure of Paul's hand was real.

They got out of the taxi, and the driver was off immediately, whirling around the corner. Nothing distinguished the headquarters of the Royal Mounted from any other public edifice. It looked like an old post office building, solid, substantial, broad, like a hippy matron. A stout stone façade, a flight of broad stone steps descending to the sidewalk, a row of lighted windows, an inconspicuous entrance discreetly marked R.C.M.P.

Someone jostled them from behind. It was more than a jostle. It was a definite push that shoved them along the icy sidewalk—away from the steps. Someone stepped between Paul and Mary.

"Keep moving," said a soft familiar voice. Paul heard Mary gasp. The row of lighted windows above cast a faint glow downward. Dr. MacGregor's eyes were sparkling, his mouth smiled gently beneath his pointed beard. Dr. MacGregor's left arm was firmly linked through Mary's. His right hand was in his overcoat pocket, and that hand was nudging Paul through the cloth. There was a gun in Dr. MacGregor's right hand.

In his sparkling eyes was an expression indicating very clearly that Dr. MacGregor was a different proposition from Alexander Campbell. A different proposition altogether. Dr. MacGregor wasn't stupid. If put to it, he wouldn't hesitate to use *his* gun.

Again Dr. MacGregor spoke.

"Don't you think yourself, Mr. Strong, it's rather late in the day for you two to be coming here? My car is at the corner. I'm anxious to have a little talk with you."

TWENTY-THREE

His car was at the corner, Dr. MacGregor had said. But he had spoken figuratively. As the doctor thrust himself between Paul and Mary, a slow-moving black car running without lights crossed the street and sidled to the curb. Almost before they knew what was happening, the Strongs were in the back seat of the car and a heavy door had slammed. Dr. MacGregor was still between them.

Paul started to look back. The gun jumped a little in Dr. MacGregor's pocket, gave Paul a gentle admonishing nudge. His face was turned, and Paul couldn't see his expression. But he had a distinct impression that the doctor wasn't smiling now.

"Just keep your eyes ahead," said the pleasant voice. Suddenly the gun was lying in Dr. MacGregor's lap. "I believe if you reach your arm around, Mr. Strong, you can pull down that curtain without too much unnecessary motion. Just give the roller a tug. There, that's better. Now, Mrs. Strong, will you oblige me with the curtain on your side?"

"May I ask, Doctor," said Paul, "what in hell is the meaning of this? Where are you taking us?"

"Not far," said Dr. MacGregor easily.

"I thought you wanted to talk to us. What about?"

"Come, come, Mr. Strong. Why not speak more frankly? There could be only one reason why I'd be interested in you and your wife, which you know as well as I do. I'm anxious to have you meet a friend of mine."

"Who is your friend?"

"I'm sorry to take such unconventional means of bringing us all together," said the doctor blandly. "Personally, I have little stomach for melodrama. I daresay I'm getting on. Still in a world that of late has gone in rather heavily for melodrama, I try to hold my own. Mrs. Strong, do you care for a cigarette?"

At that moment the car came to an abrupt stop. The doctor's extended cigarette case and the doctor's gun promptly vanished. The chauffeur sprang to the curb and opened the door.

The night was cold and dark, and smelled of snow. A raw wind blew in from the harbor the lonely sound of bell buoys. Somewhere a dog barked mournfully. Paul stared and stared again across the sidewalk. The mournful bark was Bosco's. They had pulled up directly outside 36

Canary Cage Lane.

A pathetic spray of flowers fastened to the ugly, bedraggled façade had already frozen in the winter air. The steps had been neatly swept. The parlor curtains were drawn, the shades were lowered. Behind the shaded windows, a lamp burned.

Adelbert Griggs had come home. The Royal Canadian Mounted Police were in charge of the last rites. The Mounties—no one else—must have brought the body back to Number 36. The Mounties would be inside.

Mary sat limp against the cushions of the car. Paul whirled on the doctor.

"Why, you old fraud!" he cried. "What kind of joke is this? What on earth is going on? Your friend is Major Thomson!"

The street was dark, the tonneau of the car was darker. The curious expression on the doctor's face was hidden. For once there was no malice in his voice. It sounded almost—uncertain.

"Go on in," he said. "I'll just speak to my chauffeur, and join you in a moment."

His brain was a whirl of confusion and bewilderment and, overriding both, incredulous relief when Paul walked up the familiar steps with Mary beside him. Together they passed across the threshold. Once again they smelled the mingled odors of coal gas and dirty carpets, all the odors of a tired old house. And mixed in was the sharp sickening smell of ferns and flowers. The parlor doors were closed, but someone was weeping in there. In the stillness of the hall could be heard the wretched, hiccoughing sobs of a child.

"Elsa," Mary said. "Paul, she shouldn't be in there."

She shook off her tiredness and her own confusion and braced herself and went to the parlor doors to knock. And Paul recognized one of the many reasons he loved his wife. Mary could rally herself from anything to share the sorrow of a heartbroken fifteen-year-old.

But as Mary raised her hand to knock, the sobs were interrupted and the parlor doors slid back. A red-eyed Elsa, her face swollen and contorted with tears but now painfully clean, appeared in the opening. Her dress was rumpled. They could see she had been kneeling at the coffin.

"Oh, you're finally back. Maw thought you'd gone off and stuck us with the dog. I knew you wouldn't. Maw says you'll have to pay for what he ate and for the third-floor carpet."

"Elsa ..."

"They brought Paw home this afternoon. Maw don't care. Just me."

She burst into fresh tears.

"I know, dear," Mary put her arms around the thin young shoulders. "Let's go in the kitchen, I'll help you make a pot of tea."

"Maw will make you pay extra."

"That's all right."

"Your friends," Elsa said, swallowing her sobs, clinging to Mary, "are here already. I just took them in to view the remains."

There was a stir of movement in the parlor, a muffled cough. The girls had already started toward the kitchen. Without hesitation, so sure he was, Paul moved through the golden-oak doors. He never had a chance. He felt a crashing blow. The sickening smell of flowers rolled over him like a thunderous wave, sweeping him into deep unconsciousness. As he fell, he saw the coffin across the room, and standing beside it with a strange smile on his face Baron Ludwig Hartz, sometimes known as Hans Van Anda.

Ambushed, by God, thought Paul, and, for a long time, thought nothing more. A second man, who stood directly behind the golden-oak doors and whom he never even saw, had brought the blackjack down upon his head.

Mary was halfway to the kitchen when she heard the scuffling fall. It wasn't necessary to use the blackjack on her. Something—a heavy coat—was flung over her head as she ran into the parlor.

Stupefied, Elsa saw the end of it, saw the handsome, redhaired "friend" swinging Mary's light body, twisted and wrapped in some sort of coat, from the parlor floor. The fifteen-year-old fled in terror up the stairs. The other man—the one who was carrying Paul, hung limp as a sack across his shoulder—shouted that she wasn't to call the police, raise any alarm, on the pain of death. The redhaired man said nothing at all to her. But he was the one whose face she saw afterwards in her dreams. Elsa never forgot his smile. She waited, clinging to the balustrade, until the back door banged.

Elsa ran to the front door and flung it open, and shrieked up and down the street. Some minutes passed before the hysterical screams roused anybody. The lonely block was quite deserted.

The black car in which Paul and Mary and Dr. MacGregor had arrived wasn't at the curb. The black car was several blocks away, and the doctor was speaking over a public telephone to a number he knew very well. He was just concluding his conversation "… well, at last we've put it over. Remember, you promised I could be in at the kill."

TWENTY-FOUR

Some ten miles from the little town of Sedwedge, between the prison and the Army airport, buried in the remoteness and isolation of woods that hadn't been cut over since the 1890s, was a summer hotel. Lakeside House was a luxury hotel that had been ruined by the war. Built to attract that vanished public which desired "to escape the world," cost no object, Lakeside House was too far off the beaten track to withstand the double blow of gasoline rationing and a border to the south virtually closed to tourists. The few Americans who came now to Canada with money in their pockets headed for Quebec. Or they went to Ottawa or Montreal on business directly connected with the war. Isolation had lost its charm in 1939. The owners of Lakeside House had been very happy, a few months earlier, to sell their big white elephant to Milwaukee interests.

In the summertime the small boys of Sedwedge sometimes made their tortuous way along a road which had quickly fallen into disrepair and crawled through the tangled woods to run joyously about the ruined tennis courts of the hotel. In July or June they had been known to shed their clothes and bathe in the lovely solitary lake that glistened like a jewel among a fringe of tall sheltering trees. In the bitter piercing cold of Canadian winter even the small boys stayed at home, close to the comfortable kitchen stove.

The flimsy rambling rooms of Lakeside House with the airy tower perched on top to catch the sun and summer breezes, weren't designed for winter weather. Afterwards, after it was all over, the village was astonished to learn that the place had been occupied in the depths of winter for a period of weeks. No supplies had been ordered from town, no strangers had been seen or reported. The occupants of the lonely, isolated hotel (some two dozen in number) had taken extraordinary precautions to avoid having the news of their presence spread about. When they circled the frozen lake and walked around the encroaching woods on patrol, a daily chore shared by all, they went armed. Among the supplies transported secretly to Lakeside House was a large supply both of guns and ammunition.

Mary had only a confused awareness of the endless automobile ride that carried her from a back alley in Halifax across country a hundred miles to Lakeside House.

Someone had tied her hands and feet together and flung her roughly to the floor of the car so that with every jolt, and there were many jolts, her head was banged against the metal footrest. The coat that engulfed her head and shoulders hardly softened the blows; it only served to keep her from seeing anything at all.

Back there at the beginning of the nightmare journey, back there in the alley behind Number 36, she had heard a little. Paul had been dumped into another car. Two cars had been waiting there. Only a few minutes later, a few minutes after they sped down the cobblestones away from Number 36, a brief pause had given her momentary hope, the more bitter when it left her. A coal truck that she never saw had blocked the alley mouth, and had stopped them momentarily. Shoved down there on the floor, Mary dimly heard the trucker's angry curses as he backed out to the street to let them pass. She had tried frantically to scream, to rise to her knees, and had failed in both. Muffling choking folds of cloth filled her mouth. The cords at her wrists and ankles held her to the floor.

In the hours that followed after that, she hadn't tried to scream. She had tried to save her strength for the arrival, and to swing her head free of the hammering knocks of the metal footrest. Once or twice she lost consciousness, only to awaken again to helplessness and terror, the jolting of the wheels beneath her. It had been anything but an easy or comfortable journey, that hundred miles.

Outside Halifax they had encountered storm and snow. Freezing gusts of wind blew up through the floorboards until Mary became so weak and stiff with cold that she could no longer move and twist about in the futile effort to protect her head. Sound still reached her. Sometimes she had heard the shrill blast of a horn behind them and the jolting wheels had slowed, and she had heard another car shoot past—a car whose occupants might have helped if they had only known.

It was wartime, and even in the storm and snow of the winter night there was traffic on the main road to Sedwedge. Once there had been a long delay when they had run into an army caravan. Another time a line of oil trucks had held them up. Such delays had only magnified her helplessness and despair. Any driver abroad on a night like this would be wholly concerned with problems of his own. Even when the windshield wiper ceased to whir and she guessed they had left the storm behind, she didn't hope. For now it seemed they were done with dallying and delay, done with traffic, too. She heard no other horns. Suddenly the wheels that had kept a steady thirty-five miles an hour sped up. For five miles, for ten—how could she judge?—they raced along in darkness.

About seven miles from Sedwedge, although Mary didn't know that, the two cars that had stayed together all the way from Halifax abruptly left the main road. But she knew when they left the concrete, and plunged into the woods, rocketing along a bumpy, wretched trail that dived ever deeper into the forest of spruce and pine and fir. Snow-laden branches crashed against the windows, snapped and fell beneath the wheels. Every inch of that virtually impassable road, every rut and gully, every stone, every fallen branch, defined itself to Mary in a series of sickening bumps. And then the road improved.

All at once the two cars stopped—this time for good. They had arrived. The journey was over. She was too weak now to brace herself, too weak to stir. She simply lay there and waited.

The front door of the car opened, banged. But the footsteps went away from the car and went fast. Nearby another car door banged, there were other footsteps. A little way off the retreating footsteps merged, the sound of voices was carried back. She knew the voices—Ludwig Hartz', Lisa's. So the actress had been in the second car, the car that had carried Paul. Their words were indistinguishable, the voices blown back sounded breathless, excited, urgent. At the moment apparently Lisa and the young baron had more important matters on their minds than two defenseless prisoners. Suddenly, somewhere in the distance ahead, there was noise. Many footsteps, a steadily banging door, a high excited babble; a lot of people speaking at once. The language was German. What was going on? Mary no longer cared.

Five minutes went by, ten, fifteen, before the back door of the car jerked open. A flashlight shone in. And still she didn't move.

"Is the girl conscious?" a voice asked.

At that the coat was snatched from her head and someone leaned inside and slapped her face. Mary moaned.

"Conscious, all right," said the voice in satisfaction. "Get her out of the car, and untie her feet so she can walk. Rudy and I will handle the husband."

Mary's feet were so numb with cramp and cold that she fell over the moment she was hauled from the car. She was jerked upright again. Her eyes opened.

She never forgot her first glimpse of Lakeside House. It was that strange gray anonymous hour that immediately precedes a winter dawn. The sun was not yet up. Within the hotel, behind a cold expanse of glass designed for the warmth of summer, candles and oil lamps still burned. Inside, in what had used to be the lobby of the hotel there was no electricity; just the candle glow and fugitive gleam of flashlights here and there. Powerful Aldis lanterns, set on the ground outside, illumined the clearing. Like walls of solid white, their thickly encrusted branches pressing one against the other, the trees closed in all around.

In the clearing, there in the depths of that ghastly forest, surmounted by its chill white tower, sat Lakeside House. A black arm of the lake showed beside it, frozen deep in ice. The little boathouse, half buried in drifted snow, vanished into the blackness beyond. The snow fronting the hotel, dazzling in the searchlight glare of the scattered lanterns, was chopped and hacked like a great plowed field. At least twenty cars choked the circular driveway. Their headlamps added to the icy brilliance. The scene was one of feverish activity.

Lisa and the redhaired Baron had gone inside. But fully a dozen other members of the Icarus Club, those strangers who were their followers, were violently in evidence. Men wrapped in greatcoats were rushing in and out of the lobby, colliding at the entrance, running to and fro in the driveway. They carried machine guns and carbines and sawed-off shotguns and boxes of shells and ammunition, which they were swiftly loading into the cars. The ammunition went inside on the floor, the guns were placed at the half-open windows, their stocks inside on the cushions, their ugly snouts sticking out.

In a single glance Mary's dazed eyes encompassed the scene. It meant nothing to her. The desperate urgency implicit there did not suggest another journey to her mind. Through the woods, nine miles to the west, was the camp for prisoners of war. Such things had ceased to matter to her. And then she saw Paul.

A stranger held her by the arm. Two other strangers were dragging Paul along. Blood had frozen in his hair and dried on his face. His eyes were closed. They didn't open when she called his name.

Forward they went and on into the noise and confusion of the lobby, through the lobby to the stairs. Up and up they went until at last they reached the tower. The elevators had long ago stopped working. Somehow, urged ahead by the cruel fingers at her arm, Mary walked. Paul was half dragged, half carried, his dangling legs striking every step.

In a foolish luxurious bedroom hung high in space, a bedroom with a rosy carpet on the floor and walls and ceiling in faded damask pink, once the bridal suite of Lakeside House, Paul and Mary were left alone.

The costly furnishings of the room were filmed in dust and ruined by neglect. There was no heat. Mary was flung into a chair, her feet were tied again. Paul was dumped carelessly to the bed, his head hanging limply toward the floor.

The door slammed. A lock turned. The three men who had brought them there rapidly retreated down the hall. All was silence.

And then Paul opened his eyes and slowly raised his head and managed a pale-lipped smile.

"Darling, I'll cut you loose directly I get my breath."

At once he rolled from the bed, pushed himself upright and was staggering toward her, his pocket knife in hand. Kneeling on the dusty carpet, still almost too weak to stand, he sawed away Mary's bonds. She tumbled sideways into his arms. For a moment they clung together. She felt his cheek against her tangled hair. Still kneeling, with her collapsed against him, he gently chafed her wrists. They were still together, they were both alive. She began to cry.

"Stop it, Mary."

He stood up again, stamped his feet to restore circulation. His injured head—the blackjack had struck him directly behind the ear—rocked with pain. The pain subsided to a dull throb. His eyes cleared. His feet felt less like blocks of wood. He went back to the bed, walking more easily now, spurred by a desperate inner haste, and snatched up the eiderdown comforter—there were no sheets on the bed—and returned and wrapped the comforter around her.

"Just sit still, and try to rest. You'll need your strength. I've got to figure a way to get us out of here and—quick."

She only looked at him.

"All that rushing around down there in the driveway and lobby," he said. "You and I have upset the Baron's schedule. Unless we reach help, I imagine they'll be starting for the prison sometime very soon."

Mary was silent. His voice hurried on, loud in the frigid stillness of the tower room.

"Once the Nazi pilots are out—and they've got the stuff below to overwhelm the camp defenses—they'll sweep on the airport. It's only a matter of a few hours now at best."

A few hours at best, he said. But what Paul knew in his heart was that it must be only a matter of minutes now. Automatically he glanced at his watch. In twenty-five minutes it would be seven o'clock.

He ran to the locked door and listened. In the hall was only silence— a silence that told of the desperate activity below more clearly than any sound could have done. At the moment the young redhaired Baron had no time for them. Paul and Mary Strong had interfered and they had been put out of action. At the moment, occupied with a more vital concern, the fate of the whole plot, the consummation of months of tedious thought and planning, Ludwig Hartz could well ignore his prisoners. He had no further use for them. Or had he?

There were windows on two sides of the room. Paul ran to the window which looked down upon the front of Lakeside House, at the chopped-up clearing with the ghostly brooding woods beyond. At the thicket of cars in the drive, the busy figures of hurrying men were still loading in the guns and ammunition. The Baron was not in sight. But in the midst of the active circle, surrounded by other men, stood Lisa Tennevant and, with her, Lotte. The headlights of the car were turned upon them.

From the height, the two women looked very small. At first he couldn't make out what they were doing. And then he saw. The trunk had arrived safely at Lakeside House, after all, and so urgent was the situation it hadn't even been carried inside but had been set down in the open. Lisa and Lotte were parceling out the contents, handing out those counterfeited uniforms of the Canadian Royal Air Forces, so that each of the cars should receive its allotted number. Presumably the Nazi pilots would shed their prison garb en route from the prison to the airport. Even though they must know now that Paul and Mary had been returned to Number 36 from the very threshold of the headquarters of the Royal Mounted (Where was Dr. MacGregor? Where did he fit in?), the plotters were going to carry through, just as planned. And soon. Very soon they would be starting for the prison camp. No, there wasn't a lot of time.

Paul ran to the other window. On the edge of the frozen lake, a black and huddled shape, lay the little boathouse. Unmarred and untouched were the drifts of snow below. There were no guards here! They were all in front.

He pushed up the window and leaned out. It was a sheer straight drop. The tower was not set back; it soared up from the side of the hotel, adding its height to the three tall stories below. Nothing offered the slightest toehold; there was just the sheer, blank wall.

If only he had a rope … Paul whirled around and his heart sank lower. He should have known, of course. The luxurious over furnished room that reeked of long disuse was significantly lacking in some of its appointments. There were no sheets on the bed, no blankets either. The eiderdown quilt, in which Mary huddled, was covered with delicate taffeta. Heavy draperies had been removed from the windows; only the flimsy glass curtains remained. The dressing table had skirts of diaphanous chiffon, and no cover. There was no material in the room from which one could make a long, strong rope—in a hurry. Except perhaps the carpet. He ran to the baseboard and tugged at the corner. The carpet was cemented to the floor. He fell to his knees and began working with his knife. Mary got up from her chair.

"Paul …"

His knife slipped futilely along the heavy pile. It would take hours to hack the carpet into strips and tie together a rope that was long and strong enough. He tried again and kept on trying, exactly as though the proposition wasn't hopeless. Mary went over and laid her hand against his shoulder. She gently touched his averted cheek.

"I love you, Paul."

"Go wash your face, darling, you'll feel more cheerful. We both will. Wash your face, and keep on thinking somehow we'll get out of here, get help...."

She drew courage from him and hope where none was. She went into the pink-tiled bathroom and leaned across the basin and looked at herself in the medicine cabinet mirror. Her pale, drawn face was smudged with dirt; underneath, all along her cheek and jaw and at her temple were deep-purple bruises. She was glad Paul hadn't seen the bruises. She would cover them with powder. She still had a compact in her pocket.

She twisted the water faucet. The pipes knocked and bumped and rattled. There was no heat in the tower suite but there was heat downstairs. Scalding water rushed from the faucet. Clouds of steam arose as the water poured into the frigid bowl. The steam revived and braced her. She let the water run and hung over the bowl, holding up her chilled hands, luxuriating in the warmth.

As she reached to get a towel from the rod, her hand paused. She listened tensely. She turned off the rushing water, and then was sure. Someone was in a bathroom adjoining this. Someone was rapping against the medicine cabinet, rapping lightly on the other side of the steamy mirror.

The raps increased in intensity, became a sharp insistent tattoo. The latch on the medicine cabinet jiggled. Fascinated, she stared across the basin at the jiggling latch that secured the little door. It sounded as though someone were knocking directly upon the back of the mirror.

In one quick gesture she leaned forward, unfastened the latch, and opened the mirrored door. The shelves of the medicine cabinet were still in place but the back had been removed.

She looked straight into Max's eyes.

He was in the adjoining bathroom. Two medicine cabinets, exactly alike, set in a common wall had met. Working from his side Max had removed the screws and taken out both the backs. She was leaning across a pink bowl staring at him. He was leaning across a blue bowl staring at her.

"Hello, Mary," he said. "Where's Paul? I thought I was going to have to break that mirror and be unlucky the next seven years."

"Max …"

"Quick, hand me both those towels! Oh, yes, and I'm afraid I'll have to take your coat. Has Paul got a heavy overcoat? A muffler? There won't be time to tear up his shirt."

"Max, listen …"

"I'll listen later, sweet. You listen now. I've spent the past few weeks with my own thoughts and I feel like talking. All I've got to show for my time is a rope that isn't quite long enough."

"Give your rope to me," Paul said quietly. He had come in and joined Mary at the washbowl. "Hello, pal," the men said simultaneously. In a single searching look the friends examined each other, joined forces, divided an anxiety approaching despair. All on the same light note to save Mary distress. "This will be something for our grandchildren, won't it?" Paul said. "I'm the one that's going out the window. Where's that rope you mentioned?"

"Hidden in my mattress. Look, son, I know the terrain hereabouts, and you don't. The town and nearest telephone are ten miles to the east; you strike out across the lake and …"

"Let me see your hands, Max."

"They're almost healed," Max said, and hurriedly tried to hide them. On his palms were raw ugly burns, old half-healed burns and others that were recent. He looked ashamed, almost embarrassed, as he dropped his hands below the level of the basin.

"They've almost healed now," Max repeated. "I'll admit it was a little hard to persuade the Baron and that damned woman that I wasn't going to discuss my personal correspondence. On second thought, Paul, maybe you are in better shape to go down the rope. But for God's sake, hurry back with help."

As he stepped back into his own bedroom, they saw how slowly Max moved, slowly and with difficulty. Paul's eyes were very still, with an expression Mary had never seen in them before. It was hate she saw, and savage fury. A moment later Max was back in the blue bathroom and shoving through the opening in the medicine cabinet a rope that might have made them laugh in other times—a rope that was like Joseph's coat, made up of everything, representing hours of time, days of tedious, minute stratagems.

It was a good rope. Mary recognized strips of mattress ticking; Max had patiently torn away the fabric from the underside of the mattress where it wouldn't show, from the box springs. She recognized strips of bright-blue carpet, a braided section that looked like a sweater, the vivid patch of intertwined neckties, but there were many strips she didn't recognize. Paul seized the two pink towels and swiftly added their bright lengths to the rope. He knotted her coat and his coat together by the sleeves and tied them to the end.

In thirty seconds he was across the rosy bedroom and at the open window with Max leaning out an adjoining window watching, and Mary beside him. The rope was firmly secured to the bedpost; he sent the free end hurtling through the air, a gush of crazy color. No time now to worry about possible watchers at windows below; he must take the gamble.

It was a good rope. It missed the ground by scarcely fifteen feet. Well, he must pray the snow would break his fall, that he could reach the woods and strike cross country.... Paul loosened Mary's clinging fingers.

"I'll make it. I've got to, darling."

At once he swung his leg over the sill. They had hurried, they had worked in frantic haste, but in the end there hadn't been time enough. Paul was half inside and half outside the room, when in the silent hall beyond the bedroom door there came a rush of footsteps. The prisoners in the tower hadn't been forgotten. A key grated in the lock.

Instantly Mary was across the room and at the door, trying frantically to hold it shut. It was useless. The door burst open. Lisa and Ludwig Hartz were in the room.

Mary screamed as the redhaired man swept her from the floor and up into his arms. He held the pistol to her head, but his calm eyes were fixed on Paul silhouetted in the window twenty feet away. Baron Ludwig Hartz was smiling.

"If I were you," he said, "I believe I would climb back inside. We're starting for the prison camp now. We planned on taking you both along."

Slowly Paul climbed back inside. Slowly he swung around from the window sill. The Baron nodded at Lisa.

"Tie his hands together. Rudy will fetch the chap in the next room. Mine will be the leading car; they will ride with me."

So they would ride with the Baron to almost certain death. He might live through the assault upon the prison camp, he might live to join his comrades and fly east to Halifax, he might live to drop Canadian bombs upon the convoy gathering in the harbor there, but his helpless hostages would almost surely die. Long before the last act of the tragedy was played they would be dead.

Prodded by the guns—Lisa also had a pistol—they left the pink bedroom. At the open window the useless rope blew slowly to and fro.

Max was waiting in the hall; his burned hands were also tied; Rudy, a scowling black-browed ruffian, was one of the three men who had brought them to the tower room. Again they were on the stairs and going down.

The three hostages went stumbling on ahead, with the three guns behind them. Once Paul hesitated, sagging against the balustrade, and behind them the Baron's soft voice said, "Be very careful, Strong. Any attempt to escape, and I won't hesitate to shoot."

They reached the bottom of the curving stairs, turned into the stillness and desertion of the lobby. The hurry and haste within the hotel were over now. The Icarus Club had already withdrawn, leaving ruin and filth behind. Trash and bits of paper, scores of cigarette butts, discarded cartridge boxes, littered the once imposing floor. On a leather sofa, crushed carelessly into the cushions, was a half-eaten sandwich. A pair of ill-fitting boots had been thrown toward an overflowing wastebasket. Other articles of gear and clothing lay abandoned everywhere. The Icarus Club wouldn't be coming back to Lakeside House.

The forgotten candles, the oil lamps burned on. A gilt clock above the entrance pointed to the hour. In three minutes it would be seven o'clock. The crowd was all outside. Through the lightening dusk, the men outside went streaming toward the cars that were ghostly shapes in the frigid gloom of the clearing. The Aldis lamps on the ground had been extinguished. The headlamps of the cars were still lit. The cars had been swung into position now. They stood lined up in the driveway. In a long and deadly line they would move unseen through the woods, until at last they burst into the open and hurled themselves in all their fury upon the prison gates. And then the prisoners, Nazi pilots like the redhaired Baron of so many masquerades, would come surging forth....

The doors of Lakeside House stood wide open. The excited jabber outside, the guttural German voices, had died away in this last moment;

only the distant crunch of many footsteps in the snow, the muffled clink of steel, came faintly in to them. The lobby was emptied now, or almost. The fourth hostage, as helpless as these three, had been left behind for the young Baron's disposal.

Frau Van Anda, bulky in her furs, numbed with uncomprehending terror, was tied to a chair directly beside the stairs. Above her bowed head, fantastic in that frozen setting, rose the browned fronds of a long-dead potted palm. The eyes of her one-time son flickered indifferently over the bound woman. He must have considered leaving her there. And then he jerked his head at the black-browed Rudy.

"Bring her along, too. She can go in the second car with Ferris. I'm taking the Strongs in mine."

In prompt unquestioning obedience, the other man dropped back. The party advanced a few yards farther, hesitated. The Baron lit a final cigarette. Smiling faintly, he offered one to Mary. She didn't speak. She only shook her head. In the silence the fronds of the dead palm rustled as Rudy hacked at the stubborn knots. The pistol shifted in Lisa's hand; she peered out anxiously toward the moving shadows in the driveway and the brooding woods beyond.

Behind Paul, lit by a row of guttering candles, was the deserted cashier's desk. Paul leaned wearily against the desk, in a gesture of exhausted resignation. To the casual eye, he was immobile, lost in hopelessness and despair.

Slowly, slowly, with no perceptible movement, Paul raised the hands that were tied behind him. His outstretched fingers touched the edge of the desk, crawled over to the blotter. Inch by inch, noiselessly, his fingers groped along the blotter, brushed an inkwell, crept away from it, felt warmth, the warmth of liquid wax. Higher he raised his hands. A sudden tongue of flame licked the backs of them. He clinched his teeth but his face showed no change. He had found a candle.

It burned his hands as it burned the cords; the pain was savage but brief. The cords dropped to the desk. Paul's hands were free. Slowly they closed on the heavy candlestick.

Mary was only a few steps away from him. Ludwig Hartz held her firmly by the arm. Loosely held in his other hand was the gun. The cigarette drooped from the Baron's lips. Through the windows he was watching the orderly progression of events in the clearing. The cars were almost loaded now. The Baron stood there easily, perfectly relaxed, smiling faintly, almost dreamily, to himself.

Two other people in the silent lobby—Lisa and Rudy—were also armed. Through his fractionally opened eyes, Paul made exact calculations of their positions. Rudy at the stairs, Lisa at the doorway, Hartz directly to his left. If by some miracle Paul was able to knock out Hartz in one savage blow, strike him down before he could bring the gun into play, would there be a chance? A possible chance? The luxury of probabilities was no longer his. Should he strike now? Or should he bide his time and try to take advantage of the inevitable confusion when they were herded forward through the open doors toward the cars? Instantly Paul reached decision. Now. His hands closed more tightly on the candlestick.

And then it happened.

A single shot rang out from the woods. A single shot fired into the air. They heard it clearly in the lobby. Hartz spun around in consternation. Instantly, in answer to the shot that was the signal, a deafening rifle volley filled the clearing with an agony of sound. The driveway was raked by murderous fire. Motors roared into life. In the half-darkness— it was still far from light on that winter's morning—the red flashes from the forest could be seen. The desperate men of the Icarus Club were besieged.

Car lights vanished, and snow spun under skidding tires. The closely marshaled cars were headlong in flight even as the second volley echoed and re-echoed in the clearing. Undirected but reasoned in purpose, the drivers of the armored automobiles headed for the three exits from Lakeside House: the main road, and the two woods roads. Not one of the machine guns made answer to the besiegers lest the crimson of their fire provide targets for marksmen.

Paul and Mary, as stunned and bewildered as their captors, were not to know the details of that encirclement by the Royal Mounted Police until later. But every strategic contingency had been taken care of by calm and effective planning. The initial firing had come from the forest at the right of the hotel. The rest of the clockface of the circular clearing was silent. But at the three exits that were narrow, tree-arched and gloomy, Major Thomson's machine gunners lay in deadly ambush.

Baron Hartz, forgetful of his captives, sprang to the window when the first volley announced that his deeply laid plans had gone agley. Rudy and Lisa still stood guard, and Paul, with instinctive cunning, made no move that would divulge his new freedom of action; he leaned weakly against the cashier's desk and—waited.

Hartz at the window was calm as the motor cars roared around the driveway and he was still calm and contained, minutes later, when the steady chatter of distant machine gun fire told him that his compatriots had been ambushed. He turned and spoke to Lisa Tennevant.

"Bad news," he said, and shrugged. "But always we must take those chances."

For a moment Paul was stirred by an unwilling admiration for the courage of this man whose philosophy he hated. And then he felt a slap across the face. He was slapped again and again, and he felt the blood rush into his face as anger rushed into his bloodstream. Hartz wasn't smiling now.

"I shall be able to pay you off, Strong," said the Baron, "before I take my departure. And I have a bullet for Ferris, too. *Dummkopfs*, both of you. American swine!"

The Baron cleared his throat and spat. At that moment a car pulled up with a shrieking of brakes in front of the hotel. Under the brick roof of the porte-cochere, the chatter of machine guns became raucous and deafening.

"Some of our comrades have returned," said Hartz. "Rudy and I will fight it out to the end at their side." He turned to Lisa. "But you, my dear, have more of the *Fuehrer's* work to do. Listen, closely. Downstairs, there is an underground passage which leads to the boathouse. You have a very good chance to escape. It is your duty to go. I command you."

The Baron drew himself to his full height, clicked his heels and saluted.

"Heil Hitler!" he said.

But Lisa, her gun held limply, was weeping....

Even before Hartz spoke, Paul—his hands free and hungry—had launched his flying tackle. He caught the Baron's knees and dumped him at the very moment that a grenade struck the car outside. The Royal Mounted had anticipated this return to the fortress of the hotel. There was an explosion like a clap of thunder, and the very air in the lobby seemed to be sucked by a magnet out the door. At the same time there was a hail of metal scattering, without direction, indiscriminately. Shrapnel. And then there was silence. And then after a little while there was the first licking sound of fire, and then the windswept sound of gasoline burning, and, finally, a volcanic roar as the car burst apart.

Lying on the floor, half-stunned himself, Paul felt the Baron's knees go limp; there was no more struggle. Blood ran from the top of the Baron's head, seeping through his dyed red hair and like a rivulet, down the neat, careful part the comb had made. The Baron was dead of a shrapnel wound. After a little while, Paul struggled to his feet.

There was quiet in the lobby and the acrid smell of powder and dust. There was a slow settling of plaster, and in the middle of the great room a fragment of a rubber tire had lodged itself in the wood of a mahogany table. The greater part of the front door was gone, and now the cold morning air was pouring in from the snowy outside. Paul shook himself cautiously, drowsily. Where were Rudy—and Lisa? Both were armed. Then he found them. Rudy lay bleeding and unconscious by the door. Lisa would never serve her *Fuehrer* again: she had failed to reach the underground passage because, weeping, she could not leave her lover. Her dark hair had come uncoiled and, beautiful and tragic in her last sleep, she had fallen beside the Baron.

Paul slipped to his knees drunkenly. There was something wrong with his sense of balance. His ears rang. Head bowed like an Arab toward Mecca, quite unable to rise again, he heard men enter the hotel and move around him. He struggled, felt someone thwack him resoundingly, heard a voice. It was Max.

Paul had a dream of azure-blue uniforms as he rose and then, abruptly, he was completely conscious. He saw Mary across the lobby, lying on the leather sofa. He ran. He lifted her in his arms. She was pallid, and there was a thin trickle of blood from her face. Someone touched him on the shoulder, and, his wife in his arms, he turned.

The face of the Mounted Policeman looked vaguely familiar, and then Paul knew, dazedly, it was the man who had been the clerk at Frome & Frome. His eyes shifted. Beside the Mountie stood Dr. Angus MacGregor.

"Let me take her," the doctor said.

Mary opened her eyes. Everything was very still. The doctor's fingers were gentle on her wrist. She spoke.

"Why aren't you in uniform? You—you're a Mountie yourself."

"No, Mrs. Strong. I'm only a hard-working physician, with friends in the Service. I'm just an amateur detective like you and your husband."

"How—how did you get here?"

"Don't you know?" said the doctor. "Don't you know the debt the Service owes you?"

"The debt?" she said.

"You two," said the doctor, "led us here."

And then she really fainted.

TWENTY-FIVE

"It was a curious case," Major Thomson said to them as he looked across the big, flat-topped desk, "a curious case, successfully concluded, thanks to many factors. Not the least of these," he said thoughtfully, and glanced beyond Paul and across Max's head to look steadily at Mary, "indeed probably the most important single factor was your own behavior, your—unconventional arrival here in Canada."

Three days had passed since the bloody drama at Lakeside House. The winter afternoon was clear and bright, very springlike for the season. Sun streamed in the windows. The four of them—Paul and Mary and Max and, of course, the Major—sat in the Major's private office on the second floor of the old Post Office Building. It was a cozy, informal, lived-in kind of office; not at all, thought Paul, like the cold forbidding quarters of the New York police commissioner. Comfortable chairs, a leather couch, old-fashioned bookcases that held bound records of the R.C.M.P., and, hanging on a peg beside the Major's hat, the steel helmet he had worn in the last war. "I pose in that thing with the women's clubs," he'd explained to the two journalists with a wry deprecatory grin, and hadn't added that not even the women's clubs could bully him into putting on his medals.

On the walls hung the Major's pictures—the King and Queen, an inscribed candid camera shot of Churchill standing beside a Nissen hut, a cherished picture of the St. Roch, the Royal Mounted's own and history-making ice boat, the first in the world to sail the Northwest Passage. He had courteously pointed it out to his visitors, in the strained moment of their meeting. Another cherished photograph showed a dozen Mounties on horseback, a younger Major Thomson among them, holding upraised swords in their hands. The horsemen were about to engage in a sport called tent-pegging. The point of the game was to gallop headlong upon a peg driven deep into the ground and with a single thrust uproot and bring the buried peg to the carry. "Tent-pegging is a man's game," Major Thomson had said. "We leave polo to the children."

His three visitors could well believe that. It was Major Kenneth Thomson, Superintendent of the Royal Mounted for Nova Scotia, who had masterminded the siege. In the smoke and flame and confusion they hadn't seen him then. Nor had they seen him since. Well, they were seeing him now.

Paul still wore his arm in a sling and Max's hands were bandaged. The long scratch on Mary's pretty face, where a bullet had barely missed her temple, was almost healed. Her eyes wavered a little beneath the Major's steady glance. They had been back in Halifax for three days now, residing at the Haligonian Hotel, guests, so they understood, of the Royal Mounted Police. "Guests," an impalpable, indecisive term, that had meant they went everywhere accompanied by a close-mouthed Mountie. They had appeared at the Major's private office at the Major's express invitation. "A command request," Paul had called it when the summons finally came. But he wasn't exactly joking.

There was a longish silence in the cozy office. A buzzer sounded on the big, flat-topped desk. Major Thomson flipped it off. His whole attention was centered on them. He was, however, in no hurry. He offered cigars which both men refused. Mary declined a cigarette. Major Thomson lit a cigar himself. His eyes still thoughtfully regarded the Strongs as though he found them very interesting, now that, at last, a meeting had been arranged.

"Your flight from the *Shalimar*," he said placidly, "set the key for everything that happened afterwards. It's important that you remember that."

As though, thought Mary, they could ever forget. Her mind went back and back to a darkened cabin in a blacked-out ship, with a dead man lying on the floor. Once again she heard the voice of Captain Schott accusing her of murder. Her mouth felt dry. She wished she had taken the cigarette. To her annoyance, her voice shook a little.

"Captain Schott …"

Major Thomson's face changed. His gray eyes—the distant eyes of an outdoors man penned of late years in an office—hardened. Suddenly his voice wasn't soft and pleasant.

"Captain Schott," Major Thomson said, "is locked away with the others, those who aren't already dead. It was Schott, as you've probably guessed, who advised the plotters when the convoy would be gathering in the harbor. The Captain's luck ran out," said Major Thomson, "when he tried to bamboozle the Royal Mounted by presenting a simple case of suicide as a murder."

It was Paul's turn to change expression. There in the quiet office, he had a sharp clear recollection of himself and Mary leaping from the deck of the *Shalimar*, running frantically through the rain, with the Mounties all around them.

"Then you knew all the time that Mary hadn't killed Adelbert Griggs?" Major Thomson looked surprised.

"Naturally we knew, directly we had seen the body. The nature of the wound was clear. Griggs," said Major Thomson, contemptuously, "was one of those weak sisters who can't stand up and face the consequences. A coward when the squeeze comes. In point of fact, Griggs virtually threatened suicide in his telegram to us. Naturally we knew there had been no murder."

"You—you could have arrested us that first night at the hotel?"

"Oh, certainly," replied the Major. "Once or twice," he then admitted, "you eluded us momentarily. I don't pretend my organization is perfect. You and your wife are an uncommonly agile pair. The most difficult job in police work, as you probably realize, is to shadow a pair without their knowledge. To tell the truth, I'm surprised you didn't guess that most of the time one of my men was right behind you."

Paul recalled the haunted feeling, the feeling of being pushed and crowded, that he had experienced during that frenetic investigation of his and Mary's through the streets and back alleys of Halifax. The fat man who had watched them across the lobby, the several surprising appearances of Dr. MacGregor, the trucks and lorries that had turned up in unexpected places. But he had put down all those uneasy feelings to the ever-constant presence of Alexander Campbell, the bald printer, now safely locked away with Captain Schott and the surviving members of the Icarus Club. Why had Campbell been allowed to run so long at large? Paul had no chance to ask.

Mary was speaking now. She, too, was remembering things. Her color was high.

"In New York where we live," she said clearly, "when you're unfairly accused of murder, you are decently arrested. You aren't followed about by police you don't know are following, police who don't lift a finger to keep you from being kidnapped and nearly killed ..."

And then, confused, she halted. Max, who sat beside her and knew their story well, had tried to stop her earlier. Across the desk, Major Thomson was smiling.

"In Canada, Mrs. Strong, when you are innocent you don't run away. You and your husband put yourselves deliberately outside the law, of your own free choice. Once you had done that, once you had run off, we saw a way to use you."

Mary was silent.

"Without your realizing it," said the Major blandly, "we decided to use you as our—unofficial agents. Bait to trap the big game. You made it possible, remember. In the end you led us to the hideout of the plotters, just as we hoped you would."

Again there was a brief pause before the Major resumed. He laid down his cigar and picked up a paper knife and tapped it gently against the desk.

"You see, Mrs. Strong, we didn't know where the main body of the plotters was hiding out. Nor did we know their plan of action. Our aim was to catch them all. Very soon after your own—arrival, we became aware that the plotters were after you. Very much after you. And so ..."

"Why didn't you simply tell us?" Mary began indignantly, and then stopped again. Over her head, Paul and Max exchanged one of those masculine looks. They perceived the box she had got herself in, a certain inconsistency in her position. So did the Major.

"In the first place," he reminded her, "you will recall you had made that very—difficult. Impossible, unless we had been willing to spoil everything. If Ludwig Hartz had for one minute suspected that you had talked to us, that you had told us all the things he supposed you knew, he would have called off the chase at once. Hartz had a sounder conception of the affair than did Captain Schott; he knew very well that he didn't want you to make contact with us, voluntarily or otherwise. His whole object was to prevent your reaching us; to his way of thinking you were blocked from any open appeal to us by the murder charge, but nevertheless so long as you remained at large, you represented a constant and continuing danger. There was no telling what you might discover. Somehow he had to get hold of you. Toward the end, he was growing desperate. So, I might add, were we. Your husband," said Major Thomson reminiscently, "is a man with a mind of his own."

Mary started, remembering certain narrow escapes.

"You—there were several times—when you must have thought that Campbell would get us any minute."

"We gave him every opportunity," said the Major dryly. "I will freely confess that you young people disappointed us several times. Disappointed us in ways we couldn't anticipate. In the beginning, I don't mind admitting we were hopeful of a quick finish to the drama. Dr. MacGregor, an old-time friend of mine who works with us on occasion, was exceedingly helpful and cooperative from the first. For one thing, as I daresay you will recall, he guided you to your residence at Number 36...."

Mary did recall.

"At Number 36," continued the Major, "we confidently hoped that Campbell might find an immediate chance to trap and carry you off. As he saw it, you were wholly unprotected. When he tracked you to Canary Cage Lane from the hotel, he didn't dream that we were following too! But you and your husband," said the Major with a sly glance at Mary, "stubbornly refused to stay put at Number 36, just as throughout you stubbornly refused to behave as we expected. At the theatre, for a brief time, you got away from all of us. Later at the City Market, where we picked you up again, you gave Campbell the slip. Similarly you escaped him at the printing establishment. When you took the trolley to Lotte des Brizac's country cottage, when you walked straight into the hands of the plotters, we were positive that the end was near. But then the farmer across the road …"

Again Mary started.

"Was the farmer working with you too?"

"Unfortunately, no." Major Thomson sighed. "The appearance of the farmer was an accident—a disastrous accident from our point of view. We hadn't counted on him or his wife's curiosity. In short, we had neglected to figure on country neighborliness. My men were on the scene, all right. They were …"

Mary had a sudden memory of herself and Paul standing on the snowy porch of the cottage, looking after a long-distance moving van which had moved slowly along the lonely road, turned into the woods and inexplicably vanished.

"Your men," she said, "were in the moving van."

Major Thomson nodded.

"In the van, parked and hidden in the woods, my men lay prepared and ready. They had a clear view of the cottage. They watched you two go inside. This time it seemed impossible you should get away. But then the unexpected occurred. The farmer interfered. By insisting up admission to the house, by offering the two of you transportation back to the trolley line, the farmer frightened Lotte des Brizac and Lisa half to death and threw all of our own plans completely out of gear. You Strongs were on the loose again. Frome & Frome, where you were bound to show up next, seemed to be our last chance. When we set the stage at the furniture store, put our own man in as clerk, and once again you escaped, we were indeed discouraged."

The Major paused, almost as though expecting Mary and Paul to offer sympathy. Neither commented. They merely looked at each other. Major Thomson smiled to himself.

"Now you have the time, Mrs. Strong," he said with a twinkling sidewise glance at Mary, "you should certainly give this chap of yours a lecture on caution. At every turn, by the most incautious behavior, he upset the hopes of my whole organization that the pair of you would be seized and carried off by the plotters. I've never met a man more determined to retain his freedom. It was only by the greatest good fortune that Dr. MacGregor, who never gives up and who operates always with verve and imagination, succeeded in whisking you back to Number 36 ..."

As the Major hesitated, Paul abruptly sat forward in his comfortable chair. At the moment he didn't care to discuss the little doctor's verve and imagination. He understood that, and saw very plainly how he and Mary had been used as pawns. He had another question, however.

"Major Thomson, it must have been clear to you that Alexander Campbell was one of the plotters long before Mary and I reached Halifax. The robbery of the Artillery School occurred some days before our arrival. If you suspected Campbell of being the thief, why didn't you put him straightway into jail?"

"For the same reason we didn't clap you behind bars," replied the Major suavely. "We knew, or possibly I should say strongly suspected, that Campbell was behind the robbery. We thought we would have a better chance of finding out the why of the theft, if Campbell was allowed his freedom. Unfortunately the loot had disappeared before we searched his premises. We were exceedingly anxious to find out where the guns and ammunition had gone and—why. After you and your wife showed up, we had an even stronger reason. We expected that you and Campbell together—you the pursued and he the pursuer—would lead us to the others. Precisely as you did."

"But ..."

"In jail the man would have been quite useless. His arrest would have merely alarmed those we really wanted, put them on guard. Campbell could have told us nothing of value. Actually he didn't know the whereabouts of his confederates, any more than he knew the guns and ammunition he had stolen had been transported to Lakeside House. Now, as regards you two, you and your wife—Campbell was merely instructed to lock you up in his shop until Hartz called for you. He knew as little of the plot as Griggs did, less perhaps."

With a start Paul recalled that Alexander Campbell, a mercenary acting under orders, hadn't even known the redhaired Hans Van Anda was the escaped prisoner of war, Baron Ludwig Hartz.

"Neither did we—at first," said Major Thomson quietly. He looked absently at the papers tidily arranged on his desk, papers that dealt with the forthcoming trials of the spies and saboteurs. Few of the names mentioned on those dry, legal-looking papers would be the names of living men by this time next month. Few of the one-time members of the Icarus Club would escape the gallows. The leaders were already dead and buried. It had been a mighty haul.

"Suppose," Major Thomson said, and turned his grave eyes on Paul, "I tell you what the situation was when you arrived in Halifax. From our own point of view, that is to say. I believe I remarked that it was a curious case. On the one hand we knew a great deal, on the other hand appallingly little. There were many vital gaps," the Major conceded soberly, "in our information. We knew that a convoy was endangered—Griggs had warned us before he took the coward's way out and killed himself—but we had no idea of the nature of the plot. No way of guessing what was actually in progress. We didn't know that another prison break was contemplated at Sedwedge, that Nazi pilots were involved, that an attack by air and in our own planes, was even remotely possible. We assumed the danger lay here in Halifax."

He waved his hand in the direction of the harbor and then suddenly smiled. A slow, tired and yet triumphant smile. The harbor wasn't visible from the office windows, but that morning when Paul and Mary joined Max for breakfast the three of them had stood and looked down from the hotel window. The convoy, one of the largest ever to leave Canadian shores, was gone. The choppy waters of the harbor, sparkling in the winter sunlight, that had been so feverishly filled with traffic, lay quiet now, almost emptied. Soon, within a few days perhaps, the harbor would be busy again, but now it was enjoying a tranquil breathing space.

For a moment the Major was silent, enjoying his own personal breathing space, a responsibility that was over—for a time. And then, reminded of his visitors, he picked up his narrative again.

"We had reason to believe," the Major continued, "that the plotters were members of the old Icarus Club, or intimately connected with the club. Griggs had been previously involved with them, remember. So had Campbell. After the September fiasco, after the failure of the prison break at Sedwedge, the Icarus Club disbanded and the members scattered, dropped out of sight. We believed that this dangerous group had come together again, but where? Somewhere in Halifax, we supposed. We were scouring the town for their hideaway at the time you two came here and—led us to them."

"I'm glad we could help," said Mary, meekly now. "Even though our help was quite—involuntary."

Her tone made the three men smile. And then the Major went on to tell them of another piece of information that had been in the possession of the Royal Mounted, information that at first, puzzlingly, didn't fit. The landing of a German submarine on a remote and isolated shore, many miles to the north of Halifax, had been reported by a lonely shore patrol, which hadn't been lucky enough to intercept the landing party. An exhaustive search of the beach, three long miles of beach, had at last turned up a rubber boat buried in the sand and then, amazingly, a camera belonging to an American magazine photographer. The camera was waterlogged and ruined, the metal nameplate almost rusted away. But Max's name was still visible.

"As we came ashore," Max said, "I managed to throw away my camera, hoping someone would find it."

"We didn't know that at first," admitted the Major. His grave eyes shifted to Max. "Frankly, Ferris, we weren't too sure of your good faith— at first. But then the submarine landing tied in with a confidential report sent on to us from Iceland. From the Icelandic report we were able to decide that Ludwig Hartz, five months a fugitive prisoner of war, had lain low those five months in Reykjavik and had been taken out by submarine. The blowing up of the fishing boat, the attempt to show that the passengers had perished, deceived no one."

"It—it didn't?" asked Mary weakly. She remembered very clearly how she and Paul had believed that Max was dead, drowned and lost in the cold waters off Reykjavik.

"I refer, Mrs. Strong," Major Thomson said, "to the responsible authorities. I daresay the public was deceived, but the investigatory authorities and the military saw plainly what had happened after the most cursory investigation. A search of the Thorgsens' home disclosed in the cellar a shortwave sending set removed from a Canadian plane— the stolen plane in which Baron Ludwig Hartz had flown out of Canada! Once we decided that Hartz had left Iceland by submarine, we were prepared for his reappearance here. Of course, we all know now that the plot was the personal creation of the young Baron. His were the brains that conceived it."

"Yes, his were the brains," said Max.

Max's eyes were now remembering. His thoughts had gone away from them, had gone from Halifax and traveled east to Reykjavik. He, too, had discovered the shortwave sending set, and, in advance of the official search—though, of course, he hadn't known its origin. Sitting with his friends in Major Thomson's quiet office, it seemed to Max that he could almost hear again the utter stillness of the house on the harbor on that last morning of his liberty. It had been early when he awakened, and he had been in the mood for an early-morning walk. A few pictures of an Icelandic dawn, he had thought, and got out his films and camera. He remembered how quietly he had moved about his room as he dressed, lest he disturb the pathetic youth who slept across the hall from him. But then when he stole out into the hall, the door of the other lodger's room had been ajar. As he closed it gently, Max had glanced inside. The other lodger, the helpless invalid, was not in bed. He was nowhere in the room.

"I went downstairs," Max said wryly, "to notify the Thorgsens. I still thought, if you can believe it, the kid had come to harm."

Max had been on the stairs when from the cellar of the Thorgsens' home he had heard the rhythmic hum of a radio sending set. Puzzled, unbelieving, he had paused and listened. The same repeated signal had come floating up the stairs. A single word tapped out in Morse again and then again. The word was Icarus.

"I didn't know the meaning of the word," Max said. "Of course I didn't realize that Ludwig Hartz was signaling a German submarine to meet him out at sea. But when I tiptoed to the cellar stairs and looked down, I knew it was damn peculiar that the Thorgsens' invalid was husky enough to be operating a shortwave radio."

The Thorgsens, father and son, had been there in the cellar with their lodger. Max had heard a few low-voiced words about Canada, something about a convoy. He had heard enough to send him hurrying from the house. Within the next hour he had canceled his Clipper passage, dispatched his cable to the Strongs, sent his seventeenth letter. And then he had returned to the Thorgsens' home.

"Why?"

"I went back," Max said, and, like his voice, his grin was wry, "to meet the authorities I'd phoned from town. Unfortunately they didn't arrive quite soon enough. The Thorgsens and their lodger—Ludwig Hartz, Hans Van Anda, call him what you like—were just going aboard the *Irma* and putting out to sea. I went hell for leather after them. Well," said Max, "I caught them, or you might say, they caught me. As you can see, the whole affair was reasonably simple."

The affair was reasonably simple, Max said. Somehow he preferred to leave it there. During those few days at the hotel, he hadn't cared to discuss the past. Nor had the Strongs. Even now Max didn't feel like talking about the trip to Canada aboard the submarine when he had been a prisoner, when all the cards in the game had belonged to the young Ludwig Hartz. The fair-haired boy, who later had dyed his hair with henna, had held all the cards except one.

Max had a single threat to hold over his captors—the letters he had sent to the United States to his friends, the Strongs. No threat that Hartz had offered, no torture, had been compelling enough to force Max to disclose the contents of his correspondence, to divulge what he had found out during his stay at the lodging house in Reykjavik, what information he had passed on.

"I'll admit that phase of it was less simple," Max said, and glanced fleetingly at his bandaged hands. "Hartz was damned persistent. There were times when I thought he would toss me in the sea. Also I think he considered leaving me aboard the submarine to be taken back to Germany along with the Thorgsens. But in the end, Hartz still hoped I'd talk—still figured he could persuade me—so I was dumped ashore with him. Somehow I never got in the proper mood for talking about my letters home to you."

He looked over at Paul. His grin was gay and bold now. Paul grinned back. At the desk Major Thomson flicked off a buzzer whose peremptory summons was annoying him. He reached for his cigar again.

"Your story, of course, explains why Hartz left here and went to the States, why he—guided by Lisa Tennevant—attached himself to Frau Van Anda, as Lotte des Brizac had done before him. Of course he wanted to get possession of those letters very badly."

"Very badly indeed," Paul said dryly, recalling how Ludwig Hartz had moved the whole menage, Frau Van Anda, her nurse-companion-dressmaker, and a lot of rented furniture into their apartment house. Abruptly he shifted his chair to face his friend.

"Hartz did get in our apartment," said Paul to Max, "and he made off with some of your letters—those that didn't count, those you'd sent us from everywhere except Reykjavik. By God's own mercy, Mary had the letters you'd written us from Iceland—I think there were three of them—with her in the park. I had the seventeenth, the last one, the important one, with me at the office."

"Thank God for that," said Max.

From the corner of his eye, Paul caught a stir of movement at the desk. Major Thomson was listening with great interest. All at once he laid down his cigar and stood up. There was a peculiar expression on his face.

"Have you got that letter with you, Mr. Strong?"

Paul began fumbling through his pockets. The seventeenth letter—the theatre program with the tiny pin-scratched arrow pointing to Lisa Tennevant—had served its purpose long ago. But he had it somewhere. Max was watching idly. At length Paul pulled out the crumpled leaflet. He dropped it triumphantly on the desk, and then paused in surprise. Max had got up from his own chair. He was staring incredulously at the theatre program.

"What's that thing, Paul? Where's the letter I wrote you?"

"You didn't write us any letter," protested Paul, completely at a loss. "All you sent was this theatre program, and a lot of blank sheets of paper."

"Why would I do a crazy thing like that?" demanded Max. "Of course I wrote you a letter—a long letter describing what I had seen in the Thorgsens cellar. I wrote it in a tearing hurry, but I certainly wrote it."

"We got no such letter."

"I sure as hell wrote it."

"Max, that letter never arrived."

"Oh, but it did arrive," said Major Thomson quietly. "That is to say, the letter arrived at your apartment house in New York."

Major Thomson paused a moment.

"Apparently," he said, "Ludwig Hartz was more successful than you imagined. More successful," conceded the Major and looked soberly from Paul to Mary, "than he himself realized. Your power over Hartz was always that he didn't know what you two *did* know. He stole the seventeenth letter at the apartment house—before it reached you. But you see he didn't know what Ferris had written in the other letters from Reykjavik."

It was Mary who broke the silence.

"But who put in the theatre program?"

"I fancy," Major Thomson said, "that *she* is outside now."

There was a rapping at the door, a sharp impatient tattoo. And then Dr. MacGregor's impatient voice.

"What is this, Kenneth, a private cabal?"

The little doctor jerked open the door. Together he and Frau Van Anda entered. Angus MacGregor, with his little pointed beard, looked just the same, as impudent and malicious as ever. It was Frau Van Anda who had changed. The shadow was almost gone now from her eyes.

The shackles which had held her prisoner for so long had been severed by the death of Lisa Tennevant, her evil daughter-in-law, and now she was free. She wore all her diamonds and she had rouged her cheeks; her red hair was freshly and beautifully combed. Mary ran across the room, almost as the door opened. She put her warm young arms around Frau Van Anda's shoulders.

"It's so good to see you again."

The Dutchwoman blinked. She smiled.

"Is good to see you, *liefste*. Back there at Lakeside House I think maybe we all die. Now I very much want to live. Now that the world is so much better a place, I am done with fear."

Mary held her closer.

"I can bear anything," said Frau Van Anda to Mary and her voice had strength and courage. "Now that the wicked Lisa who gives my son to the Gestapo is dead. I am willing to take what comes. I will wait until the war is over, and then I will find my son." She looked trustingly at Mary. "Tell me. Don't you think when the war is over, I will find my son?"

Tears stung at Mary's eyes. It had seemed to her that the true Hans Van Anda, the Hans Van Anda who was lost in Europe, a hostage to Hitler, must he dead long ago. Abruptly she was washed by the same wave of faith, the unreasoning but sure faith that possessed Hans Van Anda's mother. Her voice, when she spoke, was strong and steady, like the older woman's.

"Of course, of course, you will."

Mary knew well enough now who had sent them the theatre program, who had slipped the glossy leaflet in among the blank sheets of paper. It was Frau Van Anda herself.

She had done her best for them. Throughout, Frau Van Anda had done her best. Mary turned to speak to Major Thomson and then was silent. Something in the Major's eyes told her that Major Thomson himself knew that Frau Van Anda had done her best, that those many attempts of hers to help would be remembered, that it would be remembered she had acted under duress when she aided and abetted the plotters. Better to leave the situation as it was.

"It seems to me," said Major Thomson, "that about covers it. Now I'll be telling you goodbye."

Paul hesitated awkwardly. He and Max looked at each other. Frau Van Anda was now settled in a chair. Mary leaned over, gave her a last quick kiss on the cheek, went and joined the men. The three of them stood there, waiting.

"Well?" said Paul.

"Well?" said the Major, but there was a little twinkle in his eye.

"Oh, for God's sake, Kenneth," burst out Dr. MacGregor, "tell these young people what they want to know. Tell them," said the doctor, "that after they make out a few depositions they can make plans to go home."

Home, incredibly beautiful word! Home to New York, home to the apartment on Washington Square, home to Uncle Sam's own part in the war. Home! But when?

"Tomorrow, I should think," said Major Thomson.

As Major Thomson stubbed out his cigar, Paul produced one last question. How had Adelbert Griggs known so much about the Strongs on that day he encountered Mary in New York? Paul looked toward Frau Van Anda as he spoke. In that new strong voice of hers, the Dutchwoman gave him the answer he half expected.

Just as Paul had previously suspected, Adelbert Griggs had gone that day to Washington Square to call on Ludwig Hartz. Indeed he had been ordered there, had just left an interview with the redhaired Baron when Mary met him on the sidewalk in the shadow of the moving van. The plotters had no idea of allowing the man who had assisted in the earlier prison break to escape the continuing consequences of his action; for Adelbert Griggs there was to be no turning back; Hartz and Lotte could use the ex-Security Guard, or so they fancied, in the second plot. Griggs should sail to Halifax on the *Shalimar*, charged with the delivery of the trunk. He was told very little about the proposed destruction of the convoy, no more than was strictly necessary; he was merely given orders.

Frau Van Anda had overheard the short and brutal interview which took place as the first of the installment furniture was coming into the apartment above the Strongs'. Hartz had sensed at once that his visitor was wavering, reluctant. He had attempted to club Griggs back into line in the favored German way—with fear. The danger represented by Paul and Mary was not concealed from Griggs; he was shown the snapshot, he was informed of the Baron's intention to steal the letters, and then was sent away. The fear had operated, but in the one way that Ludwig Hartz had not anticipated. Adelbert Griggs had found an escape. He had killed himself.

"And very wise of him," said Major Thomson, and stood up.

It was evident that the Major was ready to dismiss his guests. He walked over to Max and clapped him on the shoulder, turned and shook

Paul's hand.

Almost at once it seemed to Mary they were out of the Major's office, running three abreast along the hall, down the stairs. Breathless, they reached the slushy sidewalk. Fast as they had gone, they were overtaken. Dr. MacGregor, his beard waving in the brisk Halifax breeze, caught up with them at the trolley car stop.

"Oh," said Mary apologetically, "we forgot to tell you goodbye. I'm sorry."

She held out her hand.

"Never mind the goodbyes, Mrs. Strong. It's a small world," said the doctor, "and I'm sure we'll meet again. But I do have a favor to ask. I'd like a memento of our experience together."

"My short-snorter bill?" asked Max.

"My autograph?" asked Paul.

"A kiss?" asked Mary.

"Bosco," said the doctor.

At that moment the demented Scotty was howling his head off at the Hotel Haligonian. In three days he had managed to demolish a bathmat, half a mattress, a pair of bedroom slippers, and a section of the plump left leg of an outraged bellboy. On the street he had also bitten a shovel-hatted Acadian friar, a Halifax policeman, a fish peddler, the Prime Minister of the Maritime Provinces, and the local correspondent of the *New York Daily News*.

"Dr. MacGregor," said Paul gravely, "you've asked me for half my kingdom, but I cannot deny you. Bosco is yours."

"Thank you," said the doctor.

"And now that the deal is consummated," said Paul, "what in the holy name of old Timbucks do you intend to do with Bosco?"

The doctor smiled and shook hands all around. He was to have the last word, after all.

"I intend to present Bosco to the Royal Canadian Mounted Police," he said. "He always gets his man."

THE END